A GENTL

"I was afraid yo[...]"
Clare reached und[...]t's bottom.

Standing on a woodland path with the woman he loved, aching with the effort to deny her what he wanted most. Lord Denzil watched as Clare brought the object of her search into view. She stood, pointing what looked like one of Edmund's engraved pocket pistols at him.

He wanted to laugh at the absurdity at being abducted, but no sensible man made light of a pistol pointed at his heart. Though, considering how that organ had suffered since he renounced Clare for her own good, a ball through it couldn't hurt more.

CELEBRATE
101 Days of Romance with
HarperMonogram

FREE BOOK OFFER!

See back of book for details.

Harper
Monogram

A RISKY
ROGUE

PAT CODY

HarperPaperbacks
A Division of HarperCollinsPublishers

For Trish Cody,
who gives caring
as well as care.

HarperPaperbacks *A Division of* HarperCollins*Publishers*
10 East 53rd Street, New York, N.Y. 10022

Copyright © 1995 by Pat Cody
All rights reserved. No part of this book may be used or
reproduced in any manner whatsoever without written
permission of the publisher, except in the case of brief
quotations embodied in critical articles and reviews. For
information address HarperCollins*Publishers*,
10 East 53rd Street, New York, N.Y. 10022.

Cover illustration by Bob Berran

First printing: June 1995

Printed in the United States of America

HarperPaperbacks, HarperMonogram, and colophon are
trademarks of HarperCollins*Publishers*

❖ 10 9 8 7 6 5 4 3 2 1

1

London, April 1811

"With the rogue returned, every heiress in Town had best stitch the hem of her shift shut." An amused feminine drawl filtered through the fitting room wall, along with the sound of a door opening and closing.

Since she suffered from a considerable fortune, Lady Clare Linwood riveted her attention on the voice next door.

"Actually, pistols might serve heiresses better than needles, with his penchant for abductions."

Clare identified the speaker as Lady Furnival, nearly as noted a gossip as Lady "Silence" Jersey herself. She leaned forward as softer tones answered her neighbor unintelligibly. A thousand pins lanced her upper body. Jerking upright, she mentally consigned to perdition this gown she had come to Bruton Street to have fitted and stepped closer to the wall, rigidly erect.

Meanwhile, Lady Furnival rattled on. "They say the papa wouldn't countenance a marriage when he caught the runaway pair. And the cit's daughter the rogue abducted later bore his brat, hair black as sin, just like his."

Clare had both a reputation and a fortune to protect, despite being as good as betrothed. And Father had warned she couldn't afford even to be seen in company with fortune hunters, after her school-girl indiscretion.

Relieved that her maid waited outside, Clare pressed her ear to the wall. Looking after one's interests wasn't at all the same thing as eavesdropping.

"When a highborn rascal is considered too wicked to repair the reputation of a tradesman's chit, the man is a complete profligate," Lady Furnival confided in carrying tones.

The soft voice sounded again and Lady Furnival replied, "With his deep pockets, naturally the papa found someone to marry the gel and claim the child. Just imagine the joy she had of that marriage, after tumbling into the den of iniquity's bed."

The odd, final phrase must designate a place where unspeakable acts occurred. Lady Furnival's rogue was the worst of bad lots, the sort who made Aunt Morrow find errands to take her out of the room when ladies dropped voices and raised eyebrows over tea. Clare set her ear firmly against the wall, listening with horror and avid curiosity.

Another soft query drew an insinuating titter. "Ruining cit's daughters would hardly get him banished from England. Sniffing round Lord Moresby's gel earned him exile."

The monster had attempted to carry off not one heiress to this den, but two! Shuddering, Clare imagined a menacing man with the hard, empty eyes of a hawk, who preyed on unmarried ladies like her. Her stomach lurched with the shamed memory of a seducer's defiling dalliance.

"He might as well stay away, now that society has his measure," Lady Furnival continued. "Every parent in the *ton* knows about Lord—"

The name merged with the screak of the door opening behind Clare. Chagrined, she leapt away from the wall, pins making the ball dress feel like a bramble bush.

"Forgive me for keeping you standing about, Lady Clare," said Madame Fanelle as she stepped inside. "The newest milliner's mannequin gets round the shop more than I do." Brandishing an elegantly dressed doll, she continued, "You see that waists are indeed cut higher this year. So if you're pleased as it's pinned, that gown can be ready for Lady Saulton's ball two days hence."

Staring at the fashion doll in frustrated abstraction, Clare saw instead a dark-haired fiend with cruel features. Had madame taken another instant to locate the mannequin, Clare would know the name of the libertine she must avoid like Black Death this Season.

Following her cousin through the thronged bystanders at Lady Saulton's ball two days later, Clare twitched her gown's waist lower. Fashion and comfort were too often strangers.

"I need a favor, Clary," Edmund said, turning to take her arm. He sounded anxious more than imploring. "I've asked an old crony to meet me here at the Saulton thing. Help me make him welcome, for I don't depend on the *ton*'s kindness."

"I'm kind to all your friends," Clare replied at once, her interest engaged more by Edmund's unease than his request. "Why beg my indulgence for this one in particular?"

"Not everyone appreciates Denzil," Edmund said, scanning the crowd round the arched doorway into the ballroom.

Clare noted the furrowed brow under the contrived disorder of Edmund's Windswept curls. As cousins pledged to each other by their fathers, they shared a special bond. Since he knew he had only to ask a favor to have it granted, she wondered why Edmund evaded her question. Though his cronies weren't all the answer to a maiden's prayers, only lack of fortune or family made unattached gentlemen unwelcome at society's routs.

"Walking about suits me as well as standing up to this indifferent orchestra, so tell me more about your Denzil," Clare invited him. At once he steered her toward a potted palm in a corner, out of the main shuffle round the dancing floor.

"He's a capital fellow, top of the trees with me." Edmund fidgeted with a silver-handled quizzing glass on a long tasseled cord. "But you know how grey-heads are. Unless a fellow is as prosey as themselves, they've nothing good to say for him."

"Present your Denzil to me if you like." Seeing his relief, her doubts about his crony returned. "If he dances no better than half your friends, you might warn me so I can be excessively thirsty when he asks me to stand up with him."

"Serve you right if he don't ask you," Edmund replied, grinning. "Denzil capers like a hop-merchant, or he did when we were first on the Town."

"Then he promises more entertainment than most of your set," Clare teased. If the man danced, he very likely retained all his limbs. The special consideration Edmund begged must have nothing to do with physical infirmity as a result of the fighting in Spain.

"Denzil isn't just any friend, Clary," Edmund said earnestly. "I don't mean to lose touch with him again, so I want you to like him, too. Most of the men I knew at Eton and Oxford are as like as fleas. But Denzil saved my groats more than once, and I'm deeply indebted to him."

Thinking wistfully of her brief stay at Miss Climping's Seminary for Young Ladies in Bath, Clare envied her cousin's school-boy friendship. She had formed few associations before her come-out and still lacked a true bosom-bow.

"We were locked into the Long Chamber from eight every night until seven next morning," Edmund reminisced. "With no masters about, high spirits sank to low hazing. The wonder is that nobody perished."

"And Denzil saved you from perishing, like Damon did Pythias," Clare teased.

"Don't know about those foreigners, but Denzil acted the best kind of friend," Edmund protested. "Canfield, the blasted bully, knocked me flat on my back one night. Meant to make me drink from the chamber pot, calling it 'home-brewed.'"

In reply to Clare's strangled protest, Edmund said,

"Don't come over missish; you don't care about plain speaking from me. As I was saying, Canfield had beaten the spirits out of enough boys that none cared to come to my rescue."

"Poor Edmund," said Clare with ready sympathy.

Sweeping a white hand toward the polished floor, he said, "There I lay, Canfield's knee in my chest, the pot tipping toward my face, when Denzil snatched it from behind. He shattered the convenience over Canfield's thick skull!"

Face alight with glee at the memory, Edmund said, "Very convenient it was, too. I'll never forget the look of utter surprise on Canfield's ugly mug as he toppled slowly off my chest, hair and shirt reeking with—never mind what."

Clare gurgled with laughter at the malodorous scene Edmund conjured, but she still harbored suspicions. "Most heroic, to be sure. Why expect such a superior person to rate the least incivility here tonight?"

As the final notes of a country dance screeched, Edmund complained, "You've kept me prosing on when I'm promised to Sally Scott for the next dance." Seizing her elbow, he dragged Clare through the jostling crowd.

"You're the one who's spent an entire set recounting odious school-boy japes," she pointed out. Edmund had looked relieved to escape further quizzing about this crony.

Though he was a decade beyond her nineteen years of age, Edmund's understanding of human nature didn't match hers. Whatever this Denzil's affliction, she could more likely help him enter into society's rounds in comfort than her cousin.

Edmund tacked through the crowd in the ballroom's

heated bedlam, towing her behind him like a scull. With unflattering haste, he abandoned Clare to her aunt.

Curtly, Lady Morrow dismissed a dandy entreating her to dance. Staring after Edmund, she said sharply above sparring notes and voices, "Hardly complimentary, when your intended hands you off like a horse to a groom."

Laughing, Clare said, "A lovesick swain would suit me no better than the role would fit Edmund."

Even as she said it, longing for ardent attentions from an impassioned gentleman nibbled like hunger pangs. She yearned just once more, before marriage with Edmund choked off any hope of romance, to feel pursued and desired by a fervent gentleman. If just once more, she could experience the singing in her soul of loving and knowing herself loved.

Except she hadn't been loved.

Realizing that she clutched her midsection with a hot hand, Clare smoothed the crumpled silk. An overactive imagination had run away with her common sense once more. Improper thoughts about improper addresses had no place in her life. She had learned the painful price of honeyed promises at sixteen.

Lady Morrow's sniff was perfectly audible above the orchestra's dissonant music. "Edmund didn't even wait to see if your next partner found you, after returning you too late for that to be likely. If he cared a snap of the fingers for you, he'd have married you by now."

Flicking open her fan, Clare plied it energetically. "Edmund and I have looked out for one another's interests as far back as I can recall. Besides, your experience of marriage generally leads you to encourage me to put it off."

Lady Morrow's lovely face stiffened and her slender form seemed diminished. She said distantly, "A monstrously cruel husband teaches caution toward men."

Sorry she had resurrected the painful past for her aunt, Clare wondered how a husband could have misused so beautiful and kind a lady. Her aunt's brown curls still glinted with golden lights just as Clare's own did, and Aunt Morrow's classical features were more perfect than hers. Though pretty Aunt Morrow flogged gentlemen with a whiplash tongue, at forty, she still fascinated them.

"You know I heed your opinions just as I would have Mama's, had she been spared," Clare said with real affection. "But you're too hard on poor Edmund as on most gentlemen. He's entirely harmless."

"My point exactly," Lady Morrow said sharply. Turning away for a moment, she assured Sir Harry Belton that she never stood up with men who wore puce coats.

To distract her aunt, Clare said, "One of Edmund's boyhood chums is to attend this ball. While we strolled during the last set, Edmund asked if he could present him."

"He should have asked my permission, not yours," Lady Morrow objected. "Who is the fellow? Why don't we know him already? Is he lately returned from Spain?"

"I didn't get the full name, let alone a biography. Edmund called him Denzil, which could be either a first or last name." Breaking off at her aunt's odd expression, Clare asked, "Why do you look as if you just smelled a bad fish? Do you know Edmund's Denzil?"

"I pray I do not," said Lady Morrow portentously. "Lord Denzil Knox was sent to his uncle in Guiana nearly ten years back. He ran with Edmund's first wild pack after he came down from Oxford." Her tone and face grew puzzled. "But the Marquess of Guilford is hardly a man to change his mind as easily as his coat. I can't credit that he would permit his son back in the country after the scandals he kicked up."

Recalling gossip about a rogue's return overheard two days ago at the mantua-maker's, Clare dismissed it at once. Her cousin would never expose her to a profligate. "Edmund's Denzil was a paragon who saved his life," she objected.

"Edmund's a fool." Lady Morrow raised her graceful nose. "Bringing him ale on a hot day would qualify in his feeble brain as saving his life. I'll soon learn the straight of this. He stands up with that flighty Sally Scott, doesn't he? Let's wait near Lady Nelle so we can waylay Edmund when he returns Sally to her."

Aunt Morrow set off at once in the direction of the ballroom's entrance, and Clare hurried to keep up. The crush of guests they pushed through must gratify their hostess. The din of music and voices overbore easy speech. The press of people hindered movement about the room to discover friends. The air was a smothering blanket, heavy with odors of hot bodies, over-done scent, wilting flowers, and dripping candles. A most successful squeeze would be reported in the *Post*'s court news tomorrow.

Minutes later, Edmund delivered a smiling Sally to her mama. Clare's two friends were well matched in fair good looks and devotion to fashionable perfection.

When he turned to seek his next partner, Aunt Morrow plucked Edmund out of the crowd like an apple off the tree. "Denzil who?" she demanded grimly.

"An old school-mate, Aunt Morrow, quite unexceptionable," Edmund said, regarding the determined grip wrinkling his sleeve with anxiety.

"I'll thank you to recall that I'm not your aunt," Lady Morrow informed Edmund. Before she could dress him down further, her attention was diverted.

A sudden hush had fallen over the guests round the door, and Edmund, too, glanced in that direction. "Denzil's here!" he cried as voices rumbled around them, rising in volume and intensity. He shot toward the door without taking leave.

Aunt Morrow stood still as an Elgin marble, though her limbs were intact. Horrified disbelief molded her features as she stared toward the door. Curious, Clare turned to follow her gaze.

"Merciful heavens!" Lady Morrow exclaimed in a strangled voice. "It's Denzil Knox indeed! I never thought to see him in England again, let alone in polite company. Margery Saulton won't gush over this guest's arrival at her ball."

As Clare wondered at her aunt's observation, a dandy close by lifted a quizzing glass, then let it fall dramatically. "So it's true; the rogue has returned," he said. "I wonder who will admit to asking old Den of Iniquity here tonight, for I feel certain our hostess did not."

The byname conferred by the dandy startled Clare. She had overheard Lady Furnival speak that phrase in the fitting room two days since. But Edmund wouldn't admire a person meriting such a sobriquet. The phrase no doubt referred to an aged roué's haunt, like a hunting box.

Clare craned to see what Edmund's rogue looked like. Her stomach fluttered at the thought of meeting a disreputable man. Proper people allowed little scope for the imagination. If Edmund's friend were a bit of a rascal, meeting him might be as exciting as seeing a villain in a Gothic novel come to life.

Near the entrance, Edmund grasped a man's hand, talking with great animation. Since the rogue stood with his back to Clare, she could form little impression of him as yet.

She could see only that Lord Denzil Knox stood above average height and filled out his evening clothes most satisfactorily. A superfine coat and pantaloons fit an impressively muscular frame as if painted on.

A weakling couldn't carry off ladies as handily. Clare quelled the warning in her head.

Most of the gentlemen wore colored coats, but Lord Denzil Knox was dressed in black. Strong shoulder blades held his coat taut across the broad back. *Like stubs left when Lucifer's wings were clipped.* Frissons of dread swept her spine.

Ebony curls tumbled onto the coat's dark collar, the sheen of the rogue's thick, unpomaded hair distinguishing it from the dull texture of close-fitted fabric. Her fingers twitched with an urge to slide into its silky mass.

The two men turned. Clare nearly laughed aloud at her fears. This vaunted rogue wouldn't look out of place as an altar boy. Edmund's fresh-faced friend looked younger than her cousin, despite unfashionably sun-bronzed skin.

As Lord Denzil Knox confronted the crowded room, Clare studied the youthful face, the forehead slightly wider than a strong jaw, the pointed chin. A straight nose stood above a mouth that almost pouted in voluptuous fullness. She traced her lips with her tongue's tip.

Even at this distance, the rogue's eyes transfixed her. Below straight black brows barely down-turned at the ends, the expression in narrow blue eyes belied angelic features. Gaze distant and knowing, Lord Denzil Knox surveyed the ballroom.

Clare felt confused, for the man's guileless good looks clashed with the wary gaze he swept past her. A mama would send a daughter to dance with this frank-faced fellow without a qualm, unless she looked into his eyes first.

Clutching her arm, Lady Morrow said, "La! Edmund's bringing the scoundrel to us. Quickly, let's make our way round the room ahead of them and escape. I can't have you exposed to Lord Denzil Knox, of all the unsuitable men you might meet."

Turning her back reluctantly on her cousin and his disturbing crony, Clare objected, "Edmund and I are all but betrothed. I can't cut his particular friend."

"You had best give this one the cut direct," Lady Morrow advised tartly. "Lord Denzil tried to elope with two different heiresses before he came of age. You hardly want to be seen in company with a fortune hunter."

Edmund's Denzil had to be the rogue Lady Furnival denounced, Clare realized with a jolt of rage against both Edmund and his rogue. Seducing heiresses wasn't romantic; it was cruel. Easy, false attentions cost the victim dearly.

Revulsion reverberating in each syllable, Clare stated, "If anyone is immune to the wiles of a gazetted fortune hunter, I am!"

Speaking to be heard against the gabble of wondering guests, Clare hurled the pronouncement into a sudden hush. A brief lull in the hubbub around them permitted the words to ring out like the peal of church bells before a funeral.

Chagrin stole her breath. Perhaps Lord Denzil Knox hadn't heard the comment reverberating in the untimely silence. No matter what he had done, she hadn't meant to humiliate Edmund's friend before the company. Clare whipped about to locate the two men.

The rogue stood close enough for her swirling skirt to brush his black stockings, close enough to make her leap back. Lord Denzil had heard, unless more ailed his ears than his muscular form. Her stomach lurched. From a cliff top of rage, she plunged into a roiling ocean of sick shame.

In one swift look upward, she saw no sign of awareness in the rogue's candid expression. But his eyes blazed singeing blue fire. Lord Denzil had heard every word, no doubt of it. And he hadn't liked what he heard.

Edmund sputtered an introduction to Lady Morrow, sounding nearly as mortified as Clare felt. She wouldn't raise her eyes above Lord Denzil's knees again. Though even this view of the man was disconcerting: The rogue's black stockings hugged a set of strong, shapely calves that no valet's stuffing could emulate.

Aunt Morrow barely inclined her head and didn't offer a hand. "So you're back in England," she said in the flat, accusing way in which she usually addressed men. "Does your father know you've returned?"

"Lady Morrow!" Edmund gasped.

Under cover of her aunt's effrontery, Clare chanced another glance at Lord Denzil, a mistake. The rogue's searing blue eyes gave nothing away now, appraising Clare as though measuring her upper form for a fitted spencer.

Gentlemen's discreet glances at one's décolletage were nothing new. But this scoundrel searched her neckline with an insinuating stare as though he had dropped something valuable down her dress. No doubt she should have devoted more concern to the gown's neckline than its waist.

Clare was both outraged and weak-kneed. Lord Denzil's regard made her feel highly insulted and dismayingly feminine. Certainly he was no gentleman, to make her feel as unladylike as Father had once called her.

Lord Denzil answered Aunt Morrow's query without removing his gaze from Clare's low, square-cut bodice. Grinning impishly, he said, "Why rush to the governor's side, when it's England's beauties I've missed most?"

Holding herself erect despite his insolent scrutiny, Clare doubted that Lord Denzil Knox referred to the scenic hills of the Lake District. Certainly his bold eyes and tone didn't match his seraphic face. She felt off balance, unable to reconcile opposite impressions of Edmund's valued friend. While Lord Denzil's features expressed innocence, his eyes promised danger.

Directing a look of anguished entreaty at her, Edmund presented Denzil to Clare. She had never let her cousin down. As Clare began to incline her head in the same chilling fashion as Lady Morrow, Lord Denzil seized her gloved hand.

As he pressed her fingers between hard brown hands, Clare felt shaken, surely because the rogue flouted convention. No gentleman touched a lady before she offered a hand unless they were betrothed or related.

Struggling to free the hand the scoundrel fondled would only create a public scene, humiliating her further. She mustn't allow this indecent contact to continue; she couldn't twitch a tensed muscle to disengage.

Babble rose about them and avid eyes stabbed from

all sides. Sally Scott watched the rogue as wildly as if the devil had come to dance, while her mama whispered behind her fan. Realizing attentions from this fortune hunter might well revive old speculations, Clare felt sick dread.

Face guileless as a choirboy's, except for the insolent eyes that searched where they shouldn't, Lord Denzil said, "I'm charmed to meet Edmund's lovely cousin after reading your praises in his letters. May I learn more for myself by leading you out?"

He gestured vaguely toward the dancing floor, or just as likely the garden. She dithered over an answer.

"Clare's card was filled within minutes of her arrival," Lady Morrow objected at once, glaring at Lord Denzil.

"Not to worry," said Edmund too heartily, nodding at Clare significantly. "My name is down for the supper dance, so Denzil can take that one. Clare don't care if she stands up with me again tonight."

Caught by Lord Denzil's insinuating grin as surely as his impertinent hands, Clare decided to refuse substitution.

Caressing her palm to disturbing effect even through her glove, Denzil spoke as if they were alone. "I'll never give up a dance with you, for friendship or civility." His quiet, emphatic voice wrapped her in the dark velvet of midnight longings, eyes glinting with sensual significance beneath coal-colored curls.

Nerves twanging like mandolin strings, Clare wavered between caution and folly. Finally she freed her hand from the disconcerting hold. With only a faint tremor to her fingers, she crossed Edmund's name off her dancing card, writing in that of Lord Denzil Knox, reputed rogue and fortune hunter.

2

Backs were turned and skirts were pulled aside
as Denzil walked with Edmund along the perimeter of
the dancing floor. He had known warmer welcomes
from Macusi armed with blowguns. Bitterness ate at his
belly at the irony of being an outcast among the very
people whose interests he served in British Guiana.

Denzil wished he could kick his younger self's back-
side from here to Dover. He must live down his wild,
youthful reputation, starting tonight in this ballroom.
And the *ton* appeared to recall every scandalous tale
ever embellished, having been reminded by Lady Clare
Linwood's scornful statement.

Not that he had let the chit see that she had stung
him. Three older brothers had taught him as a tadpole
to take a pounding, verbal or physical, with stoicism.

Edmund veered through the throng toward a doorway

and Denzil followed on his heels. This clamor of voices reminded him of the incessant din of night in the tropics, where rackety insects and croaking frogs never masked the screams of small animals being swallowed by snakes. Hissing speech on all sides put him in mind of serpents.

A path opened before them as if Denzil carried the pox. Charming his way back into society might take a bit longer than he had planned.

"We'll take a glass in the supper room while the gawkers get used to your arrival," Edmund said over his shoulder. "Let the gabble-mongers talk themselves to a standstill. Then we'll look out a few of our old set. The wives will make you known to young ladies of their acquaintance."

"Not if their mamas are close by," Denzil said, smiling as if he weren't marked like Cain, cursed to wander in the wilderness, alive, but dead to his people. "No one but you has rushed to take my hand, you may have noticed. Former friends might acknowledge me, but I'll wager not one will present me to his wife."

Denzil paused to make an elaborate leg to a dowager who seemed bent on staring him out of countenance, one bulging eye magnified by a quizzing glass. She turned a plump shoulder in the cut direct.

Short of the supper room, a man of familiar appearance stepped out of the crowd, offering his hand. "I hardly expected to meet you here. Does Bathurst know you're in England?"

Placing him as an adjutant of the secretary to the colonies, Denzil replied coolly, "I'll wait on you in chambers tomorrow to answer that. Wouldn't want to dilute an evening's pleasures with talk of cane crops and shipping problems."

"Yes, of course," the undersecretary said quickly, bowing. "Much wiser. Come at your convenience."

Catching up to Edmund, Denzil said, "Admit it; shamming my way into a ball wasn't the best way to reintroduce myself to society. I'd best climb out the supper room window and let you get back to your dancing partners."

"You can't do that," Edmund said with satisfaction. "We're above the ground floor. Besides, you've engaged yourself to stand up with Clare for the supper dance."

"I doubt the lady cares if she sets golden eyes on me again," Denzil said, wishing he had never met Lady Clare.

After the blaze of disapproval in the ballroom, entering the quiet supper room was like stepping into the shade of the homewood on his father's country estate. Alone with Edmund except for a few footmen, Denzil felt some of the starch setting his features dissolve. Facing down a roving band of runaway slaves was no more daunting than reentering that roomful of judgmental stiff-rumps again.

"Clare's eyes an't gold," Edmund assured him. "They're hazel. And you'll take to each other like a kit to a cat yet, see if you don't. We'll be merry as three mice, for Clare is a right'un."

"And every inch as pretty as you assured me," Denzil said, thinking that Edmund spoke of his cousin as if she were a favorite spaniel. He saw no reason to change the impression he had formed from correspondence; Edmund took his arranged marriage like an apothecary's dose. "Shall I see the other beauty you wrote about? A Miss Scott, if memory serves."

Edmund accepted a couple of glasses from a servant and handed Denzil one, grinning self-consciously.

Denzil resisted the urge to toss the wine down in a single gulp.

"Must meet Sally," Edmund said eagerly. "When you set eyes on the loveliest lady here, that's Sally. She's like a tiny bird, Den. A man wants to keep Sally safe."

Edmund found Miss Sally more beautiful than the lady he was to wed and exhibited a need to say her name. "So you spread a protective wing over two young ladies this Season," Denzil said. "You're a sly old dog."

Edmund actually colored under his friend's teasing. "Clare don't need my protection; she's more like to look out for the rest of us," he protested.

Denzil could believe this assessment. The young lady who announced that she stood in no danger from a fortune hunter like him had appeared capable of taking on the world. Edmund had best cry off and court his lovely Sally, unless he wanted a manager more than a wife.

"I look forward to making Miss Scott's acquaintance," Denzil said, "if you don't mind sharing her attentions."

"You'll share them with more than me," Edmund said, looking glum. "Sally's never stood out a set in her life. I beg two dances before each ball to make sure of coming near her. It's enough to give a fellow a fit of the dismals."

So the wind sets in that quarter, Denzil concluded. As he had suspected, his old friend was pledged to wed one lady while he hankered for another. "Duty is an inconvenience you first sons and heirs suffer," he commiserated.

Nodding, Edmund said soberly, "You have the right end of that stick." Putting up his quizzing glass, he studied Denzil's attire from starched neckcloth to polished pumps. "Quite natty," he pronounced. "I never thought Weston could rig you out in half the time.

Greasing fists made his needle fly, but don't fork over more blunt for a couple of quarters at least. That's how you stretch the ready."

Denzil shrugged. "I can pay my shot. When did clothes get so blasted tight? I've grown used to the freedom of loose trousers and shirt, not these sausage-skins you fops encase your bodies in these days."

"You an't scratching in the dirt of the jungle here, old thing. If you mean to make yourself as agreeable to the ladies as ever, you'll rig yourself out in civilized gear." Edmund finished off his wine. "Don't know why you had to tog yourself out in black like a chimney sweep, though. Clarence blue is all the crack."

"I didn't come home to follow fashion," Denzil reminded Edmund coolly. "Society sees me as a black sinner; why disabuse them of the notion?"

Edmund looked uneasy. "No need to rub their noses in it, Den. You'll need society's acceptance if you mean to come next to decent chits."

Denzil scowled into his glass, as empty as his hopes appeared. In British Guiana his plan had been as clear as crystal. He meant to show his father he belonged in England now, by proving he could win a wife who met even Lord Guilford's high standards.

Not that he required the old man's permission to return, or his approval of a wife. But just once in his life, he wanted the governor to slap him on the back and act pleased to see him. It was a matter of pride, not permission. If his father couldn't welcome him home, he couldn't feel at home.

Denzil looked away from Edmund to hide the depth of his need. "Keeping company with natives, I forgot how guarded pale English misses are. No matter. My sights still are set on a lady of undoubted virtue, breeding, and fortune. But getting next to one may be more of a job than I had hoped."

Taking Edmund's glass, he turned to the drinks table, where a footman dispensed punch and wines. Tawny champagne pouring into Edmund's glass reminded Denzil of glints from haughty Lady Clare's gaze. The wench wanted taking down a peg or two.

Denzil pointed to a golden-brown sherry for himself. The wine was the color of Lady Clare's hair, the weighty Grecian-bound mounds pulling her head back, arching a slender throat he could nearly span with one hand. Throttling her was a tempting thought, though he would first kiss every trace of disdain off her face.

"Will this suit?" he asked Edmund, offering the champagne.

"One wine's as bad as another at a ball," Edmund said. "Only dinners rate the best of the cellar."

"Doesn't appear I'll taste them, then."

"You're barely home," Edmund replied, cuffing his arm lightly. "The *ton* can be like a fresh mount. Give it time to dance out its fidgets before expecting a settled ride."

"You can't force me on another hostess," Denzil objected as he sipped. "If you persist in slipping me into balls on friends' cards, you'll be dropped from invitation lists."

"No such thing!" Edmund protested. "My credit is good enough for the both of us. Hostesses won't drop an heir to an earldom because he takes a friend about with him."

"Fourth sons are heir to nothing—not even a father's good will, in my case," Denzil pointed out. "And if you think anyone wants an outcast like me about, tonight's trial tells another story."

"Clare will help us," Edmund said with certainty. "She'll know how to turn the biddies up sweet."

Grimacing, Denzil asked, "Why should she help? Your cousin seemed reluctant even to stand up with me."

Edmund waved the consideration aside. "Pay no heed to that. Clare had embarrassed herself, so she acted a bit stiff in consequence. You'll soon love her as I do, and you can stay with us often when we're spliced."

Thinking love was the last emotion Lady Clare inspired in him, Denzil asked, "When may I wish you happy?"

Edmund looked puzzled for a moment. "You mean when do we tie the noose about my neck? No set time. We're merry as grigs as we are. Why shoulder the burden of setting up house any sooner than I must?"

Saluting the sentiment with his glass, Denzil smiled ruefully. Edmund's words confirmed a lack of passion for his cousin, while his features radiated fond foolishness at the sound of Sally Scott's name. Denzil stood tipping an inch of sherry idly in his glass, considering his friend's plight.

A shame Edmund was forced to marry a lady who was almost a sister. And a curst shame when he was obviously besotted with the charms of Miss Scott.

As a gentleman, Edmund couldn't draw back from even a perceived promise of marriage. Only the lady could cry off. If there were any justice in the world, Lady Clare would fall prey to another gentleman's attentions, and Edmund could follow his inclinations.

Denzil stopped swirling the sherry. That solution might permit him to remain in England, as well.

Despite Edmund's unfounded optimism, Denzil had seen enough this night to know society welcomed him about as much as it would a labarri snake. Invitations to meet genteel ladies wouldn't litter his doorstep. Lady Clare Linwood was the only proper young lady he could come near enough to court.

But she was his old friend's intended.

Even if Edmund wasn't exactly a scholar, he was the only one of the old set who had written him in exile, the only person to encourage his desire to come home to England to stay. Yet if Edmund's heart inclined in another direction, surely it was an act of kindness to help him follow it.

Denzil stared at Edmund, who named mutual friends in attendance at tonight's ball. Denzil felt little desire to meet old cronies whose company had encouraged excesses. His time was better spent pursuing proper ladies who might merit his father's good opinion. Winning Lady Clare could allow him to stay in England, while freeing Edmund to woo his Sally.

Lady Clare's affections for her cousin must also be gauged before he took a decision. He had no wish to hurt anyone, even to satisfy his deepest desire.

As the sneering speech Lady Clare had tossed into the crowded room tore through his mind again, Denzil considered the challenge. The lady fit his requirements. Her family was *haut ton* and she would inherit a considerable fortune, according to Edmund. The cool lady should impress his father as a proper specimen of British blue blood, unlike the cit's daughter he had chased in his youth.

Denzil weighed his chances with the chit. Admittedly, Lady Clare had shied away from him at first meeting as if he might lift her skirts on the ballroom floor. And while he held her hand, she trembled like a fly on a web, looking at him as though she had been presented to a hairy tarantula.

Weaving a web around the little innocent would only oblige her with behavior she clearly expected of him. A certain grim satisfaction resulted from fulfilling expectations, as he had the *ton*'s as a callow youth.

No doubt the lady would dance undressed on Oxford Street rather than come to his arms at present. But Denzil didn't enjoy easy women. The chase was the best of any sport.

Contemplating the sherry in his glass, Denzil imagined golden-brown tresses the same hue trailing glinting fire across his face and bare chest. Lady Clare might suit the purpose, indeed.

Edmund still nattered, saying Sally too would oblige him by standing up with Denzil. The lady must esteem Edmund, if he could assume favors would be granted.

Normally, honor forbade a gentleman's poaching on another's preserve, so to speak. But when a friend yearned for the bird in the bush, surely it was a kindness to relieve him of the bird in hand.

Edmund didn't show the least sign of romantic attachment to Lady Clare. All his fervor was fixed on Miss Scott. Denzil's need for a lady of family and fortune was the greater by far.

Making himself agreeable to a lovely armful of English charms was no hardship. And it could prove amusing to overcome Lady Clare's self-proclaimed immunity to gazetted fortune hunters.

*   *   *

Relieved, Clare strode off the floor ahead of Lord Denzil, joining the mob making for the supper room. Never had she enjoyed a country dance less. Even the discordant orchestra could literally be said to execute the music.

"Perhaps the musicians were invited to practice here tonight," Lord Denzil said as if he had heard her thoughts.

The music hadn't been nearly as out of harmony as Clare felt with this man. "Perhaps you should ask that of our hostess, if you recognize her, my lord," she said pointedly. Edmund might coerce her to stand up with a social outcast and seducer, but she didn't have to make pleasant conversation.

No one had looked agreeable when Clare and Lord Denzil joined the double lines of ladies and gentlemen forming on the floor for the supper dance. Performances were erratic, and Clare suspected that Lady Saulton had signaled the musicians to cut the music short.

And Margaret Atwood had acted the complete addlepate. The silly goose had gasped audibly when Clare and Lord Denzil took places as the next couple. Then Margaret had held a handkerchief over her gloved fingers when the figure called for giving hands on the diagonal, as if the rogue's merest touch would sully her like soot.

Realizing no response had followed her set-down, Clare gave Lord Denzil a sidelong look. He nodded to Sir Harry Belton, who turned away. No one wanted the rogue here.

Hardening her heart, Clare assured herself that Lord Denzil's ostracism was his own fault. No doubt the rogue had enjoyed abducting heiresses and producing baseborn brats. Now he must pay the piper.

Speaking of which, Edmund would feel the sharp edge of her tongue later, having put her out of countenance by forcing his pariah friend upon her. Clare searched the swarm of faces about them in the slow shuffle toward the supper room, looking for her cousin. Edmund had cajoled Sally into giving him the supper dance after pushing Clare onto Lord Denzil. Now the two played least in sight, leaving her to suffer alone with this man.

The rogue stood too close, his presence in black evening clothes like hovering storm clouds. Clare prayed to find Aunt Morrow or Edmund before the storm broke.

Denzil bent toward Clare, his touch on her back too much like a caress. "Edmund said he would meet us by the doorway to the supper room with Miss Scott if we became separated," he said. "If I'm fortunate, we won't find them, and I'll have you all to myself."

Frowning repressively, Clare tried to step away from the lure of his hand, all but stroking her through the thin silk bodice. The press of the crowd made escape impossible. Trapped in the throng with a seducer, she felt invisible by association with the rogue.

It was just as well Father hadn't felt up to attending the ball, though the bilious attacks that had made him miss most of the Season's events were particularly worrisome. Thinking of her father's certain disapproval of this man's reputation, Clare answered his sally sharply. "Aunt Morrow wouldn't like to find me sitting alone with a gentleman other than Edmund, my lord."

"Particularly not me," he returned at once, grinning.

So he knew he wasn't wanted here. How could he wear so artless an expression if he knew the entire company would prefer to see the back of him? Chancing another look at Lord Denzil, Clare found him staring past her, into the company that rejected him. Once again his gaze was wary, though his lips smiled faintly.

For a moment, she was sorry she had railed against him, even mentally. To give the devil his due, Lord Denzil Knox hadn't performed an outrageous deed since arriving at the ball, beyond over-warm flirtation. Instead of showing the least offense at the *ton*'s uncivil reception, he had acted as if their behavior toward him were most gratifying. A pinprick of admiration for the man's insouciance afflicted Clare.

Grudgingly, she said, "You've acquitted yourself well tonight, my lord."

"Plantation life allows little dancing, but now and again I attend Government House balls in Georgetown," he answered blandly, his gaze warming her face like flames.

"One would never realize you hadn't attended a London ball in years from your dancing," she said shortly. "Though you must know I don't refer to that." Lord Denzil danced as naturally as most men walked. If he hadn't been treated like a leper since he arrived, she would give him a set-down.

His tone dropped to velvet insinuation, stroking her ears as if he touched them. "Words between a man and a beautiful woman rarely say what they seem to, in any case."

Stifling a gasp, Clare glanced about to see if anyone had overheard. Although the word *beautiful* was bruited about too casually to have meaning, no gentleman had ever called her a woman instead of a lady. And Lord Denzil didn't say it in the way one mentioned a serving-woman.

*   *   *

Lord Denzil took Clare gently but firmly by the elbow as they gained two steps toward the supper room. He had forgotten the stifled crush of *ton*ish flocks. Above three hundred guests pushing through one narrow doorway was like a bucket's contents pouring into a small-necked bottle.

Clare tensed, tugged against his hand, then seemed to accept that he wouldn't let go. A cit's daughter would simply turn and box his ears. Pursuing a lady had its advantages. Denzil smiled without showing comprehension as she glowered up at him.

"Tell me how you occupy your days," he urged politely. "Dresses and balls can't require all your attention."

"We're supposed to be watching out for Aunt Morrow or Edmund," she said crossly. "Shuffling along in a crowd is hardly the way to carry on personal conversations."

"No reason we can't look and talk, too," he replied, standing still closer. "Besides, I doubt you'll speak with me alone, so I must seize every opportunity to become acquainted, as Edmund wishes."

"That hardly gives you leave to seize my arm as well," she said in arctic tones.

Lady Clare had the knack of looking down her lovely nose at him even though he stood nearly a head taller. Close as he pressed in the crowd, he found her outraged eyes held green depths behind the golden glints, like an English meadow strewn with spring's primroses.

Flowers teased his nose as well as his thoughts. Leaning into sweet proximity, Denzil asked, "Do you keep a stillroom, preserving petals to scent your clothing and person?"

Lady Clare flashed him a look surely meant to depress pretension. "My person isn't a subject for discussion, sir."

"Then choose one that is," Denzil said readily, appreciating the slight rise and fall of her rounded bosom against the fitted bodice. He wasn't particularly keen on this fashion that hid women's waists, but the gown's top offered undoubted compensations.

"Do you wish to discuss stillrooms?" she asked coldly.

If he could set her talking, the lady might unbend. Dancing's distance never permitted a man to thaw a lady like a comfortable prose. Brushing her golden-brown hair with his nose, Denzil murmured into it, "The air closest to you smells just like a decoction of lemons and lavender my mother made as a rinse for her hair. It is lavender, isn't it?" If he pulled her against his chest, the top of her head would fit neatly under his chin. Until she scratched his eyes out.

"The receipt is Aunt Morrow's," she said with a nod. Turning to him with a softer expression, Lady Clare said, "You can't have seen your mother in quite some time, I suppose."

Denzil let go of her elbow and erected a wall against sentiment. "Mother died four years since. She was gone before my packet reached the West India docks." And damn the old man's eyes for not sending him word to come home.

"I know how it is to lose one's mother. I'm so very sorry," Clare murmured in a sympathetic tone that made Denzil too aware of a hollow space in his chest.

"Thank you," he said briefly, not wanting pity. "That's behind me, where the past should stay. Tell me about your stillroom."

"It isn't at all remarkable," she said quietly, her close scrutiny seeming to search for a door leading inside him. "Just a plain room with a deal table and a stone floor, with shelves up one wall for my pots and baskets. I gather flowers and herbs on our estate in Wiltshire, including those my father blends with his wines."

"How appropriate, given your name," he said, thinking of clary's heart-shaped leaves and its use to flavor wines. Her delicately tinted face was faintly heart-shaped.

"Recall that clary is used to draw thorns from one's flesh as well, my lord. But I assume you're far more familiar with the herb's use in wine." The amused look she gave him indicated Lady Clare didn't lack wit.

"I've learned a bit about blending wine in Guiana, as illicit casks surface through pirateers now and again." He shouldn't have mentioned those contacts; never knew who listened. "Do you help your father blend, bottle, and bin?"

"More, just lately, since he's been ill, than he would tolerate before," Clare said. Her voice rose, as if the subject distressed her. Her eyes showed suspicious moisture.

"You must remind me to tell you about Barbados one day," Denzil said provocatively, to buck her up. "Between the troops and the tars, more rum, wine, and ale are consumed there than in any other place in the world. A sailor can swap a cask of green wine to bed a landlord's daughter for a week."

Flushing, she faced forward. "No doubt you mean to shock me, to uphold your dreadful reputation." Raising a gloved hand, she waved to Edmund and Sally, who stood to one side of the supper room door, arm in arm.

In a tone of reproof, she continued, "But Edmund thinks well of you, and I shan't believe he would choose a person as a friend whom he can't trust to observe the proprieties with his cousin."

"A lady's misconceptions of friendship can be her undoing," Denzil murmured against Clare's pink ear. "Never say I didn't warn you from the start." He meant to fight fair with the lady. This was an engagement he must win, but he didn't mean anyone to lose by his victory.

Color spread to Clare's cheek and throat as she answered the shot he had fired across her bow. "You're an incorrigible flirt, sir."

"Did you wave to Edmund just now?" he asked innocently, caressing her elbow through the transparent silk sleeve. "What a lovely young lady stands with him."

"That's Sally Scott," Clare replied breathlessly, resisting his hold. "She's a close friend to both my cousin and me. Edmund would rather stand up with her once than dance with me all night, for they move as surely together as a person with his shadow."

He must hurry; soon they would reach the other couple. "How well they look together, with the same fair curls," Denzil observed.

"Yes, indeed," Clare agreed in distraction, wrenching her arm free. "Edmund probably wishes he could wed the both of us, for he enjoys Sally's company quite as much as mine."

No female who loved a man with passion could speak that jest easily. Denzil smiled upon Edmund and Sally, wishing them a long and happy life together.

*   *   *

The mob inching into the supper room halted again, just when Clare thought to join her friends shortly. An hour for supper, safe in company with Edmund and Sally, and then she could escape this dangerous, infuriating man.

Just as he dressed in black and white, Lord Denzil seemed a puzzling mixture of midday and midnight. A sunny expression reassured her that Lord Denzil was the best of good fellows, Edmund's old friend. But at times shadows lurked in his eyes and the corners of his lips tightened with the effort to hold a carefree smile in place.

Lord Denzil's heedless air and suppressed restlessness, his personal liberties and forthright speech bordering on impropriety repelled and yet drew her to him. Clare recalled feeling much the same way when she and her cousin found an injured hawk while riding round the estate. If she dared reach out to aid Lord Denzil's reentry into society, her reputation would be slashed to ribbons by his.

Pushing the last inches to Edmund's side with a sense of saving herself from drowning, Clare greeted Sally warmly. Edmund presented Lord Denzil to Miss Scott and she stammered out a reply, pink-faced.

Clare smiled encouragement when Sally sent a sidelong look of appeal her way. Despite his facile flirtation, she would encourage Lord Denzil's acceptance by her friends. She couldn't say why she did so.

As the foursome turned to enter the supper room, Lady Nelle and Sir Richard Scott confronted them. Grasping his daughter's arm, Sir Richard said stiffly to Edmund, "You'll forgive us, but we can't stay to supper. Sally must forego the pleasure of your company this evening." Nodding abruptly to Clare, Sir Richard turned, carefully imposing his body between his ladies and the rogue.

Not once had he looked in Lord Denzil's direction, Clare thought with a spurt of anger. Sally turned in her father's grip to give them all a tentative wave, and Clare liked her the better for it.

When she looked quickly at Lord Denzil, Clare found his eyes shuttered like a seaside cottage in a storm. Though he still smiled genially, he had retreated within himself.

Lord Denzil bowed to Clare with mocking correctness, then spoke across her to Edmund, extending a hand. "You'll forgive me, old man, but I must go as well. I won't deprive you of your supper partner after all, though I thank the both of you for the dance and your company."

Indignation growing, she noticed guests giving them a wide berth as they entered the supper room. Society's civilized behavior provoked her; Lord Denzil must feel more exiled in this ballroom than in Guiana's heathen tropics.

Clare felt equally vexed with Lord Denzil for forcing himself upon her conscience, even though he hadn't asked for her help. Edmund had done the asking. But Lord Denzil had acted as if all were well since he arrived, facing down the lot of them. Now he was giving up on the threshold of the supper room, where his capitulation was most obvious.

Forming a resolution, Clare laid one hand on Edmund's arm, the other on Lord Denzil's. "You each promised at one time or another to partner me at supper tonight," she said in a gay voice, breathless with conflicting emotions. "I shan't give up the advantage of being squired by two gallants. Whatever engagement you just recalled will have to wait, my lord," she informed Denzil.

Tense muscle bunched under her fingers through his sleeve. Speaking low, she added fiercely, "You mustn't run away from a set of stuffy prigs, when you've comported yourself much better than they."

"When a lady feels at liberty to issue incontrovertible orders to a man, she must use a more familiar address than 'my lord'," Denzil said, his voice intimate as nightfall.

Laughter had dispelled the distance from his eyes, loosening the tightness in her chest. Lord Denzil's expression was openly admiring. He dropped his other hand over hers, trapping it against the solid warmth of his arm.

Clare heard a door slam upon her reputation as the three of them advanced into the noisy supper room. Heaven only knew what Father would have to say about her behavior tonight.

Arriving home with Aunt Morrow in the damp chill before dawn, Clare was out of the carriage and up the shallow steps before she noticed that the door's knocker was muffled. Father must have taken a turn for the worse while they were out. Clare's heart clenched like a fist.

Rushing into the hallway as the porter opened the door, Clare felt the changed silence in the town house at once. Normally the servants would have retired at that hour, except for those who saw them in and to bed after routs. This wasn't the comfortable quiet of a sleeping household.

"Where's Hinton?" Aunt Morrow asked, loosening her wrap.

A stair creaked and Clare looked up as the butler descended slowly, chin on chest. Chilled, she didn't want to know what made Hinton's shoulders sag and his eyes red.

"Father?" She could ask nothing more specific.

"Gone, Miss Clary," Hinton said in broken syllables.

Three simple words made the familiar entrance hall a foreign land. The same words had announced her father's departure on endless travels in the past. This time, no homecoming was possible.

A vibration hummed in Clare's ears like that of a tuning fork, and every nerve in her body echoed it. She hadn't truly believed Dr. McKerlie when he said Father could die suddenly or live for years, depending on the care he took for himself.

But tonight Father had died alone, while Clare consorted with a man he wouldn't have permitted to cross his threshold.

3

As the carriage lurched into another rut, Clare kneaded the back of her neck. Well sprung as Father's coach was, it jounced over the turnpike's gouged surface like a hay wagon crossing a field of rocks.

Only the drag wasn't Father's now, Clare brooded. As it carried the Deramore crest, Uncle Arthur must own it. Reminded of her own inheritance, she swallowed tears. No bequest offset a parent's loss, and Father had warned her repeatedly of risks to an heiress. She rubbed her neck again.

"We'll take turns with the liniment tonight, after being tossed about this coach like shuttlecocks," Aunt Morrow said.

Making an effort to smile, Clare said, "I can use half the bottle myself, though prosing about negligible pain at this time shows a lamentable want of delicacy."

"Fussing over small hurts is as good a way as any to nurse wounds you can't reach," Aunt Morrow observed, patting Clare's hand. "Your father has only been dead a week; you must expect lowered spirits for a time."

"Perhaps returning home will help," Clare said, feeling she could never be happy again. "I couldn't bear the noise and bustle of London; it's too full of life."

"We aren't precisely going home," said Aunt Morrow, looking at Clare anxiously. "You agreed that we wouldn't return to Linwood Hall. Since your father arranged for us to have the use of the dower house, I still feel it's best to go there directly. Your aunt Deramore won't want us underfoot while she establishes herself as mistress at the Hall."

Choking on tears, Clare brushed uselessly at the dust which lay like powder on their black carriage dresses. Like the dust, Father's loss overlaid her whole being. Nothing would ever again be the same. She wasn't truly traveling home, not home to the structure where she had been born, where she had awaited Father while he searched out rare vintages.

"It doesn't signify," Clare said. She didn't care where she laid her boxes or head. "Whatever Father intended is what I want to do. At Linwood Hall, I would just meet a dozen reminders of him each hour."

"A dozen!" Aunt Morrow exclaimed as dust motes swam in the air between them. "Honoring the dead is all very well, my dear, but you were fortunate to see Deramore at dinner when he was home, which was precious little. Don't paint your father different than he was, or you'll never recover from his death."

Looking out the glass in the door on her side to hide threatening tears, Clare caught sight of Edmund riding beside the coach. Dear, familiar Edmund had volunteered to see them safely into the country.

Clare fumbled in her reticule and found a black-bordered handkerchief. Scrubbing scalding teardrops from her cheeks, she rubbed in grit, welcoming the small irritation. It distracted her from feeling fully the greater pain of loss.

"Cloud up and rain when you feel the need," Aunt Morrow said in a more kindly tone. "But the sooner you remember your father for what he was instead of what you wanted him to be, the sooner you'll find peace of mind." Leaning over the cushioned seat, she enfolded Clare in a comforting embrace.

Clare hugged her aunt in return and sobbed, without its doing anything to diminish her sorrow. Though he never said it, Father had loved her. He *had*!

Feeling her orphaned state keenly, she clung to her aunt's astringent kindness. She needed Aunt Morrow's capable hands on her back, caressing and patting as they had through most of her childhood. Aunt Morrow didn't mean to distress her. She simply called a spade a spade, while Clare dreamed up terms of more delicacy.

Sitting up, Clare kissed Aunt Morrow, setting both their crepe-covered hats further awry. She mopped wet cheeks, fiercely glad for every hot tear that expressed intense grief for her father. She must never let go of his memory.

A particularly rough bump nearly knocked her chip hat against the roof, putting her in mind of life's blows. If Mama had lived, they would have formed a loving family. Father had done his best by keeping Aunt Morrow with her after Mama died. Her cousin Edmund had lived on the next estate with her uncle and aunt.

Clare had no excuse ever to have felt alone. Yet now that Father was gone, the person whose company she had most desired was forever beyond reach.

Sighing, Clare glanced through the dusty glass. The eighteen-mile stone they passed stood beyond the last house in Colnbrook, near a stream. As the road widened out again, a second horseman appeared between the vehicle and Edmund. Father would have frowned upon her traveling in company with a rogue. She jerked her head away.

"I don't know why Lord Denzil insisted on coming," she said, irritation crowding out grief. "We have quite enough outriders without him."

Peering past Clare at the men riding alongside, Aunt Morrow replied, "Better to have an extra guard than not enough, particularly on certain stretches of this road. Hounslow Heath is notorious for attacks on travelers, even in daylight, if they're inadequately guarded."

"We're well past Hounslow; he could turn back," Clare said. "Edmund can take care of me, just as Father arranged."

"Edmund couldn't take care of himself, unless his coat were in danger," Aunt Morrow said derisively. "We still have the Maidenhead Thicket to pass through. Little as I approve Lord Denzil as a proper acquaintance for you, I feel safer at inns with more than one gentleman lying near us."

Clare resented the animadversion against Edmund, whom Father himself had chosen for her to wed. Though expecting Lord Denzil to protect ladies was like setting hounds to guard hares, she resented strictures against the rogue too.

"Then you consider Lord Denzil a gentleman." Clare felt argumentative where she normally accepted Aunt Morrow's lead. "The way you spoke of him at Lady Saulton's ball, I thought your opinion was less salutary."

"Lord Denzil's father deserves the term 'gentleman' more truly than any man I've met," said Aunt Morrow flatly. "His son's actions no doubt grieve Lord Guilford, for the boy's breeding calls for better behavior. Not every gentleman lives up to the quality of his bloodlines, my dear."

Much as she respected Aunt Morrow's views and resented Lord Denzil's company on this journey, Clare heard herself speak on the rogue's behalf. "I don't mean to set up my opinion against your judgment," she said quickly, "but Lord Denzil acquitted himself in a more gentlemanly fashion at the ball than those who made him less than welcome."

"Even as a stripling, Lord Denzil behaved better in public than in private," her aunt said repressively.

"I daresay his father may have sown wild oats himself in his youth," Clare protested, another thought teasing her mind. "I don't recall meeting Lord Guilford during either of my Seasons. How do you come to know him?"

Aunt Morrow rubbed dust away from the glass on her side of the coach with a handkerchief as she decried the state of the roads. "I mislike the looks of those clouds. We could be caught in a downpour any moment, turning this dust into treacle under the wheels."

Distracted, Clare leaned forward to assess the sky from her side of the carriage and met Lord Denzil's knowing blue eyes. He bowed in the saddle, tipping his beaver to her as elaborately as though they rode in Hyde Park. The man was incorrigible, she thought, settling hastily against the squabs. Lord Denzil was as ready to flirt with a lady in mourning as at a ball. He had no sense of propriety, and she regretted that she had defended him to her aunt.

Looking through the glass on her aunt's side instead, Clare heard the first plops as fat drops struck the roof of the coach. A few uneven splats smote the carriage like a skirmish of sticks across a side drum. The rain's pace picked up until it drummed a continuous roll on the coach's varnished roof.

Glancing furtively past her chip hat's brim, Clare saw raindrops lift small dust puffs off the road as they struck. Lord Denzil urged his mount toward the postilions, and she saw with satisfaction that wet splotches marked the broad back of his dark riding coat. He moved easily in the saddle, and she shifted on the cushion, vaguely uneasy in any position she took.

The carriage slowed, jolting across ruts toward the grass verge. "Why are we stopping?" Clare cried.

"I should think the gentlemen wish to ride inside now," Aunt Morrow said in a tone of reason.

"No, indeed!" Clare said in dread. "I didn't want Lord Denzil to accompany us in the first place, and it serves him well to suffer a wetting."

"What about Edmund?" Aunt Morrow asked, giving her a searching look. "You can't think your cousin will allow his coat to be ruined."

As the coach halted, rocking on its curved springs, Clare made no response. Knowing she had sounded ungracious, she still needed to avoid Lord Denzil's company. The rogue stirred totally contradictory sentiments within her, beyond comprehension. Certainly she had found him an entertaining companion at supper during Lady Saulton's ball. His exotic stories about exploring Spanish America's interior had fascinated even Aunt Morrow.

And while she marveled at Lord Denzil's tales, Father had died alone. She stared at her black-gloved hands, wrestling in her lap, until tears blurred the view. Surely she wasn't so unreasonable as to hold Lord Denzil responsible for her choice to go out that evening.

Scolding herself sternly, Clare determined to show Lord Denzil every civil observance, just as Edmund wished. Father had chosen Edmund himself, and he would expect her to accept friends of the man he deemed a suitable husband.

The door opened beside her and Lord Denzil politely urged Edmund into the coach ahead of himself. With rain already marking his superfine riding coat, Edmund didn't hang back. The coach rocked as first Edmund and then Lord Denzil climbed in and dropped onto the forward seat with their backs to the horses.

Clare thought how spacious the coach had been moments before. Now her knees nearly touched those of the rogue sitting opposite, and no air was left for her lungs.

With the first raindrops, Clare had smelled moisture stirring hot dust. Now she caught a whiff of horse and damp wool, mingled with the bay rum scent Lord Denzil wore. Edmund used fashionable eau de Cologne, a civilized choice.

"How snug it is inside," Lord Denzil said, baring

white teeth in a predatory grin. As he leaned forward to pull his coattails from beneath him, his knees bumped Clare's. She hitched herself back instantly.

"Perhaps too snug for a lady's ease," he observed, his mocking gaze on Clare's face. "I'll give you more space." Setting a knee on either side of hers, Lord Denzil spread his limbs, tight leathers threatening to split.

Dragging her gaze away sternly, Clare felt heat climb above the standing collar of her black carriage dress. She didn't mean to appear the fast sort of female who noticed a man's form, no matter what the provocation.

The rear of the coach careened from side to side, likely sliding over a muddy patch. Lord Denzil's limbs stopped hers as Clare pitched left, then right. The contact felt as if she had slammed between gateposts.

Chagrined, Clare didn't dare look above her gripped gloves. No gentleman would sprawl in his seat wearing leathers fitted like a second skin.

Dipping her black chip hat brim, Clare glanced quickly at Aunt Morrow. From her aunt's usual reserved expression in male company, she saw nothing amiss in Lord Denzil's dress or posture. Clare gripped her hands tighter. Perhaps she was guilty of improper thoughts and should censure herself instead of the rogue.

Rain sluiced down the windows for the next half hour while the coach crawled and slid along the Bath Road. Curtains of water isolated the four within the bobbing compartment, and she thought the humid air heated noticeably. Few remarks passed among the coach's occupants, and most of those upon the weather. Clare began to feel as if she were locked in an airless cupboard.

As the carriage slithered sideways again, she held herself rigid by a hand flat on the seat at either side. Clare both dreaded and hoped that the roads would force them to take refuge at the next inn. Finishing this journey quickly meant ridding herself of the man opposite, but escaping too-close quarters appeared more desirable at this moment.

Once she and Lady Morrow reached the Deramore estate, Edmund would return to London to help complete the transfer of property to Uncle Arthur, with himself as heir. And he would take his pesky friend with him.

Lord Denzil shifted restlessly on the seat opposite and Clare held her breath. *I won't look*, she assured herself. Every muscular movement against the form-following leathers came to her ears.

"Let's do something to pass the time," Lord Denzil said restively. "Shall we sing rounds? I know several sea shanties—no, I suppose they won't do in mixed company."

"Might appear deuced odd, old thing," Edmund murmured in an embarrassed tone. "Here we are, hung about with crepe, I mean. Not the done thing to sing your way home when you've just suffered a bereavement."

Edmund cared for her feelings, Clare thought gratefully. And married to her cousin, she would one day return to Linwood Hall as mistress. Following Father's wishes was indeed the sensible course of action.

Inclining his head at her aunt, Lord Denzil said, "I beg your pardon and understanding, my lady. No offense was meant. Sitting in one place for more than a few minutes at a time simply doesn't suit my nature or body."

Aunt Morrow inclined her head in return, but Clare's pent-up emotions erupted. "You might address yourself to me as well, since my loss is the greater," she snapped. "I find your heedless suggestion most repugnant."

Leaning forward, Lord Denzil took her balled hands between his. Looking into her eyes as if reading fine print, he said, "You're first in my thoughts, if not in proper address. Your loss is indeed grievous. I can't show you the half of my sentiments."

"Jolly well said," Edmund cried. "I couldn't have made a prettier speech myself. Clare knows you don't mean any harm by a natural need for distraction. Spin us more tales of your explorations, Den. Tell the ladies about the forty-foot Cayman crocodilian."

"A difficult feat, when the largest I encountered was only twenty feet long," Lord Denzil replied. Giving Clare a coaxing smile, he said, "Would tales distract you, or do you prefer to be quiet with your sad thoughts?"

Succeeding at last in efforts to free her hands, Clare said distantly, "It's all one to me. Do just as you please." Immediately she turned to the glass, as if sheets of water coursing down it entertained her more than the company. Father would have warned her away from a man of such ready charm, with a reprobate's reputation.

Little more than patterns of color were visible as the rain's rivulets distorted the view. Were Lord Denzil not here to think it silly, she could draw pictures in the fog on the glass to pass the time.

While Lord Denzil described the manufacture of the deadly curare, which he had been permitted to witness, Clare entertained poisonous thoughts. Gradually rivulets ran more slowly down the glass, and she began to make out features of the roadside as the rain let up. Perhaps restlessness would return Lord Denzil to his mount soon. She was stiff as a poker from avoiding contact with his dangerously close limbs, and her neck ached from looking left.

At Maidenhead they stopped at the Orkney Arms to change horses worn down by the road's heavy going. Within minutes they rattled over the wide Noble Bridge spanning the Thames. The coach's pitch and sway increased as it gathered speed.

The patter of light rain gradually lulled Clare while the others conversed, though she didn't sleep. Sounds of the post horses answering others roused her from a brown study.

Then shots exploded nearby.

Clare started and immediately found Lord Denzil's steadying hand on hers. He stared at the fogged glass beside them, alert as he sat forward.

Edmund fumbled a case of overcoat pistols open.

Lord Denzil murmured softly to him, "Let me at them first. Be ready to back me up if need be."

Heart kicking her ribs while she shrank against the squabs, Clare watched her door fearfully as the coach dipped and jerked to an abrupt halt.

Rough voices sounded outside. Clare expected the words "Stand and deliver!" but heard only threats against the outriders. Vague shapes of men on horseback moved beyond the fogged glass, and Clare's stomach lurched like a boat in a high sea.

"Only three of them," Lord Denzil murmured to Edmund, whose eyes were as big as Clare's felt. Lady Morrow helped herself to the second Clark pistol in

Edmund's open case and sat quietly erect on the edge of her seat.

Outside, a harsh voice ordered, "Throw down your arms and come off the boot." The coach dipped and Clare didn't fault the guards for obeying. She could dimly make out two liveried forms stepping away from the carriage. At least no one had been shot as yet.

The hoarse voice grated, "Postilions, see only your animals, or your brains will mix with mud."

Breath light and shallow, Clare determined that she wouldn't give up her dearest keepsake to highwaymen. Stripping off her left glove, she worked an amber ring off her little finger. It wasn't a costly bauble, but Father had brought it home from a journey when she was no more than eight. She had worn it since, moving it to her smallest finger as she grew.

Clare slipped the ring free and stuffed it deep into the corner, topping it with a Morocco sleeping cushion. The thieves could take the gold signet she wore on her right hand and the few coins she carried in her reticule. Looking up, she found Lord Denzil grinning at her, eyes wicked.

"No faith in me as protector?" he murmured.

Clare felt an insane impulse to laugh but feared that once begun, she couldn't stop. The rogue relished the danger, she recognized with shock.

The harsh voice spoke from just outside her door. "We'll have her out now." Clare jerked her head toward the sound, then drew back involuntarily. She felt Aunt Morrow close behind her.

As the door was wrenched open, a huge form filled the lower part, face hidden behind a low slouch hat and a high choker like the post boys wore. Before Clare could vent the scream swelling her lungs, Aunt Morrow clutched her arm painfully.

Lord Denzil thrust forward at the same time the door swung out, planting his booted foot squarely in the face of the intruder. Without pause, he dived head first out the door onto the cursing thief. Agonized, Clare expected further shots to mark the rogue's end. She lunged toward the door.

A rough push from behind pinned Clare against the side of the coach. Above her, she glimpsed her aunt aiming Edmund's pistol through the doorway. Aunt Morrow leaned on her hard as Edmund protested in the background.

Through the open door, Clare saw Lord Denzil man-handle the highwayman, keeping the thief between himself and the two mounted hedgepads holding pistols on the servants and postilions. Following instantly on the snap of flint and the spit of priming, a shot exploded above Clare's head. Gasping in disbelief, she smelled burnt powder and knew Aunt Morrow had fired.

An unreal spectacle unfolded outside as Clare watched in horror. A horse screamed and bolted as the hedgepad astride it clapped his hand to one shoulder. The other miscreant's mount reared repeatedly, and he dropped his weapon to keep his seat.

"Give me that!" Aunt Morrow ordered Edmund imperiously. No longer trusting her eyes, Clare saw her dainty aunt drop a smoking pocket pistol on the seat and seize the other from her astonished cousin. Aunt Morrow lunged to the coach's swinging door again as the coach swayed.

Discharging the second weapon wasn't necessary,

for Clare saw only the flapping greatcoats of the mounted hedgepads as they fled the scene. Lord Denzil straddled the harsh-voiced thief, who lay on his back in the mud. Though the man outweighed him, Lord Denzil milled him down.

Then the hedgepad seized a sizeable stone from the road, clearly meaning to crack Lord Denzil's skull.

"No!" Clare screamed, surging up so violently that she shoved Aunt Morrow onto the opposite seat. "Denzil, no!" Launching herself out the open door, Clare fell heavily upon the struggling men.

Landing forcefully, Clare knocked the breath out of her body. For an interminable time, she could think only of the effort to suck air into her lungs again, though she was dimly aware of being thrust roughly aside.

When she had given up hope of breathing again, Clare finally rasped a painful breath into aching lungs. Fine rain misting her face, she made out ridged grey clouds. She lay on her back in mud, her chip hat loose. Above her, Edmund hung out the carriage door with his pistol in hand, while Aunt Morrow beat at him uselessly, ordering him out of her way.

Someone else should be there, addled wits told Clare. Denzil! She tried to sit up, slipping in the viscous mud.

Firm hands on her shoulders eased Clare into a sitting position, and Lord Denzil's face hovered close. "Can you speak?" he asked urgently. "Where do you hurt? If the blackguard harmed you, I'll burn the damned thicket to flush him out!"

"Did he get away?" Clare asked, looking about in a daze.

"Of course he got away, with you flying out of the

coach like a silly squirrel onto my head," Lord Denzil said roughly, clutching her to his muddy chest.

This was far better than Aunt Morrow's hugs, Clare thought weakly. She oozed against Lord Denzil, feeling more fluid than the mud they sat in.

"As she's dressed in black, you'd have to say Clare looked more like a bat as she leapt," Edmund protested.

Clare yanked herself free of Lord Denzil's arms, dying of mortification. "Let me up," she ordered, feeling like a prize pig in a wallow. "You ungrateful wretch, that horrid man was about to brain you with a huge stone. No doubt you would be thanking me if I had allowed him to murder you."

Standing and stretching a muddy hand down to her, Lord Denzil said with an unholy twinkle, "I expect you'd snub my ghost as readily as you do me." Severely, he added, "I fight my own battles. I don't advocate ladies leaping into the fray, or letting off pistols, come to that." Pulling Clare clear of the mud, he set her on her feet.

Then he made Lady Morrow an excessively elegant leg. "But I offer you my compliments on your aim, my lady."

"You might fix in mind that I can protect myself and my niece," Aunt Morrow said grimly, color high in her cheeks.

Lord Denzil lifted Clare into the drag as if she weighed no more than a foot warmer. His hands felt enormous on her waist, Clare thought, collapsing beside her aunt.

"You shot a highwayman," Clare said to Aunt Morrow in wonder, recalling the scramble inside the coach as Lord Denzil jumped the thief who opened its door.

Clasping Clare despite the mud, Aunt Morrow said fiercely, "We practice with pistols in order to be capable of self-protection. I would have shot all three, rather than risk harm to my girl."

"You could hardly do that, with only two pistols in my set of Clarks," Edmund protested. "And next time, give me first shot with my own weapons, if you please."

"I trust my marksmanship over a Bond Street beau's," Aunt Morrow said with a sniff.

When the servants had the coach ready to move forward again, Lord Denzil joined them. Frowning over the thieves' pistols, which he had picked up outside, he said, "This weapon is ordinary enough. But this silver-sheathed beauty was engraved by Parker of London, I'd wager. Stolen from a gentleman, no doubt." He directed Edmund to reload his fired pistol and the weapons dropped by the hedgepads at once.

"Perhaps we've seen the last of the swine, but I prefer to be beforehand with trouble." Lord Denzil looked closely at Clare. "I wouldn't have the two of you exposed to rough creatures, but it was a rare treat to see two intrepid ladies take on three bridle culls."

In Aunt Morrow's arms, Clare wondered that her aunt shivered now that danger had passed. Even her voice quavered as she said against Clare's hair, "Unlikely as it seems, one of those horrid voices sounded oddly familiar."

4

Standing on a chair to reach the corniced bookcase's top shelf, Clare studied the titles before her. Sighing, she decided that novels like *God's Revenge Against the Sinne of Murder* would give her a fit of the gapes, if not the mopes. After three months in Wiltshire, she relied on occupation to keep occasional fits of the dismals at bay.

The sound of the morning room door swinging open was followed by a gasp. Seeing Aunt Morrow's raised brows, Clare quickly stepped down while the footman disposed of the tray.

As soon as the door shut behind the servant, Aunt Morrow asked, "What's that under your skirts?"

"Just underclothing," Clare said evasively, going to the tea tray. "Will you pour, or shall I?"

"Not the usual sort of underclothing," Aunt Morrow

refuted, following her. "Standing on chairs, you display more than ankles, young lady. You're wearing pantaloons."

As her aunt seated herself upon a chintz-covered chair beside the japanned tray, Clare coaxed, "You're far too fashionable to object to pantaloons. Ladies of the first consequence wear them, even Princess Caroline."

Pouring hot water over tea leaves in the blue and white willowware pot, Aunt Morrow said, "I hope you won't pattern yourself after the Royals. As in every era, we must set an example for royalty, not be guided by it."

Clare raised tucked black skirts. "But I'm wearing a petticoat as well," she cajoled.

Lips quivering upward, Aunt Morrow waved her niece to a seat across from her at the tripod pedestal table set in the bow window. "If you mean to climb on chairs and hold up your dress like a hoyden, you may actually require such an unladylike garment. But they're said to be harmful to health, Clare. I don't forbid you anything on a whim, you will allow."

Sitting down in a swirl of black skirts, Clare said, feeling petulant, "If you're truly concerned about my health failing under a trifle of lawn and lace, I won't wear them."

"A lady of breeding never permits herself to become the subject of gossip," said Aunt Morrow reprovingly, putting a lump of sugar in a cup and pouring in tea.

"No one will remark my pantaloons in the country," Clare wheedled. "No one sees me, as little as we go about."

"You may be certain that the footman who just left has reported what he observed to half the household," Aunt Morrow said. "In ten minutes, the servants at the

Hall will know. Within half an hour, word will have reached the village that you wear this *fast* style. What will the vicar say?"

"I should hope he doesn't discuss ladies' underclothing," Clare said, playing prim as she removed her gloves and tucked them under her sash.

"Indeed!" said Aunt Morrow, laughing. "All the more reason not to tempt him to it." She handed Clare biscuits before pouring out her tea.

They sipped companionably, comfortable without conversation. A warm breeze brought the scent of newly scythed grass through open windows. Clare's spirits lifted along with the green lutestring curtains. Sorrow rarely struck her in company.

When Clare handed across her cup for more tea, Aunt Morrow said, "I very nearly forgot to tell you the news I learned when I rode over to Linwood Hall earlier. Lady Deramore had a letter from Edmund this morning. He's coming home on a repairing lease next week."

Jumping up to hug her aunt from behind, Clare said, "That should buck us up! Not that I mean to disparage your companionship, for we go on like two sisters. But you must admit that three months without any diversion but the quietest sort is enough to send anyone into a decline."

"I don't flatter myself that I offer adequate diversion for a young lady of spirit. Edmund will fetch you fashionable books and gossip." Aunt Morrow added in a disapproving tone, "Your aunt Deramore says he brings his great friend as well."

Glad she stood behind her aunt, Clare straightened and stared out at the cottage garden's riotous colors.

Her feelings were more mixed than the variety of blooms. Affecting disinterest, she asked, "Whom do you mean?"

"Lord Denzil Knox, to be sure," Aunt Morrow said, turning to stare at Clare. "The two are all but inseparable, from my friends' letters. Have you not heard the same?"

"Sally writes that she sees the two of them about Town," Clare said offhandedly, while her pulse fluttered like a duck's wings after a dip in a pond. "Lord Denzil doesn't attend *ton* parties, however, or at least not those of the first stare, so she writes mainly of Edmund."

"No doubt she keeps the other young ladies at bay for you by giving Edmund the pleasure of her company," Aunt Morrow observed with a faint lift of her brows.

"Sally and Edmund don't miss me as much when they see each other," Clare said, thinking of Lord Denzil's imminent presence in Wiltshire, within walking distance. Telling herself it mattered not one whit whether he came or stayed away, Clare resumed her seat. Picking up her cooling cup, she asked, "Does Edmund say which day they arrive?"

"He gave no certain information on that head," replied Aunt Morrow. "We shall expect them when we see them coming, if Edmund goes by his usual form."

Clare stood once more, stepping to the window, where trellised roses nodded in at her. "I wonder how we'll entertain gentlemen in the summer, and in mourning."

"Entertaining them will be Lady Deramore's duty, I'm excessively happy to say." After a brief pause, Aunt

Morrow continued, "I prefer that you spend as little time in Lord Denzil's company as is civil, my dear."

"I feel no desire to be with him," Clare denied. Lord Denzil's blue eyes were far too bold, she recalled. His presence might even be termed disturbing.

"Edmund quarters himself upon us too often," continued Aunt Morrow, brow creased. "Perhaps I had best warn him to entertain Lord Denzil elsewhere for the most part."

From wishing to be spared Lord Denzil's company, Clare turned like a weather vane to the opposite view. "But Edmund won't understand such ungraciousness from us," she objected sharply. "He made our house his own when we occupied Linwood Hall. We can't suddenly deny him because a friend comes with him."

"You don't realize how unsuitable a person this friend is for you to know," Aunt Morrow replied, coming to stand by the window with Clare. "I hope you'll allow yourself to be guided by me in this instance."

"Most men sow wild oats; Edmund did so himself," Clare protested, unwilling to lose the diversion of frequent visits without good reason. "We can't send word to the door that we're Not at Home when we obviously have nowhere else to be."

"We should have talked before, my dear," said Aunt Morrow, linking an arm through Clare's. "Had your father's death not occurred the night you met Lord Denzil, I would have warned you off more particularly. Then Edmund took it upon himself to ask the rogue's company on the road." She sounded aggrieved. "Once we were here, the acquaintance should have died naturally. I didn't doubt the rascal would batten upon the first heiress he met after returning to London."

Wishing to refute her aunt's imputation, Clare recalled instead the gossip she had overheard at the mantua-maker's. Removing her arm from her aunt's, she yanked her gloves from her sash. "How did you form that opinion?" she challenged. "You taught me not to credit tattle."

Giving her a measuring look, Aunt Morrow replied, "Lord Denzil has been the subject of talk since he was a boy. You've seen him at his best, I will allow, for he can be utterly charming. But members of his own family say he lacks self-control. *On-dits* bear out the sad truth."

"No self-control?" Clare asked incredulously, her voice rising. "If that were true, Lord Denzil would have called out half the guests at Lady Saulton's ball." Looking down, she found the first fingers of her gloves tied together.

"Naturally you wish to defend your cousin's friend," Aunt Morrow said quietly, taking the knotted gloves. "Come sit down and attend to me. You may judge for yourself whether you wish to pursue Lord Denzil's acquaintance."

Reluctantly, Clare allowed herself to be led back to their chairs. She didn't want to hear what her aunt had to say, perhaps because, despite her unusually argumentative tone, she could never doubt her aunt's word.

Working at the knot Clare had made, Aunt Morrow began, "Lord Denzil was hardly breeched when he took his riding crop to a groom. Though he wasn't yet seven, he inflicted a slashing cut across the older boy's face that left a scar."

Clare clinched her hands in distress as her aunt continued. "Guilford then sent Denzil away to school, at an earlier age than his brothers. He hoped Eton's strict regimen would teach the boy more acceptable behavior."

Anguished on Lord Denzil's behalf, Clare wanted to excuse him, as if she had done the injury. "Perhaps he had a reason for striking out at the groom," she said, pleading. "He was hardly more than a toddler."

"Twenty isn't a toddler," Aunt Morrow replied tartly. "He was all of twenty when he took his whip to a fellow in the middle of a public road."

"But what were the circumstances?" Clare cried, uneasy at further evidence of unsteady character in the rogue.

"Lord Denzil was challenged by another youth in his wild set to race curricles from London to Brighton. They meant to best the Prince of Wales's time, as I recall the story. When Lord Denzil lost the race, he whipped his opponent soundly." As she finished the ugly tale, Aunt Morrow handed back Clare's gloves, unknotted and smoothed.

Clare slowly pulled them on, finger by finger. Like her thoughts, a bee bumbled awkwardly round a rose near the window without settling. Had anyone but Aunt Morrow told her these stories, she would denounce them at once. She didn't want to believe Lord Denzil capable of cruelty.

Yet she had sensed the man's pent-up energy, had recognized the air of danger he wore like scent. Edmund had told her, even before she met Lord Denzil, of a bashed head at Eton. She had seen the rogue smash a boot into a hedgepad's face and mill him to the ground. But that force was defensive, she argued with herself. Aunt Morrow was hardly cruel, and she had wounded a highwayman.

Thoughts twisting like a corkscrew, Clare felt the full horror of the tales yet couldn't make herself accept them completely. She must learn more about Lord Denzil for herself. As Edmund's future wife, she owed his friend an open mind, if a wary one.

Smoothing her gloves, Clare recalled feeling relief when Lord Denzil returned to London three months earlier. Even in death, Father had protected her from a fortune hunter, she had thought wryly as the men drove away from the dower house. With a year of mourning to observe, she had felt safe for the first time since meeting Lord Denzil.

Now the rogue was to return, and she felt as vulnerable as a newly hatched chick below a hawk on the wing. Becoming aware that Aunt Morrow watched her anxiously, Clare wondered how long she had sat mumchance.

"I beg you won't allow Lord Denzil to sit in your pocket," Aunt Morrow reiterated. "Edmund can entertain his company with the usual male pursuits; we need do no more than sit down to dinner with them at the Hall now and again."

Her aunt's urging to avoid the rogue made Clare feel oddly perverse. "I wouldn't like Edmund to feel I disapprove of his closest friend. He means Lord Denzil to be a frequent guest in our future home, so surely I must accustom myself to his company."

"You hold to the arrangement your father and Edmund's agreed between them?" Aunt Morrow asked neutrally.

Focusing on the vine-printed wallpaper, Clare fought back tears at the mention of her parent. "The time to object to Father's arrangements was when he told them to me. It's hardly honorable to draw back from plans he laid for my future when he's no longer here to discuss them."

"You were far too young to select dancing partners at the time, let alone to choose the man who would take responsibility for your life," Aunt Morrow said vehemently.

"I was turned sixteen," Clare said at once, defending her father's actions. "You were married at sixteen, Aunt." At once she knew her unruly tongue had strayed beyond the line.

Aunt Morrow sat perfectly still while her complexion paled to paper white. "Without my informed consent," she said at last, voice harsh. "It's because of that terrible marriage by arrangement that I urge you to think carefully before you enter into one. Marriage is a lifelong sentence, Clare. Even if you're strong enough to escape a tyrant's blows and control, law usually fetters you to him still."

Sinking onto the footstool before her aunt, Clare said apologetically, "But Edmund could never hurt a flea, Aunt Morrow. The cases aren't the same. I know you endured abuses from horrid Lord Morrow that plague you even now." Taking both her aunt's hands, she continued, "But marriage to my cousin wouldn't be like that. Edmund would never be unkind, let alone lift a hand to me."

Voice grating, Aunt Morrow said, "You don't know half the horrors, child, for I wouldn't even repeat them to a married lady. And the spirit can be injured as surely as the body. A man who lives with you learns your mind well enough to devise the most damaging mental as well as physical tortures that can be visited upon a woman."

Seeing the anger and fear in her aunt's face as she

looked back in time, Clare gripped Aunt Morrow's hands hard. She hadn't considered the courage required to escape a man who could batter his wife without fear of the law. And Lord Morrow's total rights to their two sons must have made flight a last life saving resort for her aunt. Clare wondered that she had endured until both her boys were safely at school.

Visibly striving for control, Aunt Morrow continued, "I grant you that Edmund is good-natured, and kindness is a quality to be valued highly. Perhaps I've been a poor influence upon your mind, if you believe kindness an unusual characteristic in a man. Every person entering into marriage should be able to assume goodwill on a mate's part."

Aunt Morrow held up a hand when Clare began to speak. "Marriage is difficult enough between like-minded people who wish to deal well together. You and Edmund haven't a thought in common, for the boy has a dressing room for a mind."

"He does ignore the Church's Sixth Homily against excess in apparel," Clare agreed, smiling. Eager to turn her aunt's thoughts, she continued, "I know Edmund thinks more of society and cutting a dash than I. But he's never cared that I enjoy it less. We need not share interests to rub on well enough together."

"Living separate lives isn't true marriage, however fashionable to do so," Aunt Morrow protested. "You have no notion what isolation a woman feels, tied to a man who enters into few of her sentiments. With your nature, you require a gentleman with his feet firmly under him, one who challenges you to apply your excellent mind. Without an anchor, you tend to drift into dreams and fancies."

"Edmund won't care what I do," Clare said, determined to reassure her aunt. "I don't mean to sit idle at Linwood Hall while he waits upon every hostess in Town. I might start a school in the village, for example, with his blessing."

"No doubt Edmund will show you every consideration he gives his hounds," Aunt Morrow said, sounding exasperated. "But I'm not convinced either of you can ever regard the other as more than a cousin." She sat staring into the garden, brow creased. "I think I must make clear what you didn't seem to take in when your father's man of business called in London."

"Naturally I was too overset to care about consuls and mines," Clare said, clasping her elbows in grief. "I know Father left me his unentailed property. I'm as tempting a target for fortune hunters as he endlessly warned." The words tasted as bitter as they sounded.

Laying an arm about her shoulders, Aunt Morrow said, "If you're set on marriage to Edmund to ward off fortune hunters, you can send him to the rightabout. I won't permit a man to make ducks and drakes of your fortune or your heart."

Clare looked up quickly at the passion of her aunt's pronouncement. Uncertainly, she asked, "Permit?"

"You didn't take in the solicitor's explanation of your affairs," Aunt Morrow said, nodding once. "I feared as much when you asked no questions about your trustees."

"I supposed Edmund's father to be my guardian," Clare said. "Surely that task generally falls to the family head."

"Your father said Arthur had no head for business or wine." Aunt Morrow looked grim. "Thinking me unlikely to be taken in by any man after Morrow, he left you to my care."

Clare shrugged aside this consideration. "You mean you must approve my marriage until I come of age in two years?"

"The pompous phrases in your father's will go beyond that," said Aunt Morrow apologetically. "While I don't intend to be unreasonable, I must approve whomever you marry, at whatever age, in order for you to gain your full inheritance. I set your allowance until such time as you wed. After that, your father fixed a mere pittance as your yearly income if you marry a man I can't approve."

Clare tore herself from her aunt's clasp, trembling with the indignity of this arrangement. Her mind staggered between anger and incredulity. Father had built a wall of distrust about her in death, just as he had in life. She was still to be watched like a child, to insure that she didn't step beyond the bounds he had prescribed.

"My life's aim was to please Father, and he served me so," Clare said as hot anger spread over her chest like a poultice. "Couldn't he have forgiven a girl's mistake over a gentleman's affections and come to trust me?"

"I trust you, my dear," Aunt Morrow said quietly. "You have excellent judgment, when you exercise it. I'll simply act as a brake upon your sentimental nature, your impulsive and overly good heart. I desire your happiness perhaps as much as you do, for seeing you content in a good marriage, I'm compensated for my sad experience." She extended a hand to Clare. "Forgive your father, and my part in his plans."

"There's nothing to forgive *you*!" Clare said fiercely, laying her head in her aunt's lap. Aunt Morrow had offered refuge and affection when her father had been absent in fact or in spirit. "You must forgive me, instead, for a churlish outburst you did nothing to deserve. It's Father I should rail at, but as ever, he isn't on hand to hear me."

Pressing her face against her aunt's warmth, Clare assured her, "You're far more than aunt to me; you're the closest thing to a parent I have now. I couldn't ignore your opinions or doubt your good intentions. I rely on your advice utterly, dear Aunt Morrow."

Feeling her aunt's cool hand on her hot cheek and hair, Clare realized the enormity of the task before her. Despite her assurances, Aunt Morrow must be convinced of the wisdom of Father's plans.

Betrayed as Clare felt at his distrust, Father had been too strong and wise for her to overset his intentions. Marrying Edmund was the last observance she could offer her father, proving her devotion as a good daughter.

Perhaps Lord Denzil's dark presence would show Edmund to Aunt Morrow in a better light. If her aunt didn't approve Edmund as a husband, a gentleman who enjoyed the approbation of the highest sticklers, who could come close to satisfying her lofty standards?

"Where did you discover that old round gown?" Aunt Morrow asked as Clare entered the breakfast parlor next morning. "I thought it went into the ragbag last year."

"So it did," Clare said, swooping a kiss onto her

aunt's hair as she headed for the sideboard. "I salvaged it just in time, for it's quite my favorite dress for gathering my grasses, as Father called it."

Putting hot rolls on a plate, Clare took a seat at table. "This brown stuff isn't too far off proper mourning, in case I'm seen by estate people. And mended tears make further bouts with briars of no consequence."

Pouring coffee into a cup for her, Aunt Morrow said, "Don't let the Gypsies see you, or they'll mistake you for one of their own." Reaching across to brush curls off Clare's forehead, she smiled. "With your hair in your eyes, you look no more than fifteen today."

"My front hair needs trimming, but why fuss for tramping the fields," Clare said. "My maid can wash and dress my head before Edmund arrives next week."

Hardly were the words out before the door to the passage swung open. "Do I hear my name bandied about over breakfast?" Edmund asked jovially, stepping into the room.

Like a dark shadow at Edmund's heels, Lord Denzil strode into the breakfast parlor. The rogue's blue eyes flew directly to Clare's as though he had known where to find her.

The coffee she sipped went down the wrong way. *My hair! This gown!* Only the painful coughing spasm kept her from crawling under the table.

"Took you by surprise, didn't I, Clary?" Edmund crowed, coming to pound her on the back. Coffee sloshed from her cup. "No need to get all choked up at seeing me again."

Seizing a napkin as she coughed, Clare sopped up the spill. Besides looking like a scullery maid, she must act the clumsy child before Lord Denzil, who was turned out to perfection. Eyes streaming and voice a strangled croak, she scolded, "Look what you made me do, Edmund!"

"Nothing could harm that gown," he assured her, putting up his glass. "Maids must have run away with the grooms, and you've taken up scrubbing floors in their stead."

"Popinjay," Clare twitted hoarsely. "We didn't expect you this week." Though she kept damp eyes fixed on Edmund, she was too aware of Lord Denzil, whom she viewed through the wet spikes of her lashes. He stood easily in form-molding leathers, watching them with his guileless face and wary eyes.

"I meant to stay in Town for Lady Sefton's thing, but Den was over-eager for country air," Edmund said.

Lord Denzil's response to this revelation was to give Clare a mocking smile as he made his bows. She wondered if an heiress's father had made the Smoke too hot for him.

"Have seats, since you've come, and I'll ring for more coffee," said Aunt Morrow ungraciously. "I assume you've had breakfast, as you didn't send word that Mrs. Wilson was to cook for an invasion."

"Don't fuss, Aunt Morrow," said Edmund, taking a roll from Clare's plate as he sat beside her at table. "Willy won't let me starve."

Remaining where he stood, Lord Denzil addressed Lady Morrow with a smile that made Clare catch her breath. "Please forgive me for foisting myself on you at breakfast. Edmund insists that he runs tame as a pug in your house, but I can't think you feed every stray that follows him in."

"Make certain you don't act the cur," said Lady

Morrow grimly. "You might as well take a chair, too. But don't think to call me aunt like your friend."

"You're far too young to tempt me to do so," Lord Denzil assured her, eyes glinting sidelong at Clare the while.

Thinking how adroitly the rogue flirted with two ladies at once, Clare wished she had worn her best gown today, even if black was too hot for walking in the sun. Lord Denzil took the chair directly across the table from her instead of the seat facing Edmund. She gripped her wet napkin so hard that coffee dripped from it onto the table.

Lord Denzil flashed white teeth as she mopped up coffee a second time, and Clare decided that his tanned coloring had faded a shade. The force of his smile had not.

Addressing Edmund, Aunt Morrow said, "I might have known you'd descend on us like a plague of locusts, just as you did each holiday from school. Surely your mama brought her cook to the country so you could feed your guest at the Hall."

Wiping his fingers on his handkerchief in lieu of a napkin, Edmund nodded. "The one she hired as French, who hails from Yorkshire. The man is no hand at rolls, compared to Willy. And I didn't doubt you'd have a plum cake."

A footman entered with a tray, supplying the gentlemen with cutlery and plates. He set out both a cheese and a plum cake, as well as a dish of ham.

"This is something like," Edmund said, loading his plate like a school-boy and setting to. Between huge bites, he addressed Clare. "Get out of that rag and come riding round the estate with us."

"Lady Clare already has plans to replenish stillroom stock today," Lady Morrow protested at once.

Across the table, Lord Denzil watched Clare with a knowing look as he buttered a roll, a corner of his shapely mouth twitching upward. She didn't doubt he recognized Aunt Morrow's effort to keep her away from a rogue.

"What do you gather here in July?" he asked, sounding truly interested.

"No wonder you're dressed like an inmate of the workhouse," Edmund interrupted, cutting up a slice of ham. "We'll put off our ride to give you our company instead."

"I'm picking mugwort, a most unassuming leaf," she answered Lord Denzil, then turned to Edmund. "You mustn't disappoint a guest. And don't pretend you'll risk your boots on waste ground and stream banks."

"These are only my third-best," Edmund protested. "You don't think I'd hack round the countryside in my best boots, except at a house party."

Aunt Morrow looked disgusted and Lord Denzil laughed.

"Never let a lady know you aren't willing to sacrifice your finest gear to her, Edmund," the rogue said, his eyes sending Clare messages she declined to notice. "The privilege of carrying her basket is worth any cost."

"That sounds very well," Edmund said, "but Clare insists on crawling under dusty hedgerows and sliding down muddy banks. When you've been scratched and bitten in her wake as many times as I, you'll have more care for your boots."

Indicating the open window, Aunt Morrow said, "As warm as it's grown already, I misdoubt that any of you should traipse round the fields in the hot sun. By one o'clock the heat promises to be unbearable. Best stay in today, Clare."

Edmund stopped to stare at Lady Morrow, fork suspended over his decimated plate. "Clare's no delicate miss likely to come over faint in the sun. I don't doubt she could plow, if she was nodcock enough to try it."

Clare frowned at Edmund repressively. She had followed him about both family estates like a younger brother as she grew up, but that was no cause for him to put her to the blush in front of his friend. Not that she wanted to be thought missish, but neither was she a field hand.

Before Aunt Morrow could reply, Lord Denzil leaned across the table to address Clare. "Naturally your cousin will take the greatest care for you. Have you a shady bonnet?" he asked solicitously. "Perhaps if Edmund asks your cook, she would put up lemonade for you to sip when the heat becomes oppressive. I expect you'll want field daisies, too, if you mean to gather mugwort."

Surprised, Clare said, "I do mean to pick daisies. How did you know I'd need them to mix with mugwort?"

Crisp black lashes dropped like a stage curtain, but Lord Denzil's light tone didn't change. "I carried my mother's basket when I was scarcely bigger than it. One doesn't forget early joys."

An image of a sturdy toddler filled Clare's mind, black curls blowing, blue eyes intent as he carefully balanced himself and a large basket. She had been permitted to carry her dear mother's gathering basket as a child. They must share the same sweet anguish of memory, since he had lost his mother too.

What an adorable little boy Lord Denzil must have been, Clare thought, dwelling on the handsome features before her. His lashes swept up and a man's bold stare pinned her to the chair like a mounted butterfly.

Feeling stifled, Clare decided that the day must be far warmer than she had thought. She hadn't realized until now that summer's heat made it difficult to breathe, almost as if a thunderstorm threatened. If she stayed quietly at home, avoiding this rogue's company, Aunt Morrow would be pleased.

Across the table, Lord Denzil raised black brows and smiled an invitation with his eyes as much as his lips.

She was very nearly out of dried mugwort, Clare reasoned. No doubt it would be cooler out of doors than in this over-close room.

Pretending not to notice Lord Denzil's offer of a hand down the steep, grassy bank below the hedge-row, Clare stepped carefully after Edmund.

"I warned you Clare would drag us through dusty hedges in the hot sun," Edmund said to Denzil in an odiously self-satisfied way, picking his way toward the lane as nimbly as a sheep.

Clare swung her gathering basket in vexation, bumping her cousin lightly on the back. "Find a shady path if you prefer, but I'm taking to this road. I saw mugwort under the hedges just along the way not a week since."

"You think this over-warm?" Denzil asked Edmund, who had turned to swat at Clare. "English summers compare more to Guiana's late autumn, or even winter. The day isn't hot to me, but I'm dashed if I'll trudge about in a coat so tight a man can't swing his arms." He shrugged the fitted garment off his shoulders, tugging at the sleeves to struggle free.

Startled by this improper action, Clare watched as the coat came off. A light linen shirt clung to Lord Denzil's form. His coat and body's warmth had pressed the fabric close against his strong arms and torso. Unease vied with admiration as she thought of an unbroken stallion, protesting the paddock's confines. Convinced she could very nearly see through the thin cambric, she forced her gaze toward hedgerows standing high on either side of the road ahead. She hurried down the steep bank.

As they slid onto the hard-packed road, Edmund paused to speak confidingly to Denzil. "Doubtless you don't recall after years away: not the done thing, to take off your coat in company, even if it is only Clare to see your sleeves."

"I'll resume my coat, if I offend your sensibilities," Denzil said, catching up to Clare. "But the deuced thing fits more like a glove than a snyder's garment. You may have to help Edmund force me back into it." His gaze teased as surely as his words.

Against the sun, muscular contours showed plainly through the pleated sleeves of his shirt. Clare imagined inching his coat up the rogue's hard arm, her fingers brushing its flexed firmness through thin linen.

A lady of sensibility would beg him to put on his coat at once. However, the sun grew warmer by the second, and a lady was also considerate of others' comfort.

Setting a smart pace along the lane, Clare said shortly, "Please yourself. Stand arguing sartorial propriety while dust coats you like sugar does cakes, if you like. I'm gathering mugwort before dark makes this lane a cavern."

Before she had taken two strides, Lord Denzil fell into step beside her again. Grasping her basket's handle, he said, "Won't you let me carry this? You'll gather mugwort and dog-daisies the faster for free hands."

Clare yanked at the basket, shaking her straw bonnet at the rogue without risking a look into impertinent blue eyes. His strong grip didn't relax, just slipped along the handle until his hand nudged hers. She snatched her fist free, scalded by his touch even through cotton gloves.

"Thank you for giving me this great pleasure," he said, voice as silky as a dandelion's fluff. "Thoughts of walking an English lane with an English beauty occupied my mind many a steamy afternoon in Guiana."

Inclining her head briefly, Clare determined not to look at the deep-chested form of the man matching his steps to hers. No doubt Lord Denzil's reputation for seducing females of fortune was well earned, as naturally as he fell into flirtation in every circumstance. She knew from personal experience how meaningless such attentions were. Besides, the rogue knew she and Edmund had an understanding.

Looking about, she found her cousin lagging along on her left, dust rising like smoke round his boots. Edmund's lack of attention to her, which left her open to the disturbing influence of his friend, suddenly angered her. "You could carry my basket, you lazy nob, instead of leaving it to your guest to do the polite." Despite the family arrangement between them, Edmund might act a proper regard for her in company. Whether he felt it or not.

Edmund edged a handkerchief from a waistcoat pocket with two fingers. Shaking it out to wipe his face, he said, "Denzil likes to fawn over ladies, always did. I've put in my time and more fetching and carrying for you; he can take my place and welcome to it."

Turning to walk backward before her, Lord Denzil swung her garden trug and laughed with a boy's freedom. He said to Edmund in a bantering tone, "Be careful what privileges you abdicate, my friend. You could easily lose your place entirely with this lovely lady."

Clare felt as if the sun burned her cheeks, despite her cottage bonnet's brim. One swift glance at the rogue's beguiling face singed her senses. But his manner was entirely too smooth, too practiced, for her to credit the sentiment he expressed.

The sodden hem of her second-best black round gown slapped Clare's ankles as she waded the meadow's tall, dew-laden grass a week later. The gown was too fine to wear fishing, but she didn't mean to be caught out in rags again.

"The stream's just there, where the sycamores and honeysuckle hedge stand," Edmund informed Lord Denzil. Shifting the food basket, Edmund pointed with an over-large wooden walking stick. He had acted most superior, refusing to rise to Denzil's earlier baiting about fops bringing sticks on fishing expeditions.

"We're very nearly too late for good fishing," Clare complained, noting the sun's climb up the cloudless cerulean sky. "If you hadn't sat so long over breakfast, our hooks would have been wet long since."

"What an eager angler you sound," Lord Denzil observed. "Did you fish with your father as a child?"

Reminded of her loss, Clare felt momentary guilt for

the heedless joy she had taken in the morning and its outing. "Edmund was my companion far more often; Father traveled frequently in search of special stock for his cellars."

Edmund issued a warning as they approached the Kennet's banks. "Watch the rods, Clare, or you'll tangle the lines in the honeysuckle."

"Tangling lines is more often your trick than mine," she charged. "You may as well confess I generally bring home a longer string than you."

"Such an excellent angler must instruct me in the science," said Lord Denzil, giving her a look like a caress.

The rogue removed the fishing rods from her fingers, which were unaccountably incapable of resistance. Frowning at his high-handed tactics, Clare said, "Surely you fished as a boy, if not while residing in the tropics."

Lord Denzil shook his head, dark hair glossy in the sun. Holding back honeysuckle tendrils to allow her to pass before him onto the Kennet's wide, grassy bank, he answered, "Too many years have passed since boyhood fishing for me to recall the finer points of the sport. Consider me in urgent need of your most concentrated attention."

Looking at him with suspicion, Clare met widened blue eyes rimmed with pitch-dark lashes. Men shouldn't be allowed lashes like Lord Denzil's, when most ladies had to depend on berry stains for lesser effect. Accepting his word was safer than staring into his eyes during further argument.

Stopping short of the river, she said, "Surely you recall the need to stand well back from the water's edge on a bright day, when fish no doubt sun themselves near the surface. A bush may screen you from view, though if you're out of practice casting, the bush might present a hazard."

"Take your place behind a bush, as I'm certain your cast is admirable," Lord Denzil drawled. "I'll stand near you, just to the rear, so I may admire your form."

From the look he swept down her, Clare heard more than one meaning in his words. "You'll stand to my right," she said repressively. "Doubtless you bear watching."

Opening the creel with a meek air, Lord Denzil said, "Suggest a hook to ensnare an inept angler's quarry, please."

Thinking the rogue all too capable of hooking an unwary heiress with his easy address and falsely innocent air, Clare stepped to his side to peer into the creel. "What have you supplied us, Edmund? Sneck bends and limericks won't do today. Here," she said, reaching into the container's straw depths for the chamois snagged with hooks. "Bait-fishing for carp or gudgeon, I prefer the round bend."

"Which of these do you want?" Lord Denzil asked Edmund, extending the fishing rods he held.

"None of them," said Edmund smugly, fiddling with the heavy cane he carried. "This is a little trifle I won off McElvain one evening in his digs. Trust a Scot to know knacky fishing gear." While he spoke, Edmund extended a steel rod from the cane's end, complete with line and loops.

"How clever," said Clare, admiring the telescoping cane–fishing-rod. "Has it enough whip in its short length to allow you to play a fish?"

"Surely you credit a fisherman's skill as much as his equipment in playing a catch to conquest," said Lord

Denzil significantly, moving beside her to examine Edmund's toy. His gaze rested on her more than the novelty fishing rod.

Focusing on the rod again, Clare felt herself the gudgeon, with an avid angler hovering too near. She rejected the notion of being anyone's easy catch. Lord Denzil merely amused himself with any English lady at hand, just as he pursued any British pastime to idle away a long summer's day. Meanings she heard swimming lazily beneath his words were no more than foolish fancy, brought on by three months' seclusion.

Turning away from the men, Clare located a bush leaning over the water as if admiring its foliage in the mirror of the surface. "Give me your bait bag, Edmund," she said. "I prefer fishing to standing about on the bank for a jaw-me-dead."

Loosening the neck of a flannel bag hanging from his button hole, Edmund brought out a leather sack from a pocket. Clare reached into the leather bag to sand her fingers, then poked a forefinger into the flannel one.

"Intrepid lady, indeed!" said Lord Denzil, one straight brow creeping higher. "I wouldn't have been surprised when you leapt to my defense on the road had I known you bait your own hook."

Taking pleasure in even teasing approval, Clare schooled her tone to indifference. "Edmund wouldn't take me fishing with him as a girl unless I did so."

Lord Denzil joined her, taking out his bait bags. "I'll treat you far more kindly than Edmund," he said. Deftly, he removed a squirming blue-head and threaded it onto her hook.

Suspicious, Clare said, "You know the trick of leaving a worm's tail loose to move naturally in the current;

surely you've fished more than you claim. And I assure you I can bait my own hook without your assistance."

"No doubt you hook worms as readily as hearts," he agreed. "But capable as you are, isn't it pleasant to have the task done for you at times?"

Much struck, Clare considered the rogue's point, offered with a straight look of sincerity. Aunt Morrow had encouraged her to self-reliance, with Father away from Linwood Hall more often than present. Yet she had longed for the security of her father's masculine support many times. That wish felt as if it had been granted in a small way by the rogue's simple action of baiting her hook.

"You'll ruin her as a fishing companion," Edmund complained, spearing a long blue-head on his own hook.

"Not at all," Clare refuted. "You know I can't allow such indulgence every time a fish takes my bait. The two of you couldn't keep your lines in the water, for waiting upon me. Let's each take care of his own line now, in the interest of a good catch."

But Clare smiled more warmly upon Lord Denzil than she had since his arrival as she took her baited line. As she moved toward the bush she had selected as a screen, Edmund headed further downstream.

"Share Den's bait bag," he called back to Clare. "I expect the biggest fish to lie in the shade of the sycamore on such a hot day."

"No such thing," she challenged. "You simply want to stand in the shade yourself."

"Perhaps you would be more comfortable in the shade, too," Lord Denzil suggested. "Most ladies protect their complexions more than their virtue."

His gaze dawdled down the length of her form. Such

improper address and looks made keeping company with this man a constant threat to composure, if nothing more. Clare hitched a shoulder and turned away from the rogue's unabashed gaze. Looking after Edmund, she quelled an urge to follow him.

Facing the Kennet again, she found Lord Denzil much too close at hand. While she watched Edmund move away, the rogue had approached soundlessly over the grassy bank.

"You'll want to show me the proper way to cast." Lord Denzil waggled the rod's tip above his head.

"I doubt you need instruction from me or anyone else on casting out lures," Clare said severely.

"But my experience is too far in the past to serve now," he objected, a half smile quirking his lips. "Refresh my memory, so I make the proper approach to the day's sport."

"Proper approaches aren't a thing I'd expect you to concern yourself with either," she said in resignation, turning away from the unholy light in his eyes. Bandying words was useless when improper messages lurked in the depths of every speech the rogue uttered.

Bringing her rod to attention overhead, Clare began, "As you very likely know, wrist action is most important in delivering the hook to a likely spot you've chosen in the stream. Cast, then elevate the rod to limit the amount of line going into the water, so the worm descends naturally." Receiving no response, she glanced toward the rogue.

"Show me," he drawled, eyes sparkling like sun glints off the stream. "I find actions more elucidating than descriptions, if you please."

Finding her attention snagged by his mobile mouth

in speech, Clare stood staring for a moment. She wondered what his lips would feel like, moving against hers. Unnerved by the highly improper thought, she brought the wooden rod hurriedly to position over one shoulder, sending hook and sinker singing through the air with a jerk of the wrist.

No expected *plop* of the sinker parting water followed. Her line draped loosely over the bush before her; the cast must have tangled on a branch. Clare felt her ears heat under her bonnet's brim. She seemed destined to appear ridiculous before Lord Denzil each time she came near him.

Tugging on her line gently just took up the slack. Clare moved the rod's tip one direction, then another, hoping to free the line and herself from embarrassment.

Lord Denzil stepped quietly toward the bush, peering around it without comment. Had he observed her awkward cast, Edmund would be calling her cow-handed. Which she was, so Clare appreciated Lord Denzil's forbearance all the more.

"Will you wade in to free your line, or shall I?" he asked, presenting her with an innocent expression. His gaze trickled down her length as if her clothing already clung wetly. No matter how seraphic the set of his features, the rogue's eyes expressed knowing overfamiliarity.

"Neither will be necessary," Clare said stiffly. "I prefer to cut line."

"What a waste of my well-baited hook, one of the few things about me you've approved thus far," said the rogue. "*I* prefer to retrieve my handiwork."

Lord Denzil removed his coat before her as he had the previous week in the lane. Knowing how he looked in shirt sleeves didn't lessen the attention she paid to the process. Clare scolded herself roundly for her lack of delicacy.

Seating himself on the bank as naturally as if upon a drawing room sofa, the rogue tugged off first one high-topped boot, then the other. One of his stockings had slipped about a well-turned ankle. As he stripped them off, Clare couldn't look away. She couldn't recall ever glimpsing a gentleman's feet and felt stifled by the sense of intrusive intimacy the experience conveyed.

But by turning away she might give the rogue the pleasure of thinking he had discomposed her.

Lowering himself into the hip-deep water made strong back muscles flex under his thin shirt. Lord Denzil eased along the bank toward the bush without a splash. "No need to scare the fish," he explained. "Fortunately for me, British streams are free of tropical snakes and crocs."

Clare glanced downstream, where Edmund stood out of sight in the sycamores. She appreciated Lord Denzil's diplomatic handling of her bad cast, for her cousin would tease her for days if he discovered it.

Her line jerked, then the weighted end sailed over the bush. Rewinding the line, she laid down her rod and hurried to the bank. "Can I give you a hand up?" she asked as Lord Denzil waded from behind the bush.

"Actually I'd prefer to pull you in with me." The rogue grinned as he levered himself out of the water with minimum splashing and maximum rippling of muscle.

Ignoring his teasing threat, Clare said, "I'm sorry you've had a wetting over my poor cast. Let me bring you a napkin from the nuncheon basket so you may dry off before putting on your stockings again."

"I'll be dry in a trice, as warm as the sun is," Lord Denzil assured her. "If toes don't offend you, I can fish as readily barefoot as shod. It certainly won't be the first time, in England or Guiana."

"Aha! I knew you were bamming me when you said you didn't fish." She wouldn't grant permission for him to remain unshod or withhold it.

The rogue laughed. "I'm caught out, indeed. Though you can hardly scold, when I've just saved your bait and an excellent round-bend hook."

"Suffering a wetting to the waist, in consequence." Laughing, Clare gestured toward the territory she named. Her glance naturally followed the motion. She had believed fashionable fit left nothing to the imagination in men's clothing. She revised her opinion, looking away hastily.

Silence hummed like a bee's song between them. Clare felt stung by new views of Lord Denzil, both of his character and his person. Gossip labeled him a seducer and abductor. Each time they met, he flirted as naturally as he breathed.

Yet she was inclined to revise her earlier opinion of him, for he had treated her with every consideration. Perhaps she must reconsider her own want of delicacy, instead of censuring his. Aunt Morrow had never warned her about the unsettling effects of seeing gentlemen's bare feet.

Replete with rolls, chicken, and fruit, Denzil stretched at full length upon the grass, hands cushioning his head, while Edmund sat on his handkerchief nearby. Through slitted eyes, Denzil watched Clare closely.

Skirts tucked primly around trim ankles, she leaned against a sycamore tree's flaked grey bark. Twirling a five-fingered leaf broader than her small hand's span, she gazed up through the grey-green undersides of similar leaves toward the sky with an absorbed expression. Her full lips had parted slightly. He wanted her to look up at him in just this way, inviting his kiss.

He'd give a guinea to know her thoughts, much as he had endeavored to stir them in his direction this morning. The effort to win a wife to show Father he was a changed man, worthy of respect, was becoming a desire to claim Clare to satisfy quite different needs.

Edmund prodded him with a booted toe. "Ready to wet a hook again, old thing? Or rather, tangle a line?" He laughed.

Turning onto his stomach, Denzil propped his chin on his forearms and opened his eyes fully. "One bout with a bush a day is all I permit myself," he said, grinning at Clare.

Guilt flickered across her face as surely as the shadows from shifting leaves. Her lips tightened, then she spoke to Edmund. "Actually, your friend casts us both in the shade with his angling technique. My line tangled in the bush, if you must quiz someone."

A lady with a strong sense of fair play; Denzil was impressed. He blew her a kiss, smiling as a faint flush spread from her black round gown's high neckline to the obscurity of her bonnet's brim. Perhaps to hide the reaction, she poked through the food basket.

Edmund crowed to Clare, "The longer string you boasted of earlier don't come to pass, when you wrap your line about a bush like a sash."

Still pink, Clare retorted, "You lost two fish by playing out far too much line, so don't set yourself up in your own consequence."

Drawing another packet out of the basket, Clare opened the napkin. "Your cook put in cakes which I overlooked earlier," she told Edmund. "Will you both have one?" She offered the sweet to each man in turn. Edmund took three, and Denzil fumbled one free of the napkin, watching Clare.

Propped on his elbows, Denzil bit into the sweet mound, intent on her softly curved mouth. A buttery taste of currants and brown sugar combined on his tongue. "Fat rascals!" he said, pleased.

"I beg your pardon?" Clare looked at him askance.

"These cakes are fat rascals, my boyhood favorite. I haven't tasted them in years. Cook sneaked them up to the nursery when I was put to bed without supper, which meant I enjoyed them often. She called me a fat rascal, too, and kept me well supplied when she discovered I favored them."

Clare sat smiling upon him, expression softening as he spoke of his childhood. She had the knack of listening with total concentration, making you feel nothing signified to her beyond your tale. Life might have been different for him, had others been willing to listen with half the attention she generously bestowed.

Her eyes combined the warm tints of autumn chestnuts with those of both gold and green pears, but they glowed dark enough in the shade to hide multiple mysteries. Her full-lipped mouth must taste sweeter than the cake crumbs he licked from his lips.

Tongue touching her lips, too, she looked away at last. Noticing her cake, she stuffed it into the basket with the nuncheon's remains as if she had forgotten why she held it.

She wasn't entirely unaffected by him, despite her reserve.

"Shall we toddle back to the Dower House for one of Willy's excellent early teas?" Edmund's query startled Denzil; he had all but forgotten his friend's presence. "Aunt Morrow will be fretting that you're fishing in the strong afternoon sun, Clary," Edmund concluded.

Spreading a napkin over the basket, Clare glanced at Denzil and away. She probably thought her aunt's concern fixed more on a rogue's taint than the threat of spots.

"I doubt Lady Morrow wants our company for tea after seeing us over the cups this morning," said Denzil without stirring. "The lady alarms me. I'd sooner encounter a hedgehog than her barbed tongue."

Hurriedly, Clare said, "She doesn't mean her setdowns to wound you, Lord Denzil."

"What a rapper," Edmund said. "Den's a man, and she can't abide the breed. No call to wrap the matter up in clean linen with Den."

"No need to wash dirty linen in public, either," Clare said with a sharp look Denzil's way.

Swinging himself to a sitting position, Denzil crossed bare ankles. "Surely a story stands behind the lady's abhorrence of my sex."

"Certainly not," said Clare, as Edmund nodded.

"Common knowledge," said Edmund briefly. "If Den hadn't been a remittance man years since, he'd know the whole. No need to hide our teeth with him, when he can have the story from any member of the *ton*."

"Few of whom speak to him but you, rattling your

bone box like dice!" Eyes widening, Clare gasped. A hand covered her mouth as she looked at Denzil. "Oh, Edmund, see what you made me say."

Finding her capable of giving way to temper and common expressions heartened Denzil. Marriage to a proper English lady might be more than the dead bore he had dreaded after warmer tropical delights. "Speak the truth and shame the devil. Now you must tell me your family secrets to atone."

Clare subsided against the tree again, pressing her lips firmly together and looking across the Kennet's calm expanse.

"Not much to tell, but a common enough tale," Edmund said, searching the basket until he unearthed the cakes again. "Old Morrow laid about his wife with his stick or his fists, whichever was handiest, from the day they wed. Aunt Morrow had no brothers to defend her, and her papa wouldn't give her house-room again, out of fear he'd have to return the settlement he had for her." He bit into a cake.

"Lady Morrow's husband beat her?" Denzil picked up a stone and threw it into the river.

"As soon as look at her," Edmund assured him, licking crumbs off his fingers.

"I can't countenance a cowardly man who would strike a woman." Denzil yanked out a handful of grass and cast it away. "He should get as good as he gave."

"My sentiments exactly." Clare gave him an approving nod. "I never was so proud of Father as when he assured Aunt Morrow she would be safe with us, despite the man's efforts to retrieve her when she escaped to Mother."

Denzil wished he had cause to speak as well of his

old man. "Well done of him. The *ton* should censure such behavior, rather than cutting up rough over trifles enacted by youngsters with more spirits than sense."

"It was brave of Father, for Lord Morrow is a common, coarse man by all reports. Aunt Morrow must have feared for her life to come to her sister."

Despite his disgust at the tale he had just heard, Denzil saw a spot to lay a thought before the two cousins. "This is what comes of arranged marriages. They rarely prosper. The most to be hoped for is tolerance when two people come together without choice and real devotion."

Ruffling like a banty hen with chicks, Clare said, "I suppose the natives of British Guiana choose mates at will, based purely upon fancy."

The rogue grinned hugely. "Not so pure as all that, I dare swear."

Ready color rose becomingly in Clare's face, as he had hoped. Teasing her out of proper airs was most gratifying.

"Marriage is a family concern among people of *bon ton*, sir," she said, sitting to attention, "whatever heathen ways you've observed in the tropics."

"No wonder matches in England produce strange bedfellows," he drawled. "Your aunt might agree with me. A father's choice of husband for a daughter can show far from proper concern."

Clare choked without finding words, expression and bearing outraged. She seized the remainder of the cakes from Edmund over his objections, thrusting them into the basket. Rising, she said, "I've enjoyed quite enough barbed hooks for one day. Stay on to fish if you like; I'm more than capable of seeing myself home."

Edmund began gathering up fishing gear to follow Clare's stiff-backed retreat.

Denzil reviewed the exchange. He had set her off like fireworks at the prince's June fête. Luring Lady Clare clearly demanded angling of a higher order than he had experienced in a lifetime of pursuing females.

6

"*A man shouldn't allow ladies* to drag him through churches," Edmund protested as he guided his mount along the sheep track followed by estate flocks on their way to market. "Gives them notions he doesn't need them dwelling on, getting him that close to a parson."

Thinking how little he spoke like a man promised to wed her, Clare bent forward in the saddle to give him a quelling frown. "If you didn't wish to view the parish church, you might have suggested another objective for our ride."

Lord Denzil guided his mount closer to hers. "As long as it's been since I've viewed English architecture, the outing suits me. Particularly in this company."

The significant look the rogue bestowed upon her bewildered Clare. Each time they met for the past two weeks, Lord Denzil had pressed the impudent flirtation begun on their fishing expedition. Since Edmund paid them no heed, the rogue's attentions were doubtless no more than he bestowed on every lady he came near. Still, they were too disturbing to dismiss out of hand.

"Recollect, heading for church with ladies got you banished from England before," Edmund twitted his friend.

"Anvils, not alters, were my destination then." Lord Denzil's easy tone didn't match his withdrawn expression. "I hope I've grown wiser since my salad days."

Embarrassed at reference to his unsavory past, Clare hurried into speech. "You'll be struck more by the angels at Chilton Foliat's medieval church than by its alter. Angel carvings on the entrance doors, pews, and chancel ceiling make our long ride well worthwhile."

"The angel who suggested the outing for our day's entertainment makes any ride worth the effort to me," Lord Denzil said with an unserafic look her way.

Edmund hooted derisively. "If you an't learned yet that Clare's no angel, you're in for a rude awakening. The Boot at Chilton Foliat offers a special brew to settle the road's dust, or I'd never have agreed to a day in the saddle on a sleeveless journey."

"What's amiss with your mount, Linwood?" Lord Denzil dropped back from Clare's side, running a considering gaze over Edmund's chestnut.

Clare drew her mare aside to take in the prad's pace. "Lord Denzil's right; Russet's favoring his right foreleg."

Edmund halted his gelding, dismounting as the others reined in nearby. He stripped off riding gloves to feel the limb, with special attention to the knee. "No sign of tenderness," he said briefly, observing the animal as his fingers felt from foreleg to coronet.

"Want assistance?" Lord Denzil asked.

"Thanks, no," Edmund replied. "The leg seems sound enough; might be a stone lodged in the hoof." Speaking soothingly to the beast, he took the bent limb between his knees to examine the shod area closely. "There it is," he announced grimly.

"Hold on while I bring you my knife." The rogue dismounted as he spoke.

Holding out a Limeric-gloved hand, Clare said, "I'll hold your reins while you assist Edmund."

Lord Denzil placed the ribbons over her extended palm and folded her fingers round them. His gaze met hers like a kiss as he held her closed hand between both of his. The man turned the most commonplace contact into a dangerous association.

Clare nudged Gamma with a knee, presenting the rogue with the mare's flank as she led his hack to one side. From a safe distance, Clare watched the two men take turns digging at the stone. The rogue's powerful limbs strained his riding leathers as he bent over the creature's hoof. Edmund's beanpole form looked almost effete in comparison.

"The stone's too embedded for easy removal," the rogue concluded at last. "Dig much deeper, and we'll do damage. This needs removing back at the stable, where it can be fomented at once."

"Oh, no!" Clare wailed. "Our outing's over before it's begun." Lord Denzil flashed white teeth in her direction and she regretted a remark which made her sound eager for his company.

"No reason to put off visiting your precious angels," Edmund said, letting down the hoof. "If I cut across fields, I can be back at the stables in a quarter hour, get a fresh mount, and rejoin you in half an hour at most."

"You don't mean to ride Russet back to the stable on that stone," Lord Denzil said sharply.

"No, indeed," Edmund assured him. "I know you'd flay me if I dared remount a lame horse. You two ride on, and I'll be with you again presently."

"Concern for Russet is all very well," Clare said, cross with both men for arranging matters between them as if she weren't there. "But it's hardly proper for me to be careening across the county alone with your guest, Edmund."

Lord Denzil's lips and brows tilted up in unison as he gave her a lingering appraisal from riding hat to boot.

"Don't be missish," Edmund said at once, laughing derisively. "The three of us have hardly been out of each other's company these past two weeks. No one could object to your riding alone for a few minutes with a man who's very like another cousin to us both."

Eying the rogue uneasily, Clare felt quite certain Aunt Morrow would object. The way his gaze measured her was anything but cousinly. She looked resolutely ahead. "See how dark the sky looks toward Chilton Foliat. It's likely coming on to rain; we had best postpone our plans to another day."

"We'll accompany Edmund back to the stable," said Lord Denzil, a slight curl to his lip.

Feeling more than a little ridiculous in view of Lord Denzil's readiness to turn back, Clare asked uncertainly, "Edmund, are you certain you'll catch up to us before we reach the estate boundary?"

"Riding the most spavined, knock-kneed creature in the stables," he assured her cheerfully.

"If we reach the boundary marker without you, we'll wait on you there." Her agreement was reluctant. Edmund set off in a swinging stride with Russet on lead like a pug.

Clare balanced on the sidesaddle as Gamma danced nervously, seeming bent on following Russet. Perhaps her mare showed better sense than she.

Twenty minutes later, Clare was quite certain the mare had more sense than herself. They shared a severe case of the fidgets. Branches lashed like ocean waves overhead as clouds billowed toward them like racing sloops. The very air appeared sea-grey in color. Never had she seen a storm blow up with such speed or ferocity.

"We had best go back," Lord Denzil called, raising his voice above the wind's cry through the trees. He reined in, waiting for her to turn first.

More than ready to acquiesce, Clare tugged a rein. At the same instant, her newest riding hat flew off in a particularly violent gust. Grabbing at it reflexively, she jerked the bit against Gamma's tender mouth.

The mare reared once, then as lightning split the smoke-hued sky before them, reared again. A confused impression of Lord Denzil lunging for her rein was lost in the urgent need to keep her seat. A knee round a pommel and a foot braced in its stirrup gave no sense of security on a skittish mount. Jumping off her hocks at the crash of close thunder, Gamma galloped away wildly at a tangent to the sheep track they had pursued.

Rushing wind thrust savage fingers through her hair, jerking pins loose until half her back hair's heavy coil fell about her shoulders. The first sharp needles of rain slanted like darts against her face. Clare leaned low over the mare's outstretched neck, all her attention focused on keeping an uncertain seat over rough terrain.

Forcing her mind to a calm her thudding heart didn't share, Clare spoke to the mare in soothing, crooning words she hardly heard over the harsh tempest raging through tormented trees. Teeth jarring in the frantic race across grazing land, she became aware of an equine nose nodding at the edge of her view to the right as she sat sidesaddle.

Lord Denzil's more powerful mount paced her, slightly to the rear. Surely he could overtake her mare and halt the runaway. Yet no strong square hand reached for her rein.

Afraid to turn her head and risk losing balance, she clung to the leathers, repeating the same lulling words. Gamma's ears twitched toward her at last. Exerting steady pressure on the reins, she felt the mare shudder, then respond with a slight slackening of pace.

Gradually, Clare brought the shivering horse to a standstill. For the first time since the mare bolted, she realized how much she had feared a serious fall.

Lord Denzil, looking wild as the windstorm, leaned toward her from his sweating steed. "Never grab at a lost hat on horseback, no matter how fetching the creation!"

His angry, explosive tone snapped Clare's precarious control. "I suppose you've acted with perfect judgment every moment of your rackety life!"

Laughter burst from the horrid man as relief took over his features. "Cutting up rough at me again," he said. "What better proof can I have you're unharmed?"

"No thanks to you," she said, hardly mollified by his laughter. "Though I didn't require your assistance."

"So I could see," he agreed with odious readiness. "I didn't mean to interfere if you could ride her to a standstill. Far better than to have my larger mount crowding her into a stumble when she's already nervous enough to bolt."

Crowding described Lord Denzil's effect on her composure precisely. Any other man would have made every effort to stop a lady's runaway mount. She was as vexed with him for failing to rescue her as she would have been had he tried.

"Can you ride on for a short distance after your fright?" he asked. "Perhaps you know a structure nearby where we can shelter."

The downpour slicked dark hair against the rogue's shapely ears. The thought of being alone with this dangerously attractive man unnerved her more than her mare's bolting. Clare said sharply, "I can ride home quite easily from here. Finding shelter isn't in the least necessary."

"Not for you, perhaps; we can't get much wetter than we are. But your mount is shivering from more than nerves after overheating herself in that runaway."

Feeling Gamma's sides heave under her, Clare realized with guilt she had forgotten her mare's needs in a fit of temper. Being reminded of duty by a man reputedly dead to such considerations was particularly galling.

"An old sheepfold stands on the other side of that spinney," she said with reluctance. Recalling her girlhood's indiscretion, Clare shuddered without feeling chilled. She couldn't follow a known seducer into any structure.

Glance sharpening upon her, Lord Denzil said, "Let's get you and your mare under cover without delay." He gestured for her to precede him.

Strands of loosened hair whipped across her eyes and mouth, sticking like plasters. As they rode in the lee of the dense spinney, branches slashed frantic arms toward them, warning them off. As rain sluiced down her face, Clare's sense of trepidation grew with the storm's intensity.

Too soon, the light cob walls of the sheepfold loomed against the dark spinney in the glow of eerie forked flashes. Used mostly during spring lambing, the sheepfold had become a smuggler's den in childhood games with Edmund. She repudiated the very idea of entering it with a man whom gossip named Den of Iniquity.

Dismounting, Denzil turned to lift Clare from her mare. He found her landing with splash in a puddle beside him. Reaching for her reins, he said, "Get yourself inside; I'll bring the horses."

"I won't go in."

Denzil had already taken a step toward the sheepfold, which looked little more than a three-sided cart hovel, open toward the spinney. He stopped.

Clare stood, soaked from her half-fallen hair to the hem of her heavy riding dress, its long tail heaped in the puddle beside her. Rain coursed down her defiant face like tears. By a jagged crack of lightning, he saw her chin quiver.

Irritation at her continued show of distrust swamped him. Turning away, he said, "Suit yourself. I'm getting these horses inside and hope enough straw remains to rub them down. I'll do your mare too."

That very nearly brought her round; from the corner of his eye he saw her take a step after him. He turned to hand her Gamma's reins, smiling. Clare stopped again.

"When you're wet to your shift and thoroughly miserable, join us." He led the horses into the sheepfold and tied one at each end of the rick against the back wall. Shrugging out of his coat, he threw it over his black's hindquarters, removing the saddle but leaving the blanket for warmth.

As he unsaddled Clare's mare, he watched her from the corner of his eye. She stood in the downpour, lit at intervals by firebolts from the lowering sky, both hands clasping her riding crop. He took up wisps of straw from the rick and began rubbing down the mare.

As he worked, he observed Clare covertly. She turned once, as if considering the chance of penetrating the spinney's dense undergrowth to seek partial shelter.

Finishing up the mare, he stepped to the black to repeat the rubdown. He called to Clare, "I've heard geese will stand looking up in a downpour until they drown."

Putting spaces of deliberation between each word, she repeated, "I won't come in."

The stubborn chit couldn't have a dry thread on her; it hardly mattered if she chose to stand in the storm for a thorough soaking. Glancing out at Clare as he went round to the other side of his mount, he saw her shiver as she clasped her elbows.

A thunderclap sounded directly above the roof, and

she leapt, emitting a small shriek. Could she be more afraid of him than the storm? The thought lit a fire of resentment.

"Come keep Gamma company," he said over his shoulder as he set to work with the wisps of straw again. "With the thunder so close, she's growing more nervous every second."

"You come out, then."

Tossing aside the handful of straw, he turned to look at her, hardly trusting his ears. "You want me to come stand in a drenching rain, with thunderbolts pitchforking directly overhead, so you will feel safe in this sheepfold?" Anger flashed through him.

"If you were a gentleman, you'd come out, to avoid compromising a lady."

The slight quaver to her voice did nothing to calm his temper. When a cannonade of thunder had quieted, he said, "If I were cork-brained, I might stand out there for a soaking, like you. But the only thing being compromised at present is my formerly good opinion of your common sense. What do you think I am, a totally unprincipled seducer?"

Brushing back wet strands of hair turned darker by the rain, Clare said on what sounded suspiciously like a sob, "Precisely!"

Denzil stepped away from his mount in her direction, and she brandished her riding crop. He stopped, laughing despite exasperation. "Do you mean to defend your honor with that?"

"If necessary," Clare said on a stronger note.

"It isn't necessary. Come under shelter like a sensible girl. You can keep the horses between us if you don't trust my gentlemanly self-control."

"I'm not a girl; don't address me as if I were a child. I've heard about your efforts to abduct heiresses."

"I never abducted anyone," he said, indignant. "She came willingly."

"You'll find I don't come willingly or any other way, sir." Taking a step backward as if to demonstrate her point, Clare nearly fell over the wet wad of her train.

Starting forward to steady her, Denzil found himself out in the downpour. Cold rain down his collar didn't serve to dampen rising anger. Gossip-mongers had spread their tales to such effect that this silly chit wouldn't come in out of the rain if it meant taking shelter with him.

Recovering her footing, Clare wielded the crop again. "Stay back," she ordered, voice shrill.

A crack of thunder followed instantly upon a streak of fire across the dark sky. He strode toward her, rage growing against gossips and those who believed them. "Do you seriously consider yourself safer out here in this downpour than under cover in the sheepfold?"

"A lady would never put herself in a compromising situation with a man of your stamp."

"Then we'll brave the storm together," Denzil said, baring his teeth more than smiling.

He had nearly reached Clare. She raised the crop further, backing away as her free hand yanked at the water-weighted train tangling with her booted feet.

Covering the space between them in one last stride, he closed his hand over hers on the riding crop, staying her hand in midair. She stared wide-eyed, her panting breaths audible and visible through the wet habit.

"Staying outside structures won't save you from seduction," he drawled, wresting the crop away and casting it toward the spinney. Clare turned as if to retrieve it and stumbled over her sodden train. He caught her round the waist with both hands.

Through the camouflage of the habit's high waist-line he felt as trim a waist as he had expected; the curves between ribcage and hips' flare fit his hands nicely. He pulled her toward him, planting a foot squarely on her train. She wouldn't go far, tethered.

Despite the resistance in every muscle under his hands, Clare uttered not one sound. Chin set, she glowered at him.

If he were a gentleman, he would let her go now, having taught her a rogue could take her as easily under angry heavens as under shelter. But she believed him a wicked seducer, and he made it a rule never to disappoint a woman.

Folding an excessively wet Clare into his clasp, he savored the sight of her full lips, pressed together in a promise of resistance. Her sensually curved mouth looked quite as inviting within inches as from a more decorous distance. The surge of her quick breaths moved her chest against his. Heat flared in his body where they touched, and where he wanted them to touch.

Forcing himself to look away from her tantalizing mouth, Denzil searched the depths of her eyes in the semi-darkness. Clare gave him look for look, face turned up to his. Lower lashes lay against her cheeks, caught in rivulets of rain like ferns in a stream's eddy.

Her eyes normally expressed far more feeling than he had ever discovered in another woman's gaze, but in the storm's half-light, he couldn't define their message. Searching their mysterious depths, he wanted to write the response he longed to read there. He yearned to imprint her lips with a thousand kisses, for a start.

With purpose and pleasure, he touched her mouth with his. Clare pushed against his chest as she closed her eyes and sighed.

Her lips were cool and wet—and about as responsive as those of garden statuary. Setting his mouth gently to the sweet curve of her cheek, he felt an urgency to stir her to life. He kissed a path back to her lips.

Even in resistance, her mouth felt pliant under his light second kiss. He had longed to explore this territory since he first saw it. Dropping feathery kisses across her full lower lip, he gave a lingering salute to its corner. Possessing both her lips fully, Denzil knew he had never put his entire self into kissing a woman until now.

Clare's hands crept onto his forearms, up wet sleeves to his shoulders, blazing an indelible trail along his skin through the soaked linen. Denzil was washed with a torrent of tenderness at her touch.

Cradling instead of restraining her, he drew Clare against him more closely. When he covered her mouth again, he felt no further resistance, just slight trembling as her lips moved in tentative response.

Thunder had dropped out of the sky and into his chest and head, crashing against his ribs and eardrums. Through closed eyelids he could see red flashes, leaping like the flames warming his storm-drenched body from within.

She tasted faintly of fresh mint and rain, clean and wholesome as an herb garden. He needed to crush her mouth with his, releasing its sweet essence to full expression. Restraint was the hardest task he had ever set himself, as, compliant at last, she leaned into his embrace.

Rogue he was reputed to be, but Denzil couldn't take advantage of obvious innocence. This woman above all others must come to him willingly, knowing the choice she made.

Lightning illuminated the scene as brightly as a stage, accompanied by a kettledrum roll from nature's orchestra. Denzil set Clare gently away from himself. Her eyelids raised slowly, languidly, as if she awakened from a night's dreams.

"Go on into the sheepfold," he said quietly. "I'll remain here. You'll be safe from further attentions, I assure you." This statement wasn't strictly true. "For the present, at any rate."

Lightning lit Lord Denzil's face. Coal black tendrils of hair were slicked against his forehead by runnels of rain. Clare heard him speak without taking in the words, her senses strangely somnolent after the interlude in his arms. Yet the imprint of his mouth still burned on hers like the bolts singeing the sky above them.

Only a rogue could electrify a lady with his attentions and at the same time immobilize her with sweet lassitude. She wanted to press her body against him again, fuse her lips with his forever.

A crash of thunder louder than anything preceding it made her leap toward Lord Denzil. Once more, he cradled her against his chest, something of the storm's ferocity in the urgency of his clasp. She soaked up the feel of him, his wet shirt increasing the intimacy of her hands exploring the bands of muscle across his back. Then he put her away, assuming a resolute look.

"Go on into the sheepfold," he said in a new tone, without a hint of flirtation. "I'll stay out here, so you're more comfortable."

She felt bereft without his arms about her and disturbed at the desire to cast herself into them again. "Don't be a noddy; it's pouring buckets still. You could catch your death."

He cast up his hands and shook his head. "No one can accuse you of setting your mind in one direction and fixing it there. Will you lead the way?"

Feeling foolish over her earlier refusal to enter the sheepfold with him, Clare gathered up her sodden train. She ran through sluicing rain, as if she could get wetter.

Dashing under shelter, she took in mixed odors of oily wool, mucked straw, and damp horse. Lord Denzil's steps sounded behind her, bringing a new awareness of his presence.

Suddenly self-conscious with the man who had just made her oblivious to a particularly violent thunderstorm, Clare wrung out the train of her riding habit. She wouldn't rid herself as easily of Denzil's stormy sensuality.

"Get all the rainwater out of that garment in here, and the mud will be as deep inside as out," he drawled.

Searching for a response as light, Clare felt mired in dismaying emotions. She couldn't turn to face the man who had just held her close against his broad chest, seduced a response from her she hadn't intended to yield.

Overestimating a gentleman's interest and intentions was all too easy. She knew that by experience.

Lord Denzil's embraces weren't significant to the rogue or to her. She should never have challenged him by arguing the danger of a lady's taking shelter with a man. By doing so, she had spurred him to prove unwelcome attentions could be pressed on a lady anywhere. His kisses demonstrated this point, nothing more.

Certainly his attentions were unwelcome. A gazetted fortune hunter, he was a type she distrusted totally. His exploits with females were a matter of public gossip.

Worst of all, he was Edmund's close friend.

Even the sheepfold reproached her. The rick across the long back wall of the three-sided structure had served as castle, prison, and ship in childhood games with her cousin. Now she entered it with her lips swollen from his best friend's passion, even though she knew it to be meaningless.

Her tongue savored the lingering taste of Denzil's mouth on hers. But she also tasted guilt.

Turning resolutely, she said in a rush, "I hope Edmund hadn't set out to meet us when the storm began. Edmund's very likely as soaked as we are, if so."

"Do you offer his name as a shield against me?" The rogue leaned negligently against a nearby beam.

Wringing her train again with a wish it were his neck, Clare felt her cheeks flame at his insight. "Certainly not; now that you've proved your point about a lady's danger, you have no further reason to— to—" She stopped in confusion as Denzil's eyes glowed with the warmth of a forge furnace.

"No further reason to press my lips and attentions upon you?" He propped a booted foot against the rick, strong thigh muscles moving visibly against tight, wet buckskin. "You rate your charms too cheaply, sweet Clary."

Stepping away to run a hand over Gamma's shoulders and back, she said sharply, "Don't make more of the trifling tease you acted out just now than is due. You pretend to be a blackguard, but I won't believe your attentions were serious. You wouldn't abuse your friend's hospitality so far." Rumbles of thunder retreated from directly overhead, sounding like heavily loaded drays being driven away.

Lord Denzil considered, then replied, "I do indeed intend to honor my friendship with Linwood, by doing him a service of considerable value. Don't allow that friendship to mislead you, however. The attentions I pay a lady are always serious."

Distinctly uneasy as his gaze caressed her face, Clare insisted on what she must believe. "You're bamming me, hiding your meaning in what sounds like a conundrum. I shan't take you seriously, sir. You know very well I wouldn't do anything to hurt Edmund."

The rogue's smile appeared, widened until white teeth gleamed in the storm's twilight. "Actually, I depend on that affection and concern for your cousin, in the end."

Clare stared, struck by the man's effrontery. Denzil assumed she would hide his ungentlemanly behavior from Edmund, to avoid hurting her cousin.

After a moment's reflection, she admitted the rogue assumed correctly. She couldn't tell Edmund his best friend had kissed her to tingling awareness in a thunderstorm, for she had most assuredly kissed him back.

7

Riding through the homewood toward Linwood Hall next day, Clare curbed Cinder's impatience. She rarely borrowed Aunt Morrow's distinctive black, and riding a mount accustomed to another hand felt as awkward as wearing strange shoes. Her aunt had offered her spirited mare since Gamma was being shod and Clare didn't want to put off her errand.

The beaten-earth path through the wood dipped into a hollow, then rose to curve through a stand of beech and oak. A partridge rose with a whir of wings, causing Cinder to prance fretfully. Clare held her in with a stern hand.

The backstairs connection between the houses reported that the gentlemen wouldn't be home this morning, as they were riding into the market town. She wasn't likely to meet Lord Denzil today, and very glad she was, too.

Surely they must come together with feelings of constraint, after embraces which never should have happened. The attentions he paid her were too warm for civility. She whacked at a branch overhead with her crop for no reason, sending Cinder sidling.

For the man to take advantage of his host by pursuing a meaningless flirtation with his intended was deplorable. As much a sore spot was Edmund's blithe acceptance of the attentions Lord Denzil paid to his affianced. It would serve him well if she lost her heart to the rogue. Not that she was in the least danger of doing so, though it was exhilarating to be appreciated for one's wit and appearance by a gentleman.

Her riding habit snagged on a branch for a moment as Cinder brushed by too closely. Having known her forever, Edmund saw her with the blind eyes of familiarity.

Doubtless as the heir and only child, Edmund had grown somewhat self-absorbed. For example, he teased Willy to prepare his favorite foods for breakfast and tea, without thinking to request fat rascals to please his guest. She would rectify that oversight by begging the receipt from Aunt Deramore's cook on this visit to the Hall. It was a simple matter of hospitality, nothing more.

Besides, she needed exercise, and the ride to Linwood Hall gave her an objective. The beech wood's deep shade seemed like twilight. Nimble squirrels nipped out of sight around thick trunks like shy maidservants. As the high-strung black shied at a branch swaying nearby, Clare recalled Lord Denzil's pleasure in the nuncheon's fat rascals when the three of them went fishing.

The grassy ride was a few lengths ahead when a rustling in the undergrowth sent Cinder prancing, very nearly unseating Clare by an abrupt swerve. Pulling the mare's head firmly back toward the path, she controlled the nervous creature.

Nearby, another horse neighed. Too occupied with keeping her seat to look for the other rider, Clare felt a disturbing presence like a dense fog rolling toward her.

The crackle of underbrush and the clink of a hoof on stone came from the shadows under the trees to her right. With a suddenness that made her start in fright, a dark figure on horseback erupted from the trees, riding straight at her.

The menacing charge set her heart galloping. Clare laid her heel and crop to Cinder. The contrary prad whirled in a half circle rather than responding to the command.

Off balance from Cinder's spin, she caught a crazy glimpse of an enormous man in brown with his face muffled, looming toward her with a blanket in hand. Every muscle tightened to repel the approaching threat.

From the muffler's depths came a harsh voice: "You'll pay back the lost years!" As he spoke, the man reached her, swinging the blanket in an effort to throw it over her head.

Clare dodged, so he succeeded only in knocking her riding hat loose. In the midst of panicked efforts to escape, she recalled Lord Denzil's warning about letting her hat go when she lost it on horseback. She heeded his advice.

Bending low over the mare's neck, Clare sobbed with fright. Echoing her disquiet, the black curvetted skittishly. The attacker lunged at her from his saddle. But for Cinder's stiff-legged leap to one side the man would have captured her on the spot.

Heart jolting her ribs harder than she kicked Cinder, Clare urged the black toward the patch of bright sunlight ahead. If only she could make it to the open grassy ride, she should be safe. Though surely only a madman would attempt to abduct her from the homewood.

Sobbing encouragement to the mare, Clare tightened her knee round the pommel as Cinder kicked up earth in a spurt of speed. If the attacker's horse pounded close behind, she couldn't distinguish hoofbeats from heartbeats. The last of the trees flashed past, but she didn't risk a look behind.

Coming into the clearing after the deep shade of the homewood, bright sunlight blinding her, Clare tasted the relief of escape. Cinder, too, seemed affected by the changed light, hesitating in their headlong flight.

As she dared hope she was safe, a huge hand with a hairy back reached for her. She looked around into the eyes of madness just as the man with the muffled face seized her upper arm. Jerking back from him in terror, she nearly tumbled off Cinder. The attacker twisted her arm cruelly and Clare dropped her rein.

Relieved of a curbing hand, Cinder shied violently and leapt into flight. Since the attacker held her arm in a bruising grip, he dragged Clare off the saddle as her mount galloped away. The ground rushed up at her, and she banged painfully onto both knees before the burly abductor wrenched her to her feet.

Discovering she still held her riding crop in her free hand, Clare applied it with mixed fury and desperation to any part of the brown-bundled man she could reach. Breath scraping her throat in terrified gasps, she knew the satisfaction of knocking off his cap and setting a stripe across his scalp.

Cursing volubly, the man shook her like a terrier would a rat. Her arm felt as loose in its socket as a well-done fowl's leg.

Hitting out at her captor as she could, Clare heard him repeat, "You'll pay back the lost years; see if you don't." She slipped, losing her footing in the fray, but the burly man never let go her arm.

Sobbing tears of fright and rage, Clare lashed out with her crop, hitting the horse instead of the man. The agitated animal sprang into motion, dragging and bumping her alongside as it lengthened its stride.

Then the grip on her arm gave way, and Clare fell to earth like a dropped sack of grain. She hit the grassy ground with jarring impact, rolling a short distance down a gentle incline. Each turn onto her abused shoulder made her cry out.

Dimly, she was aware of hooves flashing past her head, prancing to a stop nearby. In almost the same instant, booted feet hit the ground and started toward her at a run.

Against all hope, she determined not to allow herself to be captured again. Trying to scramble away and up, Clare's feet tangled with her train, and she collapsed onto a shoulder which felt as if it were impaled on a pitchfork. When she was seized by the waist from behind, she screamed as long and loudly as she could force sound from a tight throat.

"Hush, love, hush. I've got you safe. Hush, my little love." Denzil's voice, husky and urgent, quieted her panic. Clare turned in his hands, casting both arms about his neck where they knelt, despite the sharp spear of pain in her shoulder.

Shaking and choking while she sobbed into his waistcoat front, Clare felt the relief of the rogue's arms sliding round her, gathering her to him with rough tenderness. She clung to Denzil as she would to a spar in a shipwreck.

As her gasps eased in intensity, she drew nearly enough air into her belabored lungs. Denzil took her weight on his right arm as she leaned against him. Gently but quickly, his left hand explored her shoulder and collarbone, then traveled along her left arm.

His hand settled on her hip next. Clare's sobs stopped abruptly. "Sir! I'm not a horse at a sale to be gone over at a whim!"

The wild look of concern on his face shifted toward laughter. "As long as I've wanted to get my hands on you, it's hardly a whim on my part. I'm checking for broken bones, though I'd guess from the energy with which you threw yourself at me, you have none."

Realizing her arms still curled around his shoulders, Clare flung away in chagrin. She settled herself on the ground a discreet distance from the rogue, hugging her sore arm against her side.

"Why don't you pursue the thatch-gallow who attacked me?" She challenged him as a diversion from feeling the forbidden pleasure of being in the rogue's arms a second time. "While you jest, he's fleeing." A sob broke free.

"I thought it more important to see if you were alive." Denzil eased off his knees to sit on the grass cross-legged. "The man's beyond capture by now, as is my mount. No doubt you'll say I should have taken time to tether it before coming to your assistance."

Clare looked about them, mopping wet cheeks with the back of her glove. Not a creature was in sight, just the two of them sprawled on the lush grass slope. She sat more erectly, determined not to snivel again.

Straightening her habit and resetting loosened pins in her hair became intimate actions, the way the rogue watched her every move. The mundane motions also set her shoulder aching anew.

The enormity of the attack returned with full force, and Clare found herself trembling violently. Despite bright sunlight, she felt cold to her bones. "I beg your pardon," she said. "I should be thanking you for chasing away the vile fellow, instead of cutting up rough at you."

Lord Denzil moved swiftly over the grass without rising, removing his riding coat. Kneeling before her, he laid it tenderly round her shoulders.

When she protested feebly, he laid a finger on her lips. She wanted to kiss it.

"You're badly shaken by the whole experience," he said, "probably in shock. I can't give you tea, which I understand ladies prescribe for every misadventure, but I can keep you warm." He took her hands, joining them palms-together between his, and rubbed briskly but gently.

Fighting back the threat of further tears at his tenderness, Clare voiced a question which had raced through her head even in the midst of the attack. "Why would anyone want to capture me, enough to attempt it in our homewood?"

Denzil looked grave as he continued to chafe her

hands. "A lady alone might be attacked for several reasons. In your case, the fortune you've inherited from your father could supply a motive for abduction."

Pulling her hands free, Clare clutched the rogue's coat about her. "My cursed fortune! It's brought me nothing but *mis*fortune all my life."

Eyes narrowing, he said, "No doubt that opinion explains your immunity to fortune hunters, which you announced at the ball where we first met."

Cold as she was, Clare felt a slow flush creep over her at this reminder of her *faux pas*. "I'll beg your pardon, if you'll give it. I didn't know you then, except by hearsay."

Lord Denzil reached for the dangling sleeves of his coat, pulling them gently until she felt the garment tug her toward him. "And those who hear, say plenty to embellish tales. Do you believe me as black as I'm painted?"

Though the rogue's lips smiled as he put the question to her, his eyes did not. Intrigued, Clare reflected. Perhaps this was her opportunity to learn the truth of the rumors about this man. Curiosity quelled all other considerations, even after her recent fearful experience.

"Naturally I've heard gossip," she admitted.

"And accepted it at face value, I can only conclude," he said without intonation as his gaze held hers.

Disengaging the coat sleeves from his hands to gain distance from his disturbing presence, Clare said, "I would prefer to hear your version of events before concluding anything." Perhaps this encouragement would lead him to speak openly about the shocking tales she had heard.

Looking off across the verdant hills, he said, "Someone who wishes to hear my version of events is a rarity. Why would you believe it rather than gossip?"

"Perhaps I can't. But Aunt Morrow encourages me to think for myself, so I prefer to hear all sides before forming opinions." Wincing at the movement, she gestured at the rolling hills, forsaken except for the two of them. "Our mounts bolted for the stables, so we might as well pass the time with conversation until someone comes looking for us."

"I doubt you would find the real stories behind the rumors as diverting as the gossip."

She waited, but he didn't speak further. The intimacy of their situation, as they sat alone together in a grassy hollow on the side of a slope, should inspire confidences.

Perhaps if she revealed the cloud over her own past, he would feel more free to admit the truth behind the *on-dits* about him. The rogue's rescue had given Clare a sense of closeness she hadn't known with another person. If she could speak the story of her shameful girlhood blunder to any man, Denzil had earned her confidence.

Telling anyone would be difficult, as Father had warned her the tale could ruin her socially if it got about. Yet the *ton* had already cast out this man; he knew gossip's stigma. Further, he was Edmund's old friend, a member of their future family circle. She had promised to help him if she could, and until she knew his true history, she couldn't know how to proceed.

Besides, she trusted Lord Denzil, even if he was an inveterate flirt. The thought of him repeating a story harmful to a lady was ludicrous.

"Everyone conceals actions he would prefer not to have examined under an Argand lamp," she said hesitantly. "I have my own secrets to hide."

Turning, Lord Denzil frowned. It was kind of Clare to wish to hear him out, typical of her warm nature to offer a girlhood escapade to minimize the disgrace of tales about him.

"Any secret of yours must be innocent," he said. "You haven't lived enough years to create a shocking past, and young ladies of good family hardly have opportunity to get themselves talked about as I have."

"A little gossip was stirred about me, but it ended in unconfirmed speculation." Clare looked away. "Father made every effort to keep my foolishness quiet. You see, I eloped from school in Bath before I had been there three months."

Feeling as if the hillside had tilted, Denzil propped himself on both hands in the lush grass. This was the cool English miss he had counted on to impress his father with his ability to woo and win a proper lady as his wife. The old man was a stickler for propriety. He would never countenance a lady who had attempted to elope, should any hint have reached him.

Beyond that, this was the first woman he had held in his arms and never wanted to let go. Anger leapt like fueled flames. Impossible that she had run off with another man. Probably some mincing fool of a dancing master with over-pomaded curls.

Gradually he found his way through shock to speech. "No doubt a blackguard took advantage of your youth."

Clare leaned over to pluck a spotted maiden pink nodding near her. Twirling its stem in restless fingers, she said, "I was very silly at sixteen. A girl befriended me at school, introducing me to her elder brother, inviting me to accompany them on walks when he visited her. He appeared all that was amusing and charming to me."

Noting the color mounting from Clare's curved throat to her rounded cheeks, Denzil didn't want to hear the rest. He wished the fellow and his charm at the devil. "And he persuaded you to elope with him."

"Eventually. To my credit, I argued against it at first. But he declared his devotion persuasively, and his sister painted warm pictures of our shared life once we were sisters by marriage. I had been lonely here at Linwood, especially when Edmund was off at school, one reason Father was persuaded to send me for finishing at a young ladies' academy." She brushed a palm with the pink, bending her head on its graceful stem of a throat rather than look at him.

"Sounds as if the sister courted you as assiduously as the brother." Denzil dreaded the story's ending. Obviously a brace of sharps had set themselves to take advantage of an inexperienced young heiress with no brothers to inherit the ready. He craved ten minutes alone with the knave who had put the quaver in Clare's voice.

"You need tell me no more of the tale," he said gently, wishing she had never told him any of it. Lord Guilford didn't tolerate one step off the straight and narrow. That consideration must account for the feeling of empty despair reaming out his midsection.

"I'm finding it rather a relief to speak of it. Matters seem less horrid if they can be spoken of." Clare smiled briefly at him before looking away again. Her luminous eyes appeared almost green today, in the corbeau riding habit she wore. "Margaret and I met Phillip one morning by arrangement, before the school's servants were about. He came in a coach and pair, and she waved us off toward Gretna."

Her chin rose as she talked, eyes on the pink she held. Individual shadows of lashes lay on her smooth cheeks.

"By the time we stopped to change horses and have a nuncheon at a mean little inn, I was ready to turn back. Phillip had become almost sullen at the few coins in my reticule, the remains of my pin money for the quarter."

Denzil wanted to leap up and dash away to avoid hearing more, but he couldn't abandon Clare.

"When Father overtook us there, I was actually relieved to see him at first." She grimaced and continued. "Phillip and I were alone in a small parlor—yes, I know," she said hurriedly when Denzil bit off an oath. "Quite improper. Father didn't look my way after one glance, as if he couldn't bear to see my shame. He stalked to the table and threw down a leather purse before Phillip.

"'My girl or my gold,' he said in an angry, sneering tone. 'One or the other, but not both. Make your choice, and take it and yourself out of my sight before I put a ball between your eyes.'"

Admiring her father's way with a villain, Denzil nodded to encourage Clare's faltering speech.

She continued in a small voice, "It would have been more flattering had Phillip taken a moment to consider. He swept up the purse as he rose from the bench and was out the door in the same breath."

When she continued silent for a time, Denzil said, "No blame attaches to you, given your youth and inexperience. Though I understand your father's concern over gossip, considering society's appetite for reputations."

Shredding another pink without looking at it, Clare said, "Father spoke not one word to me on the drive home. I wasn't allowed to return to school, of course. Some story of illness was put about in reply to rumors about my hasty departure."

"How did it happen your father showed up so handily?"

"Aunt Morrow told me later that Father had stopped at my school by chance, taking it in his way as he set out on another of his many journeys abroad." Pieces of the pink fell onto her dark green dress. "I imagine he escorted me home only because he had to return to replace the funds used to buy off the fortune hunter."

Her lips twisted and her tone was bitter as Clare pronounced the last two words. No wonder she had spoken with loathing at the ball where he first saw her. Little wonder he had made minimal progress in attaching her affections to himself, given the gossip about him. Little chance she would accept his version of tales about his past, even if he chose to tell it.

"The morning after we reached Linwood Hall, Father summoned me to the bookroom," Clare said. "He never looked directly at me as he spoke. 'You've learned your worth to a man,' he said in his controlled way. 'This was only the first of many fortune hunters who will see you as a road to my blunt. Be advised by this experience to repulse them. I'll make your task easy, as you appear to have no judgment of your own where men are concerned.'

"Then he took up his cellar book as if his mind already turned to more important matters and said to me, 'You will wed your cousin Edmund in time. God knows my brother was delighted to acquiesce, especially when I told him my cellars' contents come to you at my death.'" Clare tossed flower fragments onto the breeze, and they sifted onto the grass about them.

"Was Edmund equally agreeable to this arrangement?"

Looking as if she had forgotten his presence, Clare turned to him. "We've never spoken of that. Our fathers settled it between them, I daresay."

Denzil nodded. No wonder Edmund showed little eagerness to tie a knot that was not of his making. Fathers were very much the same, ready to determine your fate without a hearing.

The tale reinforced his conviction that he wouldn't be taking Clare from Edmund so much as relieving him of her. As she shifted on the grass near him, Denzil caught a delicate scent of lemon and lavender from her shapely person. He yearned to explore every inch of her until he discovered its source. The desire confused him, since she no longer fit his notion of a bride to win Lord Guilford's approbation.

Nursing her arm, Clare watched him closely in the concerned way characteristic of her. "You appear deep in thought. Have I shocked you with my waywardness?"

"Not in the least," Denzil denied, shifting toward her. He couldn't answer her wistful expression with coolness even if youthful indiscretion made her a lady unlikely to impress his father. "I could hardly reproach you for being taken in by a sister and brother obviously in league to ensnare you. A sentence to marry without your affections being engaged was too harsh a punishment."

Clare drew away. "I feel most affectionate toward Edmund, and Father merely meant to protect me."

"I didn't mean to offend you or besmirch your father's

memory," Denzil said quickly. "My governor acted in high-handed ways, settling my future without hearing a word I might offer in my defense. Maybe I judge your parent by mine."

She moved toward him. "You haven't talked of your father. Did he cut up rough over your elopements, like mine?"

Denzil dug at a tuft of grass with the toe of his boot, reluctant to speak. It was all very well for Clare to tell him her history. Women's emotions overlaid the surface of their lives. A man buried his feelings deep and didn't mark the grave. Talking about himself was as repulsive as resurrection men's work, stealing bodies.

Clare leaned over to lay a slender gloved hand on his arm. Her expression and voice bespoke real interest in him, not idle curiosity. "I know a father's judgment weighs more heavily than anyone's."

He sank into the comfort of her concern like a feather bed. Lying back on one elbow, he said, "The old man cut up rough enough. And eventually sent me out of the country. Without asking why I had a young lady in a coach I hadn't stood up with above twice." Hearing the soft intake of breath from beside him, he looked up to see Clare's eyes round.

"After dancing with you only twice, a lady agreed to elope with you?"

"Irresistible as I am, no," he said. "Though it made a better story that way, so society rejected my version. Not that I could tell it without harm to a lady's name. I came upon her at an inn and relieved her of a man's company she didn't desire. He had insisted on escorting her to Gretna, and she didn't care to see Scotland under his protection."

Clare's expression was admiring. "You rescued a lady! How grateful her parents must have been."

"Hardly," Denzil replied, recalling the caning Lord Moresby had tried to administer in the public street. "Her father was beside himself, wouldn't listen to reason. Chose to believe I was the one who had abducted his daughter, despite what the both of us said." The story became easier to spill under Clare's intent regard.

"Wouldn't he believe his daughter, if not you?"

"Said she was protecting a young rogue who had coerced her affections," Denzil replied briefly. "My father chose to believe his old crony's version." Even having gained Clare's sympathy, he couldn't reveal his humiliation and rage at being denied his father's trust.

"Father didn't want to hear anything I had to say in my defense, either," Clare said, sounding aggrieved.

Perhaps she understood the hurt outrage of a parent's lack of confidence in a child. He patted her hand where it rested on the ground between them, feeling closer to her for their shared experiences than for their kisses. She allowed the touch, but when he tried to clasp it, she tucked her gloved hand protectively under her thigh. He ached to edge his own hand under its warm pressure.

"Was the tale of your first elopement all a hum as well?"

"The one where the cit's daughter produced a black-haired brat within a nine-month?" he asked.

Flushing, probably at his overly plain speaking, Clare nodded. Choosing words with proper English ladies after the freedom of speech he had known with dark Guiana beauties was a chore.

"The girl was my calf-love, not a source of income,

as gossips prefer to say. We weren't more than seventeen when I asked her to travel with me to Scotland, then through life. Even so, her father wouldn't have caught us had I not turned back the instant she changed her mind in a flood of tears."

He turned his head at a sympathetic utterance from Clare. Ready acceptance was hardly what he had expected to gain by refuting old stories. "The cit married off his daughter at once. If her husband had reason to believe her child wasn't his, I didn't provide it."

The sound of harness and wheels jouncing over uneven ground came from behind him. He turned from Clare's blushes to see a pony cart careening in their direction. Lady Morrow reined a piebald neatly beside them.

Denzil rose from his lounging position beside Clare, brushing bits of dry grass from his buckskins.

Pitching him the reins as she jumped down, Lady Morrow knelt beside Clare. "My dear, are you injured? You're holding your arm against you. Is it broken? Can you move it?"

"Quite handily," said Denzil, clasping his hands round his neck to suggest her earlier embrace. He couldn't resist teasing Clare, since he stood behind her aunt.

Frowning repressively at him, she answered Lady Morrow, "Only wrenched a bit, I would hazard."

"I never should have allowed you to take out Cinder," her aunt fussed, feeling Clare's shoulder and arm with care. "She hasn't been ridden for a few days. I might have known, as fresh as she was, you could likely be thrown."

"I didn't come off the black," Clare protested stoutly. "I was snatched off."

Lady Morrow turned on Denzil, outrage stamped on her features.

"You have the wrong of it," Clare said hastily. "Lord Denzil rode up just in time to frighten the miscreant into releasing me. I was attacked in the homewood by a man who tried to throw a blanket over my head."

As she looked from Denzil to Clare, Lady Morrow's expression changed to one of consternation. "Hardly a highwayman in the homewood."

"Nor yet a startled poacher, more likely to carry a sack than a blanket," Denzil agreed with a nod. Though she had barely tolerated his presence near her niece these past weeks, at least the lady believed the two of them.

"What was the man like?" asked Aunt Morrow.

"Very large, dressed in brown, with horrid dark hair on the backs of his hands. I can't tell you more, for he was muffled to the eyes. His voice was gruff and rasping."

"What did he say to you?" Denzil queried.

Clare concentrated, bringing back the confused kaleidoscope of events in the homewood. "Something like 'I'll make you pay for the lost years,' I think. It made no sense whatsoever, but the man must have been mad to attack me on home ground in the first place."

Lady Morrow had gone very still, staring blankly.

"Promise me you won't ride out alone again," Denzil urged. "Wait for me to accompany you, or take a groom with you if you must ride without me."

"No doubt Edmund will see to my safety, if I need protection," Clare reminded him stiffly.

"I'll satisfy myself on that head," he answered grimly.

8

Hearing steps strike stone, Clare glanced up from the volume she read. Under the pergola, Lord Denzil followed Edmund toward the bench she sat on at the bottom of the garden. Her lungs felt as if her sash were too tight. Sitting straighter, she laid aside her novel.

In the last three days, meeting Lord Denzil should have become easier. After the attack in the homewood, he had visited the dower house daily to inquire for her health and help Edmund entertain her.

The men stepped alternately from sun to shade as they approached under vine-covered supports. She steeled herself against the consideration Lord Denzil had shown for her in recent days. It was far easier to ignore the rogue's constant flirtation, as she had his meaningless kisses, than his solicitous mood.

*I*f you
have a passion
for great
historical
romance,
here's an offer
you'll love...

Introducing
The Timeless Romance

Passion rising from the ashes of the Civil War...

Love blossoming against the harsh landscape of the primitive Australian outback...

Romance melting the cold walls of an 18th-century English castle —— and the heart of the handsome Earl who lives there...

Since the beginning of time, great love has held the power to change the course of history. And in HarperMonogram historical novels, you can experience that power again and again.

Free introductory offer. To introduce you to this exclusive new service, we'd like to send you the three newest HarperMonogram titles absolutely free. They're yours to keep without obligation, no matter what you decide.

Free 10-day previews. Enjoy automatic free delivery of three new titles each month — up to four weeks before they appear in bookstores. You're never obligated to keep a book you don't want, and you can return any book, for a full credit.

Save up to 32% off the publisher's price on any shipment you choose to keep.

Don't pass up this opportunity to enjoy great romance as you have never experienced before.

Watching her cousin reach up to strip off woodbine flowers, Clare compared his graceful saunter to Lord Denzil's purposeful pace. How easy it was to undervalue years of affectionate association when a new acquaintance took one's fancy. Novelty was no reason to abandon comfortable companionship. She would devote herself to Edmund anew, treating Lord Denzil with no more than common civility.

Every storm eventually subsided, as would the one the rogue had stirred in her composure. Father's wishes must be honored. She was pledged to life with her cousin. Lord Denzil must remain only a friend.

Her greeting to Edmund was markedly the warmer when the two men reached her.

"Why sit here alone, when you could have joined us for the morning's ride?" Edmund demanded, dropping onto the seat beside her and offering her a honeysuckle flower.

Clare was too aware of Lord Denzil taking up a leaning stance nearby, a boot on the bench beyond her book. "I don't ride every day, Edmund. Since I've hardly cracked one of the volumes you brought me, I decided to spend the day getting acquainted with the newest novels."

"Minerva Press, I presume," said Lord Denzil, picking up the volume she had laid aside. "I've never quite understood ladies' preoccupation with romantic books, or any other for that matter. Reading means sitting about too long for me."

"I've read no more than the first fifty pages," Clare said, "but *Sense and Sensibility* is like no Minerva Press novel I recall. The lady who wrote it appears to be a keen observer of human nature."

He turned to the title page. "The author conceals her identity. Is this because she thrills you with no more than the usual abductions and false heirs?"

"Hardly," Clare said, meeting teasing blue eyes with reluctance. "The anonymous lady describes quite ordinary situations and people, though with extraordinary perception. For a man who professes not to read at all, your superior tone toward ladies' novels is unaccountable."

"Well defended," he said, laughing. "I own it's infamous to denounce such books, when a romance can't take place in life or novels without males as well as females."

"Indeed, men play the active role," Clare insisted. "Surely you don't imply a lady could put herself forward so far as to solicit a gentleman's attentions?"

"Personally, I'd welcome a lady's pursuit, whatever form it took. I give you leave to practice on me at will." Lord Denzil bent toward her, elbow braced on bent knee.

Clare snatched her book from where it dangled from his hand. Remaining civil with a gentleman bent on offering provocation was beyond her. "Fast females are hardly ladies, sir."

Taking the book from her in turn, Edmund leafed through the pages she had cut so far. "What is this tale, to stir up a brangle? I told them at Hatchard's to put up a parcel of books suitable for a young lady. Have you found anything indelicate in these pages?"

"Not at all," Clare cried in vexation at Lord Denzil's relentless flirtation and Edmund's obtuseness. "It's your friend who's indelicate, not this novel."

Reading, Edmund said absently, "Denzil? Best of good fellows. Trust him with my wife as readily as my mount."

Edmund's faith renewed Clare's unease about her

dealings with his friend. Within moments of resolving to concentrate more on Edmund when the three of them were together, the rogue had tempted her into debate over reading tastes that left her cousin far behind in understanding.

Unable to suppress a guilty look toward Lord Denzil, Clare met a quizzical gaze. Pressing her lips together tightly, she determined to stop snapping at the conversational bait he dangled before her.

"Looks a dull enough thing to me," Edmund said about the book he still examined, following words on a page with one finger. "Can't do any harm I can see, if you don't waste time reading it when you could go about with us instead."

Putting down the maligned work, he stood. "Think I'll toddle round to the kitchen to see if Willy's started tea. If I'm in good time, she might stir up a lardy cake."

Clare watched with exasperation as Edmund skirted the curved pergola dividing the flower garden from the kitchen garden. Giving him most of her attention was difficult when he spent more time with Cook than with her. When she turned back, Lord Denzil had seated himself on the stone bench at her side.

"Tell me more about this sensible story you're reading," he urged. "Perhaps you'll inspire me to read it."

"I would prefer to inspire you to act sensibly around me, instead of playing the mooncalf. I don't require every male who comes near me to flirt, you know. Being friends is far more comfortable."

"But I don't mean you to be too comfortable with me. Though you may love me as a friend. For now."

"I don't love you in the least," Clare said, finding herself on her feet at the outrageous suggestion.

He took her hand at the wrist, laughing and tugging her toward the bench. His broad thumb stroked the exposed area above her pulse in a compelling circle, spinning warmth through her limbs. Clare sat down, rather than sink at the rogue's booted feet from weakening knees.

The sense of safety she had felt with Lord Denzil after the attack on her in the homewood fled. Any man who inspired extreme reactions each time he put his hands on her person was a man who could cut up her peace forever. With her future settled firmly in her mind, such complications were unwelcome and unwise. Clare pulled back at arm's length from the rogue and pulled her hand free.

Gesturing toward the book lying between them, he said, "I'll wager a love story marks the plot between these covers, no matter how unconventional the novel. Surely you wish for a romance of your own, or you wouldn't read such tales."

"Fustian!" Clare cried. "Ladies enjoy glimpses into other people's lives, no matter how suitable their own connections. Reading about others' experiences is a natural enough pleasure for anyone with an interest in people."

"'Suitable' seems a sad word to use about your future marriage," Lord Denzil said. "If the woman meant to wed me said it, I'd be forced to kiss the notion out of her head."

Offended, Clare sprang off the bench once more. "You'll never be put to the trouble, as 'suitable' is one word no lady would use to describe a union with you."

The rogue leaned back and gazed at her from under lazy lids. "You look like a lovely jack-in-the-box. Surely a brave woman exists who will risk her fate with me. It's not my idea of wedded bliss, to bed an unwilling bride. I never have understood the appeal of abductions and forced marriages in those books you ladies moon over."

Picking up her novel and seating herself again, Clare reproved him with a look. "Perhaps we need to believe love can improve any situation. Or we may enjoy the thought of being persuaded to love a man who's a bit more outrageous than society's rules allow us to know normally."

Denzil grinned, watching Clare with interest. Clearly awareness of her speech's application to herself and a rogue who plied her with attentions soon entered her pretty head.

"Not that I care for that sort of book in the least, personally," she refuted.

He chose not to fill the silence that ensued, just allowed his disbelief to show by grinning more widely.

A note of challenge energized her tone. "Despite explaining away the stories about the ladies you're said to have abducted, you must have a history as a philanderer for such tales to be generally accepted."

Stretching long legs before him, Denzil gripped the front of the bench as he leaned back. "Would you prefer that I be an experienced philanderer when I take you in my arms, or that I come to you an innocent?"

"I prefer you reserve your attentions for ladies who show you they welcome them," she said at once, turning to look at him over one shoulder.

"I never press attentions on ladies who fail to respond to those I offer them," he answered as readily.

Her pretty lips parted to reply, then she took the full

lower lip under her teeth as she frowned. No doubt she had intended to state she had never invited his attentions, until she realized he had forestalled that comment.

The mulish look she cast his way warned him Clare was ready to roll out the heavy artillery.

"Very well; I accept that abductions aren't in your style, as you've explained away two elopements laid at your door. Gossip attributes other incidents to your discredit as well. Would you care to explain stories that put a whip in your hand?"

Denzil no longer felt like bantering. Old anger reared like a wave in a stormy sea. Obviously Lady Clare hadn't found him as guiltless in the gossip she had heard as he had liked to believe.

Deliberately, he said, "I choose not to justify the behavior in such tales. You'll have ample opportunity to know me before the summer's past. Form your own judgment about my character."

Movement from behind the pergola interrupted Clare's search for a reply. Edmund walked toward them, munching, a napkin-wrapped packet in his hand.

Holding it out as he advanced, he called, "Raided Willy's kitchen to good purpose. She's made fat rascals for tea, from a receipt Clare begged from our cook for you, Den."

Denzil felt sweet hope. Rather than reaching for a cake, he clasped Clare's hands. Only a rosy chin was visible of her down-turned face under her cottage bonnet's curved brim.

He couldn't resist teasing. "My favorite cakes. Never say you don't love me a little, to put two cooks and yourself to extra effort on my behalf."

Clare showed him a pink face briefly, snatching her hands free. "I merely wished to express gratitude to you for coming to my rescue on the grassy ride."

Denzil grinned. Clare's continued show of indifference must be an act. Though the pleasure this brought him made little sense, if her girlhood scrape made her ineligible to win his father's approbation as his proper English wife.

No longer inclined to smile, he felt the ambivalence which had plagued him since they had traded stories about their pasts. He should be making his excuses to Edmund and fishing in another pond for a dull English miss. Yet here he was three days later, making a cake of himself because Clare had arranged for his favorite tea cakes to be served him.

A shadow shifted across his abstracted view. Edmund stood before them, offering the napkin of fat rascals.

Edmund looked between his cousin and his friend, wearing an expression very like a basset hound's.

On the ride back to Linwood Hall, Denzil found Edmund unusually silent. A fine mist had settled in during tea at the dower house, and now it laid surface dampness over their shoulders and hats. Edmund hadn't grumbled once about damage to his clothing.

They put their mounts over a low stone wall easily, taking a shortcut across fields to the Deramore seat.

Settling onto his saddle again after the jump, Edmund looked at Denzil earnestly. "You and Clare are getting on terms at last, wouldn't you say?"

"Quite." His friend's query put Denzil on guard.

"I an't what you would call the most knowing of fellows. Not exactly overstuffed in the cockloft. But Clare's my responsibility, and you're my friend. I want the two of you on good terms so we can all be comfortable together."

Denzil appraised Edmund's creased brow and earnest expression. "The three of us have spent a good deal of time in company, and we enjoy smooth sailing for the most part."

Edmund nodded once. "My opinion exactly. Today I saw something between you and Clare. Can't say what. Like a strong undertow, roiling sand out to sea under the waves. I may seem like a care-for-nothing, but I worry about the old girl, you must know."

Shifting in his saddle, Denzil switched the reins from his right hand to his left, threading the ribbons through his fingers with deliberation. "I appreciate your concern for your cousin's well-being, Linwood. Her welfare is uppermost in my mind, too, especially after the attack on her in the homewood. I mean to do everything in my power to help you protect her from further danger."

"Goes without saying, old thing. You'd do as much for my sake alone, even if you didn't appreciate Clare on her own merits."

For a few minutes, only muffled hoofbeats on the grassy meadow filled the air around them. Then Edmund spoke again, avoiding Denzil's eyes. "Don't want to interfere, you see, but I'm pledged to look out for Clare as well as wed her. Way I see it, abduction isn't the only threat to her peace. She's soft-hearted and full of dreams, easy to wound as a kitten. Don't want to see her hurt."

"No more do I, old friend." The depth of that sentiment took Denzil by surprise. Intense feelings about
Clare had shaken his composure repeatedly since he'd
come to Wiltshire.

In London, he had seen her as a means to an end, a
way to show Lord Guilford he was a son to take pride
in. In Wiltshire, he had come to respect Clare's proud,
independent spirit. He had recognized her need to be
appreciated and supported; he empathized with her
desire to be understood and loved for who she was.
No, he couldn't see Clare hurt.

Clearing his throat noisily, Edmund reclaimed
Denzil's attention. "My mind don't work like a mantrap,
but it holds fast to what it grabs. And one thing I know
is, ladies hurt easier than we do. Just think what water-
ing-pots they are. Stands to reason. Ladies cry; men
don't. Must be more tender in their sentiments."

His confused quandary since hearing about Clare's
painful experience with a fortune hunter made Denzil
doubt Edmund's assessment. Surely no female could
feel more anger and anguish than he had over what
had happened to her. But nodding agreement was easier than expressing strong emotions.

"Don't take me wrong, Den. I know you just naturally
tease and carry on with ladies as a matter of form.
Don't mean to accuse you of the least impropriety with
my cousin. Farthest thing from my mind." Edmund cast
an apologetic look at Denzil. "Thing is, I also know
you're hanging out for a wife, and getting next to a suitable lady don't come easy. I'd even help you snare a
different bird. But Clare's my cousin, Den. I wouldn't
want to see her affections abused. Now, if you want to
call me out, get on with it."

"Putting a bullet through as poor a shot as you would do your coat no good and give me no satisfaction," Denzil said with a jocularity he didn't feel. His friend's earnest concern put him on his mettle, made him face thoughts he had pushed to the farthest reaches of his mind.

He hadn't wanted to deal with his conflicting feelings about Clare. Surely her girlhood elopement made her ineligible as a proper lady to win his father's approval. Yet he hadn't even considered calling an end to his visit with Edmund and riding away to seek a bride better suited to his purpose.

Clare's concern and warmth were too comforting to give up easily. Sparring verbally with her was too enjoyable to abandon. The sight of her heart-shaped face, changeable golden-green eyes, and tender mouth was too entrancing to ride away from. The lady was too much woman to leave without more regret than he could endure at present.

Whatever he felt for Clare, it was a new experience for him, one he wasn't ready to give a name. Neither was he prepared to reveal his feelings to her, without knowing how to define them for himself. He most assuredly wouldn't show Edmund the muddle rioting through his mind.

"Don't mean to press you, Den," Edmund interrupted his musings. "But I give you fair warning. I won't see Clare's affections trifled with by you or any other man. If you love her, that's one thing. If you go after her as a matter of convenience, I'll have to put a spoke in your wheel."

The word *love* made Denzil as skittish as an unbroken steed. "Given my reported record with ladies, I don't hold your warning against you." He made more of guiding his mount's steps through a small stream than the passage required. "You've stood my friend too long for me to be less than honest with you, Linwood. You imply a question by what you say, and I'll answer you with another question. How would my making a marriage of convenience with your cousin differ from your doing so?"

Looking much struck, Edmund dropped his hands, causing his chestnut to break stride. He gathered the reins and control again before saying, "Damned if I know how to put it into words, but it's different. I love her like a sister, and you can't give her that, if you wed her without the regard a man usually gives a wife."

"Brotherly love strikes me as a poor gift to any woman except a sister," Denzil said, smiling at his old friend.

"That's just the kind of sharp thing you and Clare say that I don't have the wit to match," Edmund said, shaking his head. "But I can enter into her memories, Den. I remember when she learned to walk and when she sat her first pony. You don't. Married people settle down into comfortable ruts anyway, so they might as well be like two carriage tracks, stretching back as well as onward."

"I don't mind settling into a comfortable coze with my lady," Den said, surprised his old friend had thought about marriage so deeply. "But I hope to fan a blaze between us first. One that may burn down to embers at times but can be kindled to flames again when we choose."

"Flames and embers sounds like something out of those books Clare reads too many of. I just don't want her getting burnt, Den. Particularly not by my best friend. Deuced uncomfortable thing, I vow, when friends and flirtation mix."

Edmund's protective stance toward Clare stirred Denzil's admiration, though it complicated his purpose. If he continued his pursuit of Clare, he did so under his friend's watchful eye. Only honesty would serve now—honesty with himself as well as Edmund.

"I don't mean to hurt her, Linwood. I doubt I could bring myself to do so. I don't believe the two of you suit as mates, and I mean to win her if I can. But if you and Clare love each other in the right way for marriage between you to work, my efforts will fail."

"Don't know that I find much comfort in that assurance," Edmund said morosely. "You always won all the females, Den. But I warn you, I won't see her give her heart to another man unless she's paid in like coin. And if we all wind up in the basket, I can only blame myself for bringing you to Clare's notice in the first instance."

Honor forced Denzil to make an offer he didn't want to act on. "Do you want me to leave Linwood Hall?"

Sighing, Edmund said, "Too late for that. I've seen how she looks at you, and how you look at her. The two of you had best run this hare to ground and see what hole it bolts down. But keep this in mind: if you break her heart, I'll have to live with it for the rest of my life. You won't be around to see the damage, for you won't be welcome here again."

As a shadow fell across the deal table, Clare looked up to find Edmund standing in the stillroom doorway. "Come in," she invited. "You've been a stranger for the last two days."

Unusually for Edmund, he leaned against the door-frame instead of coming in to claim the room's single stool. "Thought you wanted time to catch up on your reading," he said. "Den and I have visited every stable in the neighborhood, sizing up horseflesh. Didn't think you'd care to go along."

"You guessed rightly. A horse is no more than trans-portation to me, but I know men are in transports over their points and paces." At least she no longer had to wonder why the rogue had halted daily inquires into her well-being. The encounter with the abductor in the homewood had occurred five days since; no reason in the least that Edmund, let alone Lord Denzil, should feel continued concern for her.

Clare jerked a vase from a shelf and set it sharply on the table. Pouring water from a pitcher into the blue oriental vase, she took a sheaf of yellow and white ra-nunculus from her garden trug.

"You can't do that," Edmund protested, leaving the doorway. "White does well enough in that bowl, but yellow flowers with blue offend the eye." He took the sheaf of blossoms from her and began picking out the yellow ones.

Taking her bouquet back again, Clare said, "I like the mix of colors, Edmund. I'm arranging these flowers for my drawing room. Go home and tear apart your mother's floral arrangements to suit your over-nice tastes."

"Bet you'd wear yellow gloves with a blue spencer as well," Edmund said darkly, drawing up the stool to the table opposite her. He watched in brooding silence as she stood daisies in the vase in a loose arrangement to hold the more showy globe flowers in upright positions.

Since her cousin's mood rarely sank into the doldrums, Clare watched him as she inserted the yellow and white blossoms into the bowl. He fingered his fob, opening and closing his mouth more than once without finding words.

Finally, he blurted, "You in love, Clary?"

Feeling frozen where she stood, except for a heart that hammered like a woodpecker, Clare consciously resumed the business of placing ranunculus in the arrangement. "What a silly question between us, Edmund. You know I love you."

His face was a study in confusion. "Love me? Of course you do. That's not what I'm asking. Are you in love with Den, is what I'm getting at."

"Hardly. He's the greatest out-and-out flirt I've ever had to endure." Hearing too much heat in her tone, Clare continued matter-of-factly, "Why would you entertain such a want-witted notion for two minutes? Making up to ladies seems to come as naturally as breathing to your friend, but I'm not likely to be hoaxed by his gammon."

Sticking his knuckle in his mouth, Edmund stared at her for a few uncomfortable moments. Taking it out again, he asked, "Do you want to marry me?"

Laying down the flowers she held, Clare leaned on the table to look directly at Edmund. "I'm quite determined to follow Father's wishes. Unless you want to be free of our parents' plans for us, of course. Is that what this natter is about? Do you feel parson's noose pinching at your neck?"

Sighing heavily, Edmund said, "A man don't fly from the scent. Can't leave you unprotected. I'll hold to it buckle and thong if you're set on us being leg-shackled."

"Very kind of you to oblige me," Clare said waspishly, feeling uneasy about their arrangement for the first time. "You might improve your addresses to ladies by paying more heed to Lord Denzil."

"Don't take a pet. Never had to mind how we talked before. Little late to expect Spanish coin from me now." Edmund drummed on the table with the fingers of one hand. Teeth clenched, Clare considered giving him the vase to hold.

"You hardly sound like a man who wants a wife," Clare said shortly.

"Never said I did," Edmund returned. "Might not wear the willow if we didn't wed, but duty's duty. If you want to hear flummery, you'd best listen to Den."

"I have little dependence on a man's sincere regard when he ladles pretty speeches with a shovel," she said, and jammed three yellow blossoms into the vase in quick succession. Realizing one entire side of the arrangement blazed gold, she began yanking them out again.

"Den don't pay out false coin. He's honest in his dealings to a fault. And I want you to be the same." Edmund laid a hand over hers as she snapped a stem in tensed fingers. "Be honest with yourself, and be honest with me, Clary. If you find your affections engaged, tell me."

Snapping another stem, Clare said in exasperation, "My affections aren't engaged by any man, Edmund. Stop worrying the subject like a dog at a bone. You asked me to help your friend find his way into society again. I can hardly do so if I don't know him well enough to understand why he's at odds with it in the first place."

Frowning, Edmund said, "Any gossip-monger in the *ton* can tell you why he an't received. What's to understand?"

Clare recalled her aunt's stories about Denzil's violent nature and the rogue's refusal to explain his overuse of the whip. Perhaps it wasn't quite honorable to pry, but Edmund very likely knew the right of it. "For example, I've heard disturbing tales about Denzil marking a groom with his whip as a child, then setting about another gentleman on a public road after he lost a curricle race."

Poking in a basket at the end of the table, Edmund scoffed. "Those tales are so old they wear beards. Can't believe you listen to such rumgumption."

"I didn't say I believed the stories," Clare disclaimed. "I want to understand how they got started, so I know how to defend him among my friends if I hear them repeated. Aunt Morrow says even his family considers him unsteady."

"If that don't beat all hollow," Edmund said. "It an't unsteady to lay a lash on a groom who's doing the same to one's first pony for no reason. A boy's attached to his first pony, don't you know."

The tale of Denzil's boyhood violence was just as Clare had thought, a bag of moonshine. "What about the roadside whipping he's said to have administered after losing a race? Might that be explained away just as reasonably?"

"Can be, to a reasonable person. Dillingham crammed his team along the entire route to Brighton, just to set a pace outdistancing Den every step of the way. Den's got a soft spot for horses, you've seen that for yourself. Can't abide to see them abused." Edmund's observation reminded her of the day his mount had gotten a stone in its hoof.

"When Den caught up to him, Dillingham's leader had burst his heart and dropped in harness on the road," Edmund continued. "Den lost his temper and laid about Dilly with his whip." Edmund picked up a daisy and considered its petals. "Like to think I'd have done the same, though Dilly was a big brute. Outweighed Den, too."

Clare stood stroking the globe of a ranunculus. Far from appearing unsteady of character, Lord Denzil appeared to think just as he ought on every subject. She wondered that his father had given Aunt Morrow another impression.

"Why didn't Lord Denzil go home and engage his father's intercession with society's leaders on his behalf? Do you know what's amiss between the two of them?" Clare was glad to direct Edmund's mind to others' relations with the rogue and away from her own.

Scraping the stool against the stone floor as he drew it closer to the table, Edmund said, "His governor was too stiff-rumped to hear a word Den offered in his own defense over that business with the Moresby chit, just ordered him out of the country like he was shamed by him. Can't blame a man for not turning to a cold fish like that for a favor."

"Lord Guilford may be cold, but Aunt Morrow thinks well of him. And she has no opinion of men in general, you will agree. I wonder which view is nearer the mark."

"Surely a man knows his own father best."

Thinking of the chasm between her late father and herself, Clare wasn't convinced. "If we could get the two of them on terms again, surely the *ton* would look more kindly upon Lord Denzil in Town."

"I'm the best friend Den's got, but he don't listen to me on the subject of approaching his old man."

"Because a man hasn't listened before is no reason to assume he's deaf." Responding to the second part of Edmund's speech, Clare focused on the first part.

Her cousin need not fret that her intentions to marry him would alter. He had just stated the strongest reason why she was in no danger of loving the rogue: she could never permit herself to come between such old and devoted friends.

9

Morning sun slanted across the table, setting a cut-glass dish of lemon marmalade aglow. Clare pushed bites of ham about her plate, brooding on Edmund's uncharacteristic observations in the stillroom yesterday.

If she discovered a way to demonstrate her concerned friendship for Lord Denzil, her cousin would be reassured no warmer sentiments existed, however much the rogue flirted. If she found ways to promote Lord Denzil's acceptance into good society once more, he would spend less time in company with Edmund and herself. Inexplicably, that desirable outcome lowered her spirits.

Spooning out a dab of marmalade, Clare dipped ham into it, spreading the sticky mass over her plate's surface.

"Do you mean to eat that concoction, or do you merely make extra work for the scullery maid?" Aunt Morrow broke into her thoughts, speaking with asperity.

Uncomprehending, Clare looked at her aunt, who nodded toward her plate. Seeing the unappetizing smear of sweet mixed with ham for the first time, she laid down her fork and pushed the plate away.

"You don't appear peckish this morning," remarked her aunt. "Do you feel quite the thing?"

"I'm fit as five-pence. Forgive my distraction; I must be a poor table companion to you."

"Not only at table," said Aunt Morrow, signaling the footman to remove the plate. "I hardly see you, with Edmund and his guest monopolizing most of your time. You'll be burnt to the socket, racketing about with those two."

Guilt nudged Clare at the truth of her aunt's plaint. She didn't find frequent jaunts tiring in the least, but Aunt Morrow lacked companionship the better part of the day. "I'm sorry, Aunt," she said at once. "How thoughtless of me to abandon you to solitary pursuits. Surely you know we welcome your company on our outings."

Aunt Morrow waved the assurance aside. "I find company enough at Linwood Hall or the village. By the by, Mrs. Grayson asked after you yesterday, when I called in with a restorative jelly for her."

Clare felt both defensive and guilty; normally she visited the sick with her aunt. She had allowed Lord Denzil to tempt her away from duty. "I hope you said all that was proper to her on my behalf. Are you vexed with me for neglecting neighborhood calls, especially on my old nanny?"

Shaking bright curls at Clare, Aunt Morrow said, "Not on my own account. Mrs. Grayson isn't the only one who has asked pointed questions I had to turn aside, however."

Taking a roll, Clare broke it in half and surveyed the tender texture inside. "I know I've neglected Nanny shamefully since Edmund returned. Surely you expressed my concern for her, however."

"Her questions had nothing to do with that topic. She's heard through the village grapevine that Edmund's friend grows most particular in his attentions to you. Naturally she's concerned about a stranger's intentions, especially one with the reputation Lord Denzil has earned."

"Nanny always appeared to have eyes in the back of her head, but how does she know the particulars of Lord Denzil's behavior toward me, whatever its nature?" Being the subject of local gossip discomfited Clare.

Aunt Morrow looked pointedly toward the footman moving quietly round the dining room. "You must be aware her son is our undergardener, a nephew serves as estate gamekeeper, and a granddaughter is our parlor maid. Very little the family does escapes observation or comment."

Living with servants constantly about afforded one little privacy, though one tended to forget their presence. She and Edmund had never gotten into mischief that word of their scrapes hadn't reached home before them. "Gossip makes over-much of it, to call Lord Denzil's gallantries anything but meaningless," Clare protested. "From what Edmund lets fall, his friend charms any lady in his company as naturally as most men inquire for their health."

"The amount of time you're together inspires speculation. I still can't like your association with a man who has been the subject of unsavory stories." A vertical line between her brows marred Aunt Morrow's perfect features.

"How can what time I'm in company with Lord Denzil cause comment, when Edmund is always with us?" Breaking off bits of bread, Clare rolled them between fingers that refused to remain still. "Lord Denzil poses no threat to my heart or reputation, you must apprehend. And I'm not convinced his dubious reputation is earned, from what he's said about the elopements laid at his door."

"You know we disagree on that subject, so I won't lick that calf over." Her aunt poured tea for them both. "You've been closeted in the country over four months since your father's death. Naturally you take advantage of any available company and diversion. Perhaps we should take a house in Bath, where we can pursue quiet entertainments, within the bounds of propriety, during the remainder of your year's mourning."

A refuge for invalids and dowagers offered little appeal. Clare said quickly, "Appearing in Bath just four months after Father's death must surely look nohow. I want to honor him with every proper observance, you must know."

Aunt Morrow regarded her skeptically from under long lashes. "I don't doubt you're most observant these days, but I question the real object. No good can come of trusting your affections to a younger son who has given his just to ladies of fortune in the past. You know I only speak out of concern for you, my dear."

"I'm in perfect control of my affections," Clare insisted. "You and Edmund make too much of nothing.

Even if I were hanging out for a husband other than my cousin, Lord Denzil is no more than a friend."

"What has Edmund said to you?" Aunt Morrow took her up at once on the remark.

"Nothing of consequence. He lacks common understanding, or he would never have inquired into my sentiments toward his friend. He merely mentioned our arrangement to wed, asking that I tell him if I should change my opinion that we suit. His determination to do his duty by me was hardly flattering." Clare heard the aggrieved note in her voice.

She hurried to add, "Edmund trusts his friend, I assure you. He described Lord Denzil as honest to a fault in his dealings. That being so, he could hardly expect the man to trifle with his good friend's cousin."

"Lord Denzil makes a long stay, even for a country-house visit," Aunt Morrow pointed out. "It was past time Edmund took notice of his friend's preoccupation with you. As for control over your heart or mind, you appear perfectly distracted more often than not. For instance, I haven't seen you play with your food since you were confined to the nursery."

Clare looked down at a pile of bread pellets on the table's smooth mahogany surface. "How silly, to be sure," she admitted. "Nanny would make me gather them all up and take them outside to feed the birds, rather than waste food. Come out to the garden with me, and we'll see how close we can entice a fat robin to come."

"Just consider my suggestion to remove to Bath," Aunt Morrow requested, sliding back her chair to rise. "A change of scene and company would give your thoughts a far more suitable direction."

*   *   *

"Calling on Zeus for favors?"

Clare started at the unexpected sound of Lord Denzil's teasing voice. Turning away from the statue centering the garden, she found Edmund and his friend nearly upon her.

Constraint fell over her, due to both Edmund's and Aunt Morrow's strictures about the rogue. Pegging a smile in place, she determined to act in the same civil manner she had cultivated toward him before break-fast today. "I'm considering how to create a setting suitable to his eminence," she answered the rogue's sally, in an equally light tone. As the men came up with her, she continued, "Nothing too formal, befitting the dower house's style, yet appropriate to the classical nature of the statue."

"Best plant climbers to hide it," Edmund advised, raising his glass to study the John Cleeve lead figure.

"Great-aunt Linwood could have chosen statues of shepherds and shepherdesses instead, which would have outraged your delicate sensibilities still more," Clare twitted her cousin.

He shuddered, dropping his glass.

Walking away as if to survey the figure from a better perspective, Denzil said, "Old Zeus isn't that objection-able. His weathered grey surface is more appropriate than pale marble, outdoors in England's damp climate. Why do you choose to change the plantings? These grassy wedges seem restful to the eye after the cottage garden's chorus of color." He gestured toward a half cir-cle of paths radiating from the statue like the sun's rays.

"Restful to the point of giving me a fit of the gapes,"

Clare assured him. "I look down on this area from my chamber window, and a more stimulating view would be welcome. Perhaps I'll edge the paths with rosemary and heartsease."

"A suitable selection of plants," Denzil said from the opposite side of Zeus. "Rosemary for remembrance, and heartsease is an even more obvious choice."

"I don't follow you," Clare said.

He turned toward the lead statue. "Zeus is the father-god in Greek mythology. I assume you mean to honor your father's memory by replanting this part of the garden."

Much struck, Clare considered the notion. "Perhaps you're right, though I didn't realize what lay beneath my plan. Father was the all-powerful figure in my life."

"Don't want your old man taking too much notice of you." Edmund shuddered. "Dashed uncomfortable when he does."

"Zeus took as little notice of his children as most fathers, stepping in only when their escapades outraged his notions of suitable behavior," Denzil assured his friend. "Protecting his power occupied him far more."

Clare protested, "No one could ask for a more attentive parent than my father, when he was home."

"Don't remember it like that," Edmund contradicted her.

Aunt Morrow had said very nearly the same thing, Clare recalled, feeling aggrieved. "Allow me to know my own parent best, Edmund."

"Don't know that you do. Him being around so little, you couldn't know him much better than me. Foolish as you were about him, maybe you didn't see him as well." Edmund looked much struck by his observation.

"Girls are naturally much attached to their fathers, and losing Mama before I was barely out of leading strings gave him even more importance in my affections." She turned to the rogue. "You haven't seen your father in years. Yet I daresay you feel you know him quite well."

"Don't appeal to me for arbitration," Denzil said, walking away down another path. "I have little enough opinion of my own father."

"Why is that?" Clare asked, following him.

"The topic is too dreary for a day in a garden with a lovely lady as company." He spoke without turning, and she wished she could see his expression.

"Told you he don't talk about his old man," Edmund said with satisfaction.

"Nothing to talk about," Denzil said, frowning over one shoulder at Edmund. "Ten years since, my father believed his life would be more comfortable without me in it, and I hardly require him in mine now."

"What a pity," Clare said, thinking how alone in the world she had felt since her father's death. Even if he hadn't been a part of her everyday life, he had held a special place in her thoughts daily. Lord Denzil must be far more lonely, outcast from both family and society.

"Not at all," said Lord Denzil with cool finality, though he stopped, waiting for her to come up with him on the path. "I manage quite well without him."

"Odd you should say I wish to replant this garden to honor Father, though," Clare said, hoping to approach the subject of Denzil's relations with his parent from another path. Her father's death had taught her that not only was he lost forever, but what might have been between them was gone for all time as well. She wanted

Denzil to make peace with his father while it was possible. "When I was a little girl, I came here often because I thought this statue had a look of him about the nose and mouth."

"Not surprising," said Denzil. "Half England resembles classical statues, since much of the population inherited the straight Roman nose and full lips. In Guiana, native faces look quite different, even though many people in both countries have full lips and prominent noses."

"Don't see the sense in conversation about noses and mouths," Edmund said, shaking his head. "How the hair is dressed or how a lapel is cut are subjects of consequence, since those features can be altered for the better, with taste. Can't improve facial parts."

"Quite right," agreed Denzil. "Far too much bad poetry is written these days about ladies' eyebrows and lips, for example. If you don't salute the loveliest of features with kisses, words are a paltry substitute."

The rogue's appreciative gaze on her mouth made her lips tremble with remembrance of his kisses. His expressive features disturbed her far more than pretty words. Needing to escape from traitorous thoughts, Clare said at random, "Lavender is just what's required here."

Both Edmund and Lord Denzil looked askance.

"In the borders. Lavender provides a nice transition of height and color between rosemary and heartsease."

Denzil grinned as if aware of her uneasy response to his warm glances. "Lavender's scent seems timeless as well. It might indeed inspire special communion with your father as you stroll here."

Looking up at the lead figure, Clare was reminded

that her father would hardly have approved of the rogue. Yet Denzil understood her need to maintain a connection to her parent. "'Commune' is a fitting word. I held many a conversation with my father during his absences, here in this garden. Since his death, I've found myself doing the same thing, speaking to him as if he were simply away on another voyage. Doubtless that sounds touched in the upper works to a sensible male."

"Not at all," Denzil assured her. "Whatever gives comfort must have merit."

"Sounds deuced odd to me," Edmund protested.

"As a girl, I rode over especially to make speeches to this statue, expressing thoughts I wouldn't have dared address directly to Father. Speaking my mind, even to an inanimate work of lead, affordred satisfaction."

"Maybe that's what you should do, Den," Edmund said, staring up at Zeus. "Pretend this statue is your old man, and put a flea in his ear."

"I have nothing of consequence to say to Lord Guilford, in pretense or in person," Denzil said, his tone putting distance between them as he set off down the path again.

Unhealthful as night air was considered, Clare could no longer bear the stifling stillness of an over-warm bedchamber. She slid off the high bed, bare feet landing on the strip of carpet on the floor.

Groping toward a chamber window's faint rectangle, hands extended to find the way, she felt her thin muslin nightrail clinging to damp skin as she moved.

Outside air would offer relief, even if she caught her death.

Sleep had eluded her like a restive lamb veering away from a herding dog. Her thoughts had been just as unruly, as she sought a workable plan to aid Lord Denzil.

Reaching the window, Clare eased off the latch and pushed at the sash. The window opened with a shriek that shattered the dark silence of the night.

In the garden below, a figure by Zeus's statue swung toward the house. Clare dodged behind the drape's protection at once, peeking round its edge to discover who lurked in her garden after midnight.

Heart bumping, she recalled the burly man who had attacked her in the homewood. She wished she hadn't opened her chamber window, even if it stood well above ground level on the first floor. Aunt Morrow's room on the other side of the house seemed leagues away.

The silhouette was most assuredly masculine, wide at the shoulder and narrowing to lean hips. Despite the figure's muscular outline, this man lacked the hulking threat of her attacker. He stood staring directly at her window as if he knew she hid in the shadows within.

Clouds scudded across the sky like dim sails against a darker sea, and moonlight gilded the scene below with silver. At this distance, she could discern the man's features no more than she could China, but she knew beyond question the person who stood with Zeus in her garden was Lord Denzil.

What her eyes couldn't tell her, intuition spoke with full certainty. Her pulse fluttered in her throat, as happened whenever Denzil stood nearby. Her breath grew quick and light, just as when his eyes made nameless promises. Every nerve in her body responded to the figure backlit by moonshine, as if to a physical challenge. No doubt this was the rogue staring toward her window as if capable of penetrating walls as easily as her defenses with his gaze.

Clare pulled the banded ruffle of her nightdress away from her constricted throat, feeling greater warmth than with the window closed. She stood staring into the darkness, her mind painting each feature on the still form below. Seeing the rogue didn't depend on eyesight alone.

A breeze whispered into the room from his direction, and she felt its caress on her skin like his tantalizing touch. Without feeling chilled in the least, she knew the prickle of bumps rising along her arms and clasped her elbows, leaning for support against the wall by the window. Wrapping her arms around herself didn't satisfy a need to be held, which burned deep inside with a heat different from that of the stifling room.

Remembering the dark menace of a thunderstorm and the rogue's disturbing presence, she relived the pressure of his hands seizing her upper arms that day. His fury had rivaled the storm's, and she had felt it in each finger separately as it pressed into her flesh.

Then his expression and hold on her had changed as he stared, claiming every feature of her face. She had feared the hunger of his gaze, exulting in it at the same time.

Caught more surely by the force of his wanting than his hold on her arms, she had stood transfixed, feeling his hands loosen so his arms could slip about her, trapping her against the broad expanse of his chest. Thunder and lightning and slashing rain had receded from consciousness until nothing existed but a rogue's face coming nearer, a rogue's mouth claiming hers with an insistent demand that gradually gentled into searching need.

She hadn't chosen to answer the sweet torment of his lips; indeed, she had formed an intention to refuse him that satisfaction. But treachery from a secret place within had molded her mouth and wet body against his shamelessly, until only his setting her away from him had ended the embrace.

Standing at her chamber window in the sultry darkness, Clare knew an urge to turn from the window, run down the passage to the stairs, flee into the garden on bare feet. Her body thrummed its need to meet Lord Denzil for another embrace out of doors, out of time, out of reality.

She was clearly out of her mind.

Only the lateness of the hour and the heat of a summer's night could account for mad thoughts totally inadmissible in the mind of a lady. Beyond the still shape of Lord Denzil loomed the figure of Zeus that put her forcibly in mind of her father. And Father meant her to wed Edmund.

Clare burned with shame at the mental images she had allowed to possess her. Neither her father nor her aunt could approve of a man who inspired such improper thoughts. And Aunt Morrow's approval was required for her to marry Edmund or anyone else.

Regretfully, Clare admitted Aunt Morrow was right about removing to Bath. She must turn her thoughts in a more seemly direction.

Backing away from the window, she felt her way across the room to the bed. Climbing onto the crisp linen sheets, she mused that Lord Denzil's shirt linen would feel soft under her hands. His chest would offer the warm wall of strength she had felt through his wet waistcoat outside the sheepfold.

Calling her imagination sternly to heel, Clare blotted out the image of Lord Denzil's person. She must forget that he stood motionless in her garden in the moonlight, staring up at her window. He hadn't come out in the night's heat to torment her, no matter what his disturbing effect on her wayward thoughts.

The question of why he had come out distracted her from unwelcome sensations at last. Clare sat up as the afternoon's conversation repeated itself in her mind.

She had revealed her childhood habit of addressing her father through the statue of Zeus. Edmund had even suggested that his friend try the same means to speak his mind to his father. Perhaps Lord Denzil's appearance in the garden after midnight indicated he was more ready to confront Lord Guilford than he admitted. She smiled into the darkness.

Lying back on her pillows, Clare outlined an argument to win Edmund's assistance with her plan. If Lord Guilford were reconciled with his son, surely he would help Denzil reenter society. But the two of them could hardly get on terms again unless they came together. She must bring them face to face.

To that end, she formulated a letter in her mind to Lord Guilford. At first light, she would rise and pen it, ready to go off in the first post.

Putting the letter on paper wasn't possible at present, for Lord Denzil might still linger in the garden. She wouldn't want him to know for a certainty, from a candle's glow through her window, that she had observed his presence.

Still less would she want him or Edmund to suspect her unseemly reaction to seeing him there.

A screak sundered the silence in the dark garden like a gunshot. Turning to search the sleeping dower house's face, Denzil spotted an open window on the first floor. Lady Clare had said her chamber overlooked Zeus's garden. Almost, he could persuade himself he had glimpsed a pale shape flitting to one side behind the glass.

He wanted to believe she stood looking down at him from the window, connected to him by the night's mystery. The desire made him wonder if he had indeed come here to figure out his father through communion with Zeus's statue, as Edmund had suggested, or whether he needed the lady.

Either way, sensing her presence as surely as if he could see her made him long to fold her in the protection of his arms. Not that she would be safe there, in the conventional sense of the word.

Moonlight laid the shadow of the statue alongside him at the convergence of the garden's paths. The king of gods had appreciated mortal females as keenly as he, lending their proximity here an ironic aptness.

Straining to discern further movement behind the glass gilded by the moon's glow, Denzil's mental image of the lady grew too real for comfort. He pictured her standing to one side of the window in the heated darkness, clad in a nightdress dampened against her smooth skin by the warm night's humidity. If he stood in the darkness of her chamber with Clare, he would clasp her delicate wrists gently, setting her hands against his chest as she had herself twice before.

Touch would link her once again to his quickening heartbeat. Odd, how the slightest physical contact between them joined him to Clare as he had been united with no other woman. The connection was one of spirit as well as body. He had embraced enough women to wonder at the difference he experienced in holding this one.

In fancy, he touched her silken cheeks, traced the line of her chin as her face lifted to his, held her in his arms, pressed her against his needy length, claimed the generous curves of her lips with his. Yet sweet sensuality was just one of the ways he wanted to know her.

His hands clenched and unclenched. Often as his senses had been stirred by females of various ages, stations, and nationalities, none but Clare had spoken to his mind as much as his body. None had offered him acceptance and understanding, challenged his wit, exasperated his patience, called forth his protective instincts like Clare.

Little as he knew what to name the sentiment she branded across his soul, he knew enough not to deny its existence. Much as he had hoped to inspire a *tendre* in her strong enough to woo her away from Edmund, he had recognized her reserve. She resisted his practiced flirtation, suspected every lure he cast her way. Clare's heart hid like a shy woodland creature, frightened by a fortune hunter's cruel misuse and a distant father's indifference.

Yet she lavished warmth and concern on a man she must have been warned repeatedly to avoid. She chose

to believe his version of tales vilifying him. She stood
staunchly his friend, even as she resisted warmer ad-
vances.

Staring sightlessly at the window far above, he no
longer knew if he wanted to win Clare as his wife. His
first assurance had been shaken when he learned she
had been led into a girlhood elopement by a bounder.
Though this made her an unlikely candidate to impress
the old man with his reformed character, his doubt
grew out of more than this consideration.

Wooing women he could lose without regret had
been a pleasure. Ensnaring a lady whom he didn't want
to suffer through association with him grew increas-
ingly painful.

Hearing about her elopement as a school-girl, he
had assumed Lord Guilford wouldn't think highly of
her. Without putting the matter to the touch, he could
guess his father's caveats against Clare. Still, he hadn't
ridden away from the estate to seek a bride more likely
to gain his father's approbation. He had gone on flirt-
ing as avidly as if her past were all a father could desire
to graft onto the family tree.

Not that her innocent girlhood mistake made her
unfit to wed a royal duke, if one of that disreputable lot
deserved her. Angrily, he repudiated the strictures of
those who ignored the inner worth of a person, judging
one over-harshly for reported youthful actions. Clare
deserved his father's full approval. So did he. The realization angered him still more.

However, Lord Guilford probably wouldn't listen to
him any more now than he had ten years since. He was
foolish to ride here in the middle of the night on a
sleeveless errand. If he couldn't communicate with the

starched-up tyrant in person, he certainly couldn't expect to reach a better understanding of him by talking at a leaden statue.

A cacophony of emotions came at Denzil like jumbled sounds from the jungles during missions to Angostura. If he were to deal with clamoring sentiments he mistrusted, he must tune out most of them to identify the threatening ones.

The feelings that menaced his peace of mind all centered on Clare, up there in darkness, as he was. He doubted she could help him win his father's good opinion and reclaim his self-respect so that he might remain in England. Yet he couldn't leave her to seek another lady.

Denzil shifted uneasily on the path. An alliance with him must expose her to gossip. Separating her from family—a certainty, from her aunt's obvious disapproval of him—gnawed at his conscience. He knew the loss of a family too well.

Despite a desire to carry her back to British Guiana, he doubted the wisdom of that mad course. Clare's comfort and well-being were too vital to him now. He couldn't expose her to the dangers inherent in his pursuits in Spanish America.

Staring at a window that gave him back nothing but moonshine, Denzil knew only confusion from his soul searching. He should go away, but he couldn't bring himself to depart. He must give up all thought of claiming Clare, but he rebelled at the very notion of relinquishing her. An alliance between them would ruin her life, but he didn't know how to endure the rest of his life without her.

Pulling down his waistcoat, Denzil strove to get a

grip on a tormenting whirlpool of emotions. Consorting with statues in an effort to make sense of his sentiments had reduced him to this muddle of the mind. Emotions were better banked down, not fueled by over-indulgence. Feelings let out of strict control were as dangerous as a candle carried into a hayloft.

His midnight visit to the dower house garden had brought him no nearer to dealing with his feelings about his father than with those he had for Clare. Just one overwhelming sentiment fought past his need to stifle plaguey emotions.

Turning to glare at Zeus's statue, he saw in its rigid form his father's implacable posture toward himself. Through gritted teeth he said aloud, "Approve or disapprove of me as you choose. But look down your proud nose at the lady I value above all others, and your disapproval be damned. I find I require her good opinion above yours."

10

Holding her breath to avoid inhaling its odor, Clare sipped the warm, metallic-flavored fluid. Drinking the Pump Room's vaunted waters certainly provided incentive to recover from any illness, in her considered opinion, simply to avoid continuing the cure.

After a fortnight in Bath, her nerves required more treatment than the waters. Aunt Morrow seemed in spirits, talking avidly with acquaintances this morning as if she hadn't taken leave of them mere hours before at an evening musicale. Close enough to her aunt's Chippendale chair to enjoy her protection, Clare stood behind the group of ladies to escape inclusion in their talk. Aunt Morrow's friends were pleasant, but *on-dits* failed to hold her interest. Watching out for Lord Guilford, as she had each day for the past two weeks, required full concentration.

Writing and suggesting he come to Bath if he wanted to meet his son again had seemed reasonable in Wiltshire. In penning her early-morning missive, she had failed to take into consideration the minor problem that she had never met him. Now she awaited his arrival without a hint as to how she would recognize the man she had invited here with such hopes.

Further, she suffered agonies of doubt that he would appear at all. Perhaps he was as disinterested in his son's welfare as Lord Denzil believed.

To lower her spirits even more, Edmund still had not brought Lord Denzil to the spa town as promised. Her cousin had expressed doubts about luring his friend to Bath if his father's presence was so much as hinted. And keeping secrets had never suited Edmund's simple, open nature. He was hardly the best co-conspirator in a matter of delicacy.

Perhaps Lord Denzil had refused to accompany him and returned to London—or worse, to British Guiana. Refusing to entertain this daunting prospect further, Clare surrendered her nearly full glass to a passing servant.

More likely, the two friends had stopped along the way to take in a mill or visit stables of exceptional repute. Edmund was quite capable of allowing her to cool her heels in company with a crowd of invalids and gossips, while the two men toddled along the road to Bath, taking their pleasure.

Out of sorts, Clare eyed the milling midday throng. At least Aunt Morrow supported daily visits to the Pump Room. Anyone arriving in Bath came here at once to sign the subscription book and see who among their acquaintance might be present in the town. Her best chance to meet with the mysterious Lord Guilford was at the Pump Room, if she survived daily doses of its vile waters.

A flock of new arrivals crowded through the entrance, their coiffures and clothing showing evidence of the mizzling rain that matched her mood this morning. Clare eyed them, wondering if a Friday-faced gentleman shuffling in on two sticks might be the rogue's father.

An elegantly dressed gentleman broke to the side from the group, stepping round them deftly to advance into the room. *Denzil!* thought Clare with a throb of the pulse, before realizing this man's dark hair was liberally laced with grey. Otherwise, he hardly looked old enough to have fathered a son with nearly thirty years on his plate.

The man who must be Lord Guilford stood for a moment as if looking out acquaintance. The haughty lift of his head was quite unlike Denzil.

Surveying the room's numerous occupants, he didn't appear to meet anyone's eyes. The familiar yet strange features were devoid of expression. She wondered how Denzil had ever discerned his father's disapproval.

Then Clare realized Lord Guilford was staring directly at her, with no more expression than he had shown before. Purposefully, he strode toward her, neatly avoiding bystanders and Bath chairs without acknowledging their existence, as he cut his way through the crowd without a wasted step.

"Lady Clare Linwood, I don't doubt," he informed her, bowing correctly, with an economy of motion. "I knew your father slightly; good chap to have on one's side in a battle of wits. Sorry to read of his death in the *Post*."

"Thank you," she replied, daunted by the man's aloof air. "Yes, I'm Clare; but how, in this packed room of people, did you guess who I am?"

"Not difficult. A most attractive young lady, looking anxious," he said. "Besides, you hovered too near Lady Morrow to be anyone else." He eyed her aunt's graceful back.

"Aunt Morrow has indicated the two of you are acquainted, but I don't comprehend the rest."

"Acquainted, indeed; I should say so." He laughed briefly without appearing amused. "As for the rest, you would watch for the person you summoned to Bath with an air of anxiety, as you hadn't the least notion of my appearance. I, on the other hand, knew to expect exceptional beauty in any young lady involved with my fourth son."

Neither features nor inflection gave her a clue to the man's sentiments about that son. No wonder Denzil had spoken of his father with such cool hauteur. He had very likely learned it from the man himself.

Clare heard a chair scrape back abruptly. She turned to find Aunt Morrow standing, hands extended toward Lord Guilford, eyes glistening with a suspicious sheen. "Ben! I couldn't credit my ears when I heard that laugh, but it is you, indeed. What brings you to Bath? Surely not ill health."

Both hands flew to her mouth as Clare looked a frantic appeal to Lord Guilford. He noted her reaction with a raised eyebrow before stepping away to take Aunt Morrow's hands. The other ladies gaped astonishment from their arc of chairs.

Lord Guilford's tone almost registered emotion. "Anna. I don't have to ask if you're here for your health, for you look in far better curl than last time we met."

"I should hope so, indeed, considering that occasion. How very happy I am to see you again, under far more pleasant circumstances. Or at least I hope they are, unless you do come here to take the baths or waters."

Clare drew in a sharp breath and held it. As many questions as this meeting of the rogue's father and her aunt raised, the most pressing one at the moment was whether Lord Guilford would reveal her shocking impertinence in writing to a man she had never met. Aunt Morrow wouldn't like it, recognizing the action's link to Lord Denzil.

"I gathered from certain information which came into my hands that I might find you here, my dear," he said. Though the words were complimentary, Lord Guilford delivered them in a tone as dry as unbuttered toast.

Aunt Morrow nodded comprehension. "Still at the old occupation, I collect."

"Quite, though this is hardly the place to discuss that subject. May I give myself the pleasure of calling upon you and your niece at your convenience?"

"But of course." Aunt Morrow turned to her briefly. "You've presented yourself to Clare already, I presume, since you were talking when I turned round?"

"Yes, indeed, by her proximity to you, and by the chestnut curls so like your own. I knew you instantly, of course. I can't say the same for Lady Clare, who has changed past all recognition since my last view of her."

"We've met before, sir?" Though Clare had invited Lord Guilford to Bath, she felt no control over ensuing events. The sensation was like reading a part from a play and finding everyone else held a different book from hers.

"You saw him fifteen years back," Aunt Morrow answered her without looking away from Lord Guilford's arrogant face. "He brought me to my sister when I finally fled Lord Morrow."

"Your head wasn't as high as the bannister," Lord Guilford put in, "as you peered at us from above stairs. Perhaps the sounds of our arrival brought you from your nursery."

Memory opened a fogged window on the past, and Clare recalled dimly an early morning arrival at Linwood Hall, attended by distraught voices. Mama had stood in the entry hall in her wrapper and bare feet, holding a cloaked lady closely to her. Both women cried in duet, and the show of adult distress had terrified Clare.

Father had hovered nearby, speaking with a dark gentleman in a greatcoat who raised a grim face to stare at her. Following his gaze, Father had spotted her, ordering her back to the nursery in stern tones.

Evidently, Lord Guilford was the grim man in the greatcoat. Clare noted that he still held Aunt Morrow's hands, in the middle of the Pump Room. Glancing about uneasily at inquisitive faces turned their way, she said, "Aunt Morrow and I shall enjoy renewing acquaintance with you, sir. Won't you join us for tea this afternoon?"

"Nonsense," said Aunt Morrow. "You'll take luncheon with us, Ben. I can't promise you more than cold meat, as we didn't expect guests, but you're a most welcome one."

Unable to credit her ears, Clare reflected on the sharp set-downs her aunt normally delivered upon every encounter with a male. Unaccountably, she had invited this haughty gentleman to join them at table, an invitation ladies living alone extended only to males who were family members.

The proposed luncheon provided no further opportunity to speak with Lord Guilford out of her aunt's hearing. Clare required a few minutes apart with him to explain Lord Denzil's situation and enlist his assistance. Since Aunt Morrow's intention in coming to Bath was to separate her from the rogue, she would hardly applaud Clare's machinations on his behalf.

"Perhaps Lord Guilford prefers to lunch at his hotel," Clare suggested. She might slip out with her maid to gain a private audience with him in a public room there.

"Cold meat in warm company suits admirably," said Lord Guilford to her aunt as if she hadn't spoken. "Give me your direction."

"We're in Green Park Buildings, number twenty-six," Aunt Morrow said, gazing into Lord Guilford's eyes like a green girl. "Hardly the most desirable or convenient address, but coming without forethought, we were fortunate to secure a house at all, in August."

"Just so," replied Lord Guilford. "Let me put you into a hack, and I'll be with you presently."

"Come with us now," Aunt Morrow urged.

Clare wondered at her aunt's tenacity. She still stood hand-fast with the rogue's father, as if she couldn't allow the man out of her sight. The gabble of voices had risen in level about them as interested onlookers took in the scene. The public behavior of these

two middle-aged acquaintances bordered on the unbe-
coming, if not the scandalous.

"Let's discuss it as we walk outside to find a hackney," Clare urged, embarrassed on their behalf.

Lord Guilford looked at her blankly, as if he had forgotten her very existence. The man's indifference to
her, when it was she who had brought him here, was
vexing. Since he was already this much in Aunt
Morrow's pocket through their past association, her
chances of influencing his attitude toward his son
looked dimmer than a moonless night.

Clare put off her spencer and bonnet as a footman
buffed Lord Guilford's splashed boots with a leather.
She might as well not have been present on the ride to
Seymour Street, for all the attention the other two had
paid her.

"Let me step belowstairs to consult with Wilson
about luncheon a moment. Clare will see you settled in
the drawing room," said Aunt Morrow, handing her
bonnet to the butler.

In relief, Clare led the way abovestairs. The brief
time afforded for private speech was hardly adequate,
but beggars couldn't be choosers. Showing Lord
Guilford into a sitting room half the size of the same
apartment at the dower house, she indicated a seat
upon the sofa and took a chair nearby.

"What's this you write about Denzil requiring my
assistance?" he asked directly, before she had her
skirts arranged, let alone her thoughts. No wonder
the rogue disconcerted her with his plain speaking,
he had learned the habit growing up under this man's

influence. Perhaps other fine qualities had been absorbed from the same source, and Lord Guilford shared Denzil's compassion.

Taking her courage in hand, she plunged in with equal directness. "Lord Denzil isn't accepted by good society, sir. You could clear his path back into the *ton* by showing you accept and support him, now that he's returned to England."

"His return at this time isn't particularly convenient to me," Lord Guilford said with no more emotion than he had shown on any other topic. "I prefer he remain in Guiana."

"Convenient, sir! This is your son we speak of, a man who has been deprived of association with his family and countrymen for close on ten years."

Lord Guilford leaned back on the sofa and set one knee over the other. "Naturally I recall the relationship. Has Denzil enlisted your intercession on his behalf? I must commend his choice of ambassador, if so."

Feeling almost bereft of speech at the man's cool aplomb, Clare replied with asperity, "Approaching you was my idea entirely. Lord Denzil assured me he had no more need of you in his life than you have of him in yours. I couldn't credit that you were so unfeeling a parent, however."

"I'm gratified at your kind thoughts, particularly since we're so little acquainted. Denzil is unwittingly correct in his assessment of our need for one another. Has he followed you to Bath as yet?"

"Not that I'm aware of," Clare said, wondering how the man knew his son hadn't come to town at the same time as her aunt and herself. "If you have no intention of seeing him, it hardly matters if he's arrived or not."

"I didn't say I wouldn't see him. Reports of his health have been excellent over the years, but I don't mind reassuring myself on that head at first hand, if discreetly."

"Then you at least show enough concern to desire information about Denzil's welfare." Clare heard scorn in her tone and didn't apologize for it.

"Don't assume you see an entire situation from one vantage point," he answered without inflection.

Recognizing she had invited the set-down, Clare was aghast to find Denzil's father more unfeeling than the rogue had painted him. Holding herself stiffly erect in her chair, she said, "You might take your own advice, sir. Had you learned your son's full situation rather than listening to gossip, you need never have banished him."

Lord Guilford's slight smile didn't light his eyes. "But it was vital that Denzil leave the country at the time. You must trust a father's judgment on this matter."

Lord Guilford's detached pronouncement put Clare forcibly in mind of her father as he sat in his study, settling her future without regard for her sentiments. With reluctance, she admitted she had known her father little better than she did this stranger who sired Denzil. A flash of anger toward them both ignited a lump dark as coal within her mind.

Shaken, she said, "When a parent doesn't trust a child enough even to hear his version of an event, he can't expect trust in return. Denzil didn't elope with Lord Moresby's daughter, sir. He rescued her from the reprobate who abducted her, and you made him pay for his kindness with exile."

Uncrossing his legs to lean forward, Lord Guilford rested his forehead on his fist for a moment before looking at her again. "Den has found a ready champion in you, Lady Clare. Despite being an heiress yourself, you're convinced his tale of events is the true one. He must find your support a source of considerable satisfaction. I hope you continue to offer it to him."

Clare felt as if she had leapt at a branch and caught only the shadows of leaves. Lord Denzil's father said nothing she could take hold of, yet underneath the surface of his words lurked substance, like colorful carp in a dark pool.

"You show understanding of the importance of support to a person in your son's circumstances. Can you not look upon Denzil with compassion this many years after his youthful escapades? Even if he were guilty of more than gossips charge, he doesn't deserve to live apart from family and friends for a lifetime."

Lord Guilford sat back and bent back his head, contemplating her from half-closed eyes, as Denzil did at times. "I can assure you my son won't remain in Guiana for a lifetime, unless he chooses to do so. He isn't unprovided for there. When I may encourage his return to England is a matter I can't discuss with you. It must suffice to say I hear the force of your argument and will consider what might be done on his behalf."

Ready to battle for more than the slight ground she had gained, Clare leaned forward in her chair.

Aunt Morrow stepped over the threshold, her gaze going directly to Lord Guilford. "Wilson will have luncheon ready for us by half one. Will you take a glass of wine to stay your hunger until then?" She walked to the cut-glass decanters standing on a side table.

As Lord Guilford accepted her aunt's offer and then a glass from her hand, Clare regretted Aunt Morrow's interruption. Surely she had begun to thaw the man's cool disregard for his son's plight. Given more time, she might have won his support for Denzil's reentry into good society.

She watched Aunt Morrow settle on the sofa by her old friend, wondering at the difference in her aunt's reception of him compared to other men. Disliking Lord Guilford was all too easy, when she considered his show of indifference to his son. Further, he side-stepped issues she laid before him with equal impassiveness, on the surface.

Yet something made her wonder at the evasive answers he returned to her pleadings. Nothing concrete in his words or expression gave her reason to doubt he cared as little for Denzil as his son thought. But her intuition caught hidden meaning in his speech. She sensed a careful tension on his part as they conversed that led her to hope he could be persuaded to reconsider his attitude toward his son's return.

Clare came out of her musings to hear Aunt Morrow say, "Elizabeth's death was a sorrow to me, Ben. You must have had a time of it, adjusting to life without her."

"Your letter after I lost her was a haven of warmth in a cold lifescape; thank you for writing it." Lord Guilford smiled at her aunt. "Elizabeth had read me parts of your correspondence over the years. I missed knowing about your thoughts and activities firsthand once it stopped."

"It would hardly have been proper for me to continue writing. Though I confess to gleaning word of

your welfare where I could, from mutual acquaintances." Aunt Morrow's expression had softened,
probably from thinking of the loss of her friend Lady
Guilford.

"I used every resource to acquire information about
your progress after you left the county," he admitted.

"Not inconsiderable means." Aunt Morrow smiled.
"Though my doings must have made for dull reports,
as I've preferred to stay quietly in the country for the
most part, to avoid attracting Lord Morrow's attention.
I hope Elizabeth conveyed my gratitude to you for your
rescue from the nightmare I lived when we were neighbors."

Clare focused on the conversation between her aunt
and Denzil's father with renewed interest. If Lord
Guilford had rescued Aunt Morrow, he had risked
being called out by a violent husband. She could only
admire his courage, when she wanted to dislike him for
banishing Denzil.

Aunt Morrow hadn't revealed the particulars of her
early life. Perhaps this was an opportunity to learn
something of it, if she remained quiet and listened.

"I never had the opportunity to thank you properly
after you delivered me to my sister," Aunt Morrow continued in a low tone.

"I didn't rescue you," he replied. "You saved yourself by leaving Morrow's house and asking for the assistance you required."

"How can you say so, when Elizabeth and you stood
staunchly my friends during the years until my boys
were both at school?" Aunt Morrow laid a hand on the
man's sleeve. "Public opinion is against a wife who
leaves her husband for whatever reason. The support I

felt from the two of you was hardly what I could expect
from the world at large."

He covered her small hand with his broad one.
"Elizabeth shed tears over your bruises at times, but I
told her we couldn't interfere before you were ready to
help yourself. As long as you tolerated the beatings, no
one could step in to protect you."

Aunt Morrow withdrew her hand to cover her
mouth for a moment. "I was so ashamed, Ben.
Ashamed that I merited no better treatment from my
husband than to be brutalized. It seemed entirely my
own fault at first, and Lord Morrow encouraged me in
that belief."

"No one deserves the disrespect of violence, no
matter what they do or don't do. I will confess that
once, when Elizabeth told me the child you carried had
been lost to his madness, I spoke to him. He accused
me of improper relations with you, warned me that
should I interfere again, you would pay for both
events." At last, Clare saw emotion register on Lord
Guilford's face as his jaw tightened.

Aunt Morrow looked mortified. "As if either of us
would dishonor our marriages, let alone hurt Elizabeth!
But the man was quite mad."

"We could only wait until you were ready to break
free of his abusive tyranny." Lord Guilford patted Aunt
Morrow's hand where it lay on her lap. "Though I
wouldn't have grieved had the man broken his neck in
the hunting field."

Aunt Morrow laughed harshly. "Don't imagine I
didn't harbor similar thoughts. Finally I realized no
miracle would change him, or my situation. I had to
take my life into my own hands, if I were to save it."

Head to one side, she asked, "Do you recall that your butler very nearly turned me away from your door when I finally found the courage to escape?"

"Little wonder. With blackened eyes and a swollen jaw, you were hardly recognizable." He smiled without mirth. "Had you not gotten control of your voice enough to speak up, our butler would have sent you round to the kitchen entrance. Elizabeth never allowed anyone to be turned off who required assistance."

"Then how did you persuade her to allow her son to be banished?" Clare demanded, unable to remain silent.

Once more, she saw a shadow of emotion cross Lord Guilford's taciturn face. "With great difficulty, my dear," he said. "That part of it was more painful than any other."

Aunt Morrow frowned at her. "You sound quite the rudesby, challenging Lord Guilford on personal matters."

Hardly hearing her, Clare sat back again, mystified. Lord Guilford had taken action toward Denzil he found disagreeable, if she were to believe her assessment of his reactions. She could think of no good reason he should have done so. Yet during his last speech, she had felt almost sorry for him.

Against all odds, Clare was of two minds about Lord Denzil's father. He appeared to be more feeling than she had believed upon first meeting him.

Confronting Lord Guilford about his lack of trust in his son had let loose emotions hidden since her father's death. Her anger was very like that she felt toward her own father. Neither man had listened to his child's side of events, let alone heard that child's needs. Neither father showed trust in his child. Both settled their offsprings' futures out of hand, without reference to their desires.

Clare faced her resentment and anger toward her father for the first time, recognizing it for what it was. Her father had been no better than Lord Guilford. The parent she had idolized hadn't deserved blind adoration.

Yet Lord Guilford had shown compassion and understanding for Aunt Morrow, helping her to escape inhuman treatment at the hands of a brutish husband once she had chosen freedom for herself. She sensed that he cared deeply for her aunt's welfare still. Without obvious evidence of his regard for her aunt, she felt its existence.

It was equally possible he cared deeply for his son, without acting it out like a stage performer so it could be recognized easily.

Clare wondered if the thought might be carried a step further. If Denzil's father loved him, yet had shown so little evidence of it, surely it was at least possible her father had loved and trusted her. Even if he hadn't shown it.

Reluctantly, she accepted a new view of her father, not as a paragon, but as a man who could make mistakes like any human being. She felt closer to him than she ever had during his lifetime.

While her aunt reviewed the past with an old friend as if turning over the pages of a book of days, Clare ached for the words and embraces she and her father had never shared. If she could spare Denzil this remediless sorrow by encouraging father and son to forge a connection while it was still possible, she must do so.

"I'm delighted government affairs brought you to Bath," Aunt Morrow murmured to Lord Guilford. "Though I know I mustn't ask for particulars."

He took her hand, merely holding it in a firm clasp rather than kissing it. "The opportunity to renew our acquaintance is one I couldn't allow to pass."

Clare sat, ignored by her elders. Bringing father and son together in a new understanding appeared doomed from the start, when Lord Guilford had come here on government doings more than in response to her letter.

11

Clare followed her aunt and Lord Guilford across the wide expanse of the Pump Room's polished floor two days later, feeling invisible. Certainly her two companions saw no one but each other, no matter what the company.

The room's visitors saw no one but these two middle-aged friends, for every eye fastened upon and followed them. A rise in the gabble's level renewed her conviction that gossip rather than the healing waters brought people here. Having been reared on warnings against inviting public scrutiny, Clare was nonplussed that her aunt permitted a gentleman to be so particular in his attentions.

The three of them reached the shallow curved alcove along the wall beyond the fountain. A long-case clock and Chippendale chairs furnished the area, along with paintings and a statue in its high niche. With one of the room's three-tiered crystal chandeliers casting light into the space, it took on the character of a stage setting, with Aunt Morrow and Lord Guilford the principle actors. Clare played no more than a walk-on part. "Shall I procure glasses of the waters?" she asked when her seniors continued their conversation as if they inhabited the private drawing room on Seymour Street.

"Instruct a servant to bring us three glasses, if you will," Aunt Morrow said before turning back to Lord Guilford.

Giving up on sharing sensible converse with two people old enough to act in a more seemly way in public, Clare moved apart, looking over arrivals who had followed them into the room. When a servant came near, she requested just two glasses of the Pump Room's vile mineral waters.

The man had no more than walked away when the entrance of the gentlemen she awaited riveted Clare's attention. Her cousin and the rogue had come to Bath at last. A quick glance confirmed that Lord Guilford had failed to notice his son's arrival. He had eyes only for Aunt Morrow.

The babble of voices soared to the vast height of the vaulted ceiling as heads turned toward Lord Denzil. Clare paid the rogue's familiar countenance close attention, his arrival causing her pulse to flutter like a hummingbird's wings.

Raising a gloved hand, she signaled them; as the two friends responded to her cue, her sense of taking part in a play increased. If dramatics were to ensue, she could do nothing to halt them now. Better to get this meeting between father and son over, even if she would have preferred that it not take place in full view of a Pump Room crowd.

Watching Lord Denzil anxiously, Clare decided he hadn't spotted his father as yet. He advanced toward her eagerly, his gaze sliding from her face to her feet and back again, making lingering stops along the way. She insulated herself against the warmth his appraisal trailed in its wake. Having observed his father with her aunt, she now knew this ability to embrace a lady with his glances for a family trait.

With the moment of meeting at hand, anxiety nipped at Clare's nerves. She wished she had never written Lord Guilford in her high-handed fashion. This wasn't the way she had envisioned father and son reuniting, a significant family event turned into a public spectacle.

Near panic, she realized that too much of Denzil's life had been bruited about by the public. If only she could take back her letter and send Lord Guilford back to his estate. The last thing she wanted was to put Lord Denzil at risk of rejection before a staring herd of gossips.

Locking her gaze with the rogue's, she willed him not to look away and discover his parent standing nearby. As Lord Denzil reached her, Clare gave him both hands. Stepping to one side, she maneuvered him into a half-around dance step which positioned him with his back toward his father.

"What a delightful surprise to see you in Bath," she said too brightly, breathless with dread of the meeting ahead. "What persuaded you to come in oppressive summer weather?"

"By Jove," Edmund said. "Strange thing to ask a fellow, when you gave me strict instructions to get him here."

Feeling matters proceeded from bad to worse, Clare frowned on her cousin repressively, then turned back to the rogue at once, fearing he might look about him. "Edmund means I expressed a hope that you might both visit Bath, to relieve the tedium of the town for Aunt Morrow and me."

"Not what you said in the least," Edmund argued. "You said I must bring him here without fail."

Lord Denzil's grin stretched wider as he waited on her reply to her cousin's revelations. Even in her chagrin, she noticed how his eyes appeared to dance with drollery at the same time they stroked her face tenderly.

Still clinging to the rogue's hands as if the two of them stood on the edge of a cliff, she stepped back a pace, bringing him with her. Perhaps by degrees, she could put enough space between father and son so they never realized they had been in company here.

She addressed Denzil in desperation. "Tell me how you left matters at the estate. When did you depart? Was your journey a pleasant one? Were the roads passable?"

The rogue disengaged one hand to lay a long finger against her lips. Clare felt an overpowering urge to press her mouth upon it in a lingering kiss.

"I've never heard you this voluble," he said, laughing. "If I'd known you were starved for conversation, I'd have left Edmund to his race-meet and hurried to you without him."

"Do the races continue?" Clare seized on the thought. "Please don't feel you must hang about on my account. You must leave on the instant, if more sport remains to be seen."

"But the filly whose paces I prefer to watch is in Bath," said the rogue, exerting a meaningful pressure on her hand.

Looking away from the provocative expression he bent on her, Clare realized the Pump Room's guests gave them greater attention than an audience normally devoted to a theater performance. She feared this occasion would as likely prove to be a tragedy as a farce. Much as she desired it, she had no notion how to conclude this act without disaster.

"Come with me to the fountain, and I'll procure you a glass of the famous waters," Lord Denzil said, tugging on her gloved hands.

Seizing on the suggestion with relief, Clare said, "Oh, yes!" Then realizing they couldn't walk to the fountain without Denzil passing by his father, she exclaimed, "Oh, no! I find I can't stomach the waters. They quite disagree with my tastes and constitution."

"Something agrees with you here, for I've never seen your color so high." The rogue's teasing comment was accompanied by an appraising look that appreciated more than the visible portions of her.

Clare breathed deeply, feeling she might faint if she didn't get herself and Lord Denzil out of this place at once. Then Edmund dished her.

Pretending a discovery all too obvious in its fakery, her cousin announced in overly loud tones, "Zounds! I'd swear that's your governor standing behind you, Den."

Dropping her hands as if scalded by them, Lord Denzil swung about. Lord Guilford chose this precise moment to tear his gaze away from Aunt Morrow.

Clare couldn't see Denzil's expression, and Lord

Guilford never wore one. In an agony of suspense about the outcome of the meeting between father and son after almost ten years' separation, she stepped forward, looking up into the rogue's frozen face.

He showed no more reaction than his father; only the jut of his jaw showed her that Denzil had his teeth clenched shut. He stood still as the statue of Zeus in the dower house garden.

"So you've returned to England," Lord Guilford said flatly, speaking from where he stood by Aunt Morrow.

"As you see," said Lord Denzil with no more tone to his voice.

The crowd in the Pump Room paid hushed attention.

"Do you make a long stay?" asked Lord Guilford with no show of interest in the reply.

"That depends entirely on the welcome I'm accorded," said his son at once.

"A short visit is in order, I should say," Lord Guilford stated without emphasis. "You will no doubt wish to return to Guiana almost immediately to assure yourself of the progress of the crops on your plantations."

Clare's heart plunged into her slippers. She had dared hope Lord Guilford would make it easy for Lord Denzil to remain in England.

"I have no desire to make a long stay where I'm not wanted," said Denzil, only a faint flush betraying the hot sentiment beneath the cool words. "Not that I came to Bath to give you my company."

"Don't allow me to detain you here in any case," Lord Guilford said as if he commented upon nothing of more import than the weather. Every kind thought

Clare had bestowed upon him was swept away in a
whirlwind of anger.

Edmund spoke up as he took a stance on Denzil's
other side. "But you did come to Bath to meet your old
man, Den. You just didn't know it when we set out."

"Keep out of what you don't understand, Edmund,"
Clare said sharply, dreading what he might reveal next.

"I an't awake on every suit, but I know what you told
me," Edmund assured her. "You said if I got Den here,
and you persuaded Lord Guilford to come, all would be
right and tight between them. Don't think it's working
out that way, Clary. You're the one who don't understand. Can't interfere in a man's private affairs, like I
tried to tell you."

Against all inclination, Clare looked at Lord Denzil.
He fixed an accusing gaze on her, expression coming
alive with an anger that made her step back from him.

"So this little set-piece is your contrivance, is it?" he
asked through shut teeth. "You wished to set me dancing
like a trained bear, as my father has done my whole life.
To think I fretted that he might not find you everything he
desired in a daughter-in-law. Indeed, the two of you have
much in common. My mistake was in thinking a lady who
suited my father could be the right woman for me."

Feeling cold as a frozen pond despite the room's
heat, Clare stood shaken by Denzil's statement. The
rogue had thought of her as a daughter-in-law to Lord
Guilford. As his wife. The attentions he had shown her,
the constant flirtation, the kisses he had pressed upon
her in a thunderstorm, all had been genuine efforts to
fix her interest. Her heart flew to the heights of the
curved ceiling before plunging through the polished
floor as the rest of his speech registered.

Turning to his father again, Lord Denzil made a coldly proper bow. "I'll relieve you of my company at once. You won't be embarrassed by it again."

Before Clare could do more than put out a hand toward him, Lord Denzil had turned away, stalking toward the crowd with a fine disregard for the onlookers. They scattered before him like leaves before a blast of wind.

With Denzil's departure came an overwhelming rush of emotion she couldn't deny. Now that it was too late, she realized a truth she had hidden from herself for weeks. She loved the rogue.

Her love for him was nothing like her affection for Edmund. Her cousin had been a brother too many years for a passionate sentiment to exist between them. And now the only emotion Lord Denzil felt for her was revulsion.

Raising her chin against the curious stares of onlookers, Clare refused to allow a tear of the flood threatening her composure past her eyelashes. Love was misrepresented in novels as the most pleasurable of sentiments. No one would choose to love knowing he could drown in this torrent of despair and self-recrimination.

Dimly she was aware of Aunt Morrow beside her, putting a glass into her hand. She drank deeply before realizing her aunt had pressed a glass of the Pump Room waters upon her. She forced herself to swallow the rest of the vile fluid. The waters couldn't heal a broken heart, but the horrid taste might distract her from the knowledge she had brought down her troubles upon herself.

Feeling both numb and miserable, Clare admitted she

had been too set on pleasing her father, even after his death, to see the difference in her sentiments for her cousin and the rogue. The cold comfort of an arranged marriage was now all she could expect. By trying to resolve Denzil's problems with his father rather than her own, she had alienated the one man she loved with every true emotion a woman could bring to matrimony.

Turning to face Edmund and their joint future like a visit to a tooth-drawer, she discovered him still facing the entrance. He wore an expression of pure joy.

"Look!" he announced in delight. "It's Sally, with Sir Richard and Lady Nelle. Sally's in Bath! Glad you made me come here after all, Clare. Thought it would be a dead bore, but now it's the very place I most want to be." He set off at a pace to match Lord Denzil's precipitate departure.

Clare stood staring after him, feeling absolutely alone in the world. Realizing at last the true nature of her feelings for the rogue, she recognized the significance of Edmund's eager gratification at seeing Sally.

Walking up and down the confined spaces of the small drawing room in Seymour Street next morning, Clare squeezed her hands together painfully. Edmund sat eyeing her, gnawing on a knuckle. He had appeared for breakfast as usual, except for Denzil's absence. He had devoured Willy's plum cake with dispatch, as if Clare's heart weren't broken.

"Don't like to see you unhappy," he offered now.

"It isn't your doing," she replied, stopping by his chair. "You warned me about interfering in Lord Denzil's affairs, but I thought I knew better than you."

"Most people generally do," he agreed without rancor. "Sally don't think I'm hare-brained. Sally thinks I'm top of the trees."

"And so you are. Sally's quite right. She'll help you to find far greater happiness than I ever would." Clare forced herself to speak bravely, despite the bleak future stretching before her, an empty life alone without reciprocated love.

Edmund sat staring, mouth open. "What do you mean by that flapdoodle?" he asked uncertainly.

"Just that we don't suit. Our fathers never should have put us in the position of having to marry in the first place." She perched on the edge of the sofa nearby, leaning toward her cousin as she offered him freedom.

Brow furrowed, he stared at her in deep concentration. "Are you jilting me?"

"I wouldn't use that term, precisely. Say instead I'm releasing you from an agreement neither of us was party to."

"Wrap it in roundaboutation if you like, but you mean you don't want to marry me?" He sounded incredulous.

"That's what I mean." Resigned to her lonely fate, she drooped on the sofa.

Edmund leapt from his chair to grasp her hands. "Much obliged! You've made me the happiest of men!" He had the grace to look abashed. "What I mean to say is, sure you won't make the best of a bad bargain and wed me after all?"

"No need to ruin both our lives, though it's kind of you to offer," Clare said, smiling wryly at his expression of obvious relief. "If you have the slightest hope of securing the affections of the person you feel a true attachment for, don't let it slip away." As she had done.

"Never thought you was romantical about me, but you won't go into some curst decline and bring the governor's wrath down on my head, will you?" He watched her anxiously.

"I love you most sincerely." She had to laugh as fright molded his features. "But I love you as the brother I didn't have. I've seen how you look when Sally's about, and to hold you to a family arrangement when you and she could make a happy life together isn't the part of a friend." She reached for his hand. "I'll remain a friend to you both, you know."

"Don't know that she'll have me." He sounded morose. "Can't leave you unprotected."

"You can look after me just as well as my friend, perhaps better. You'll have Sally's help, for I know she cares for you, too, from the way she looks at you. And Sir Richard is hardly likely to turn down an offer from the heir to an earldom. So I'll gain a sister as well as a brother."

Seating himself again, Edmund said, "Know what you mean about looks, for I've seen you and Den eye each other too. Why don't you leg-shackle him, and then I won't have to fret about you."

She sprang up and paced to the window overlooking the wedge-shaped park. "Lord Denzil can't wish to speak to me again after yesterday's public humiliation. I've killed all hope of friendship between us—let alone warmer feelings."

"That don't sound like you," Edmund rallied her. "Giving up don't suit you, Clary. You're bound to come about again. Maybe you can tell Den it was all a hum gone awry. Always ready for a lark in the old days, was Den."

"This is life, not a lark, and I provoked him past bearing. He can't forgive me, whatever I might find to say." Despondent, she leaned her forehead against the cool glass.

"You won't know if you don't try. Let me bring him along and see if he refuses the fence," Edmund urged.

Wanting to be convinced, Clare considered. "Where could we seem to meet naturally? I doubt you'll persuade him to Seymour Street if he refused to accompany you this morning."

"I'll coax him out for an airing in the Crescent fields after church tomorrow," Edmund proposed. "Unexceptionable thing to do. Everybody goes there. He can't object to stretching his legs after sitting through a service."

"And I'll meet you, as if by accident," Clare agreed, feeling her shoulders straighten at the prospect of seeing Denzil again. She had no notion what she could offer by way of excuse for her interference between father and son. But surely if she could just gain his attention for a few minutes, inspiration would attend her efforts to win his understanding and forgiveness, if not his love.

Tugging his beaver firmly onto his forehead, Denzil felt the wind freshen as it rippled grass on the Crescent fields hillside. A similar wind would soon billow sails, taking him back to British Guiana. Back to serve the interests of the society which rejected him. The thought gave him bitter satisfaction, as it had over years of exile.

He noticed Edmund looking about them anxiously. No doubt he was oppressed by furtive looks sneaked their way. Tongues naturally wagged after yesterday's scene in the Pump Room, brought about by Lady Nosey-Parker Clare.

Denzil felt a restless need to be gone from society's tattling and restrictions. Give him the jungle's certain dangers any day, threats he could meet head on with cutlass and gun. He didn't want to deal with one meddlesome English Miss in particular.

"There's Sally," Edmund announced, grinning like a red howler monkey as he looked down toward Queen's Parade.

At once Denzil spotted Clare making her way up the hill toward them, arm in arm with Edmund's shapely little lady. His teeth clenched against a surge of joy at sight of her. Traitorous feelings didn't change the fact that she'd betrayed him to his father. Setting him up to suffer the old man's cool rejection in full view of Bath society was unpardonable interference. He should have put an ocean between them weeks ago.

Greeting Miss Scott with warmth, he frosted Lady Clare with a bow of cold correctness.

Barely looking his way, Clare spoke at a great clip to Edmund and Sally about the church services they had just left. "This breeze is most welcome after a stuffy sanctuary," she said, tawny curls blowing against her cheek. "Speaking of windiness, why don't you bring Edmund up to date on the latest *on-dits* from London, Sally?"

Letting go of her friend's arm, Clare calmly set her hand on Denzil's sleeve. His hackles raised at having her intentions imposed on him a second time in two days.

Edmund availed himself of Miss Scott's company with every display of agreeable pleasure.

A tremor communicated itself from Clare's slender fingers to his arm. Denzil's righteous indignation nearly deserted him. Recalling his father's indifference in the Pump Room, he stoked the blaze of his fury toward this meddling baggage in order to set her at a distance.

The quaver in her voice was equally unnerving as she addressed him. "I must beg your pardon for yesterday's scene. I never meant for you and Lord Guilford to meet again in such a public way."

"The choice of when and particularly *if* we met was mine to make, not yours," he said, taking deadly aim at her tender feelings. It was past time to end their association. He would be leaving the country as soon as he could book passage. Any sportsman knew a quick kill was kindest.

"I only meant to mend the rift between you," she said, her speech gaining steadiness. "As I've come to terms with my father's death, I've hoped to encourage you to make peace with your parent while he lives."

"Have the goodness to permit me to deal with my parent as I see fit," he said, his ire rising. Lord Guilford's rejection was nothing he could put right, and he resented her implication that he could fix matters with a little effort.

Quite humbly, she replied, "You have every right to cut up rough at me, and I offer you my head for combing, if it will mend matters between us. I hope we can regain our former footing with each other."

"Nothing exists to be mended," he assured her, determined to put an end to relations with Clare, as he should have done long since. "You've viewed me as a fortune hunter, set on seducing you into marriage for what I could gain. My fortune was made in Guiana. I don't require a bride to bring me wealth. The only footing we are on is that of two people who have a mutual friend in Edmund and the memory of a pleasant summer's acquaintance."

His pronouncement brought a flush to her face under the straw basket-hat's brim, and her lips firmed together. Good; he had angered her. He preferred to leave her ranting rather than entreating, since he must leave her behind in England.

Stiffly, she said, "Naturally you're incensed at me after yesterday's events. I'll overlook your insulting presumption that I formed improper expectations of you. Aunt Morrow never encouraged me to entertain notions of—of a closer connection than friendship between us."

"Then you're quite in charity with your aunt," Denzil assured her. "You won't be losing her good opinion by receiving the attentions of a man she doesn't approve."

Clare recoiled as if she had been struck, her face now as pale as her color had been high before. No longer conciliatory, she snapped, "I didn't encourage your attentions, and far more than her opinion was at stake. Had I foolishly credited your undeniable flirtation, I would have whistled an inheritance down the wind. Aunt Morrow has full say over my future and fortune. You may be certain she wouldn't approve the suit of a rogue like yourself, and very right she was to warn me away from you."

"I've made no offer for her to refuse—or you, either," he retorted, growing angrier as this woman who had meddled in his affairs now took him to task. She walked so close her faint floral scent tormented his senses. Even her skirts, billowing against his boots as they walked, entangled him.

"I should hope not," she said, yanking her hand off his arm to clutch her reticule's strings as if cut-purses worked the crowd. "I chose to believe you didn't abduct those heiresses. But if you pretend you didn't offer me every attention a gentleman can show a lady, plus many no gentleman should, I shall wonder at your veracity after all."

Knowing Clare spoke the truth, that he had set himself to attract her and win her affections before he knew he could only ruin her, Denzil's guilt brought out an unconsidered utterance. "My attentions were hardly the first you had entertained. You should have known how to deal with them, if they offended you. At the time, I thought you a proper English miss with an unblemished past."

"Oh!" Clare exclaimed, stopping dead on the grassy slope, hands gripped into fists at her sides. "How dare you throw that girlhood indiscretion in my teeth! I was a fool to believe you innocent of gossips' charges, when you don't credit my innocence. You had two elopements on your plate to my one, and very likely they both happened as reported. No doubt you wielded the whip as viciously as is said, too, for you don't scruple to do worse violence to a lady's feelings."

Angry that he had allowed himself to be provoked into flinging improper and untrue charges at Clare, Denzil stared out over the popular view of Bath. Deserving her animadversions didn't reduce his feelings of ill-use at her counter-charges.

Before he realized her intention, she had stalked away from him, hastening back to Sally and Edmund, who had dallied behind in the Sunday crowd. Now he truly stood alone among the strollers on the Crescent fields hillside. He had alienated Clare as he had set out to do, and the resulting sense of loneliness and loss overwhelmed him.

Clare already had Miss Sally by the elbow and was dragging her down the hill toward the line of waiting carriages. The piteous looks Miss Scott cast back toward Edmund as she stumbled along in her friend's clutch would have been amusing, had he felt the least inclination to smile.

Denzil cursed himself for an insensitive clod. Then, recalling Clare's revelation about Lady Morrow's control of her fortune, the inheritance of which obviously depended on her approval of Clare's future mate, he choked off self-recrimination.

Clare might as well part from him in fury, as part they must. Lady Morrow had set her face against him from the beginning. And his circumstances no longer allowed him the hope of offering for any English lady of family, since he remained exiled from his own.

For Clare's own sake, he had best let her go. Allied with him, she would lose family, fortune, and reputation. The money wouldn't have mattered; he had brass enough for them both. But he knew at first hand the unrelenting ache of being closed out of the family circle and the society of one's own kind. Clare had too recently lost her father to bear up under the loss of her aunt's affections and the *ton*'s approbation.

Just as well it had ended here, their sweet connection of the summer swept away like dead leaves before the gusting wind on this Bath hillside. Both family and society had rejected him again. At least he didn't have to live with the anguish of making Clare an outcast as well.

12

The door into her room crashed open far too early next morning, considering that Clare felt she had no more than fallen asleep. Echoes of Denzil's hateful utterances had kept rest at bay most of the night.

Pulling a pillow over her confused, aching head, she protested, "It can't be time to rise. Drink my tea yourself."

Before she could hitch the covers under her chin again, she was seized by the shoulders and shaken. "Get up, Clare," her aunt ordered breathlessly. "I need you to come with me. Oh, please, just get up!"

The urgent anxiety in Aunt Morrow's voice brought Clare from under the pillows, awake if not alert. "What's amiss?" she asked, squinting at her aunt. It was hardly half-light as yet, and they rarely went out before eleven.

"You must dress in all haste and accompany me,"

Aunt Morrow said. "No time to call your maid, I'll help you do the necessary."

As Aunt Morrow pulled at the covers and urged her out of the bed, Clare took in her scrambled appearance. Usually precise to a pin, her aunt looked as if she had dressed in the dark, then pushed through a bush backward.

"Are you ill?" Clare asked, taking in Aunt Morrow's feverish looks as she held out light stays.

"Not I, but Lord Guilford," Aunt Morrow said in a rush. "A message was just delivered from the Sidney Hotel. He's stricken seriously ill and needs me. I can't go alone, and I don't want a servant along on a matter of such delicacy. Hurry; he must be in a bad way, to send for me to a hotel."

Seeing her aunt was worried to distraction, Clare wasted no more breath on questions, simply put on the first garments to hand. While she pulled on pink stockings and tied them, Aunt Morrow caught up her back hair and pinned it.

When she had finished, Clare reached for her reticule and headed for the door without looking in the mirror. She preferred not to know how she appeared, having dressed in such a harum-scarum way.

Hinton waited at the entrance, fully dressed. Closer inspection revealed he hadn't combed his hair or shaved, but Clare couldn't fault his solicitous manner. "Don't you fret, Lady Morrow," he said as he opened the door. "I sent young Bobbit out to fetch you a hackney, and he came upon one not a block away. You'll reach the Sidney in good time."

The junior footman handed them down the steps toward the hackney coach. Through the light morning haze, Clare made out a pair of horses and a burly coachman hunched into a dark coat on the box. A gaunt man held the door to the hackney ready for them to enter. Hackneys didn't normally provide an outrider's services, Clare thought, pausing on the street.

Then Aunt Morrow urged her up the step and through the door of the coach, following on her heels with all haste. Clare sank onto flat cushions, thinking the last occupant appeared to have cleaned his boots on them.

Hardly had the door closed with an odd scraping noise than the coach set off with a lurch, spilling Aunt Morrow onto the seat beside her. A whip cracked and the coach gained speed until it traveled entirely too fast for town streets.

From behind them Clare heard a shout, and she tried to let down the side window to see what transpired. The window wouldn't budge. As the hackney jerked round the corner from Seymour Street into Kings Mead, she caught sight of the gaunt man running after them, shaking his fist at the vehicle.

"What ails the jarvey?" she asked Aunt Morrow as the coach rocked over the street's uneven surface. "Surely he isn't jug-bitten so early in the day."

"Bobbit must have explained the nature of our call at the hotel," Aunt Morrow said, leaning forward as if to urge the hackney to still greater speed. "No doubt the man is putting his team along in consequence."

"I hope we arrive with our teeth intact," Clare said. Gripping the seat's edge despite its dirt, she held on as the coach swayed through the square and onto Westgate. Through the glass behind the box, she noticed the driver touch up his leader with a sense of

disquiet. Unable to identify the source of her apprehension, she watched round the coachman's broad
body as they turned left onto High Street soon after.
Only a couple of blocks further, Bridge Street led onto
Pulteney Bridge and thence to the Sidney Hotel near
the gardens. They would arrive in record time.

Two minutes later, she sucked in the stench of wet
straw from the hackney's floor in a gasp of surprise.
The enclosed bridge flashed by on their right as the
coach plunged ahead up Walcot Street.

Turning to Aunt Morrow in alarm, Clare found her
looking outraged. Leaning forward, her aunt slid back
the panel behind the driver. "Turn about!" she called.
"You've missed the turn to the Sidney. Turn about at
once!"

The burly driver appeared deaf, as the hackney actually picked up speed. Clare studied his menacing
breadth with growing suspicion and horror. The
brown stuff of his coat looked alarmingly familiar, as
did the hulk of his shoulders. A cold slime of dread slid
over her skin.

The driver's whip hand raised to flail the horses and
her worst fear was confirmed. Springing from his
hand's broad back was coarse, dark hair. Just as on the
hands of her attacker in the homewood. She was being
abducted, most likely for ransom, and Aunt Morrow
was at risk too.

Crying out in panic, Clare lunged across her aunt to
the coach door. Wrenching at it frantically, she slid to
her knees in the noisome straw as the hackney fish-
tailed.

Pulling her back onto the seat, Aunt Morrow asked,
"What's sent you into such a taking? The horses must

have bolted, but the jehu will get them under control in a trice."

Panting in an excess of terror, Clare gasped, "His hands! This is no ordinary jarvey, he's the man who attacked me in the homewood!"

Thrusting her out of the way, Aunt Morrow staggered across the intervening space as she transferred herself to the forward seat. Pounding the glass with both fists, she ordered the driver to halt at the top of her voice.

Meanwhile, Clare wrenched at the door with renewed strength. It didn't budge, as if it were wedged shut from the outside. Furtive looks from the gaunt man who had waited outside the hackney as they entered now held sinister meaning. The scraping sound when he shut them into the coach must have been made when he secured the door.

She couldn't think why he had been abandoned by his cohort on the box, unless their abductor wanted no one to know where he delivered them. Denzil had warned her that her fortune made her prey to abduction.

Aunt Morrow still called to the driver, pounding the glass with gloved fists. For one awful instant, he turned to peer down at them, mouth gaping in mad laughter, before devoting full attention to his pair once more. The man's features, which Clare hadn't seen clearly in the homewood, could pass unnoticed at any rout, except for an obsessive intensity about the pouched eyes.

Recoiling as if struck a blow, Aunt Morrow fell back onto the seat. Supporting her aunt in her arms, Clare braced her boneless form against the coach's bucking progress. From fear for herself, her feelings veered to concern over her aunt's pale, lifeless features.

"Without doubt, I'm done for," Aunt Morrow finally gasped through stiff lips. "That's Morrow up on the box!"

At the White Hart Inn, Lord Denzil woke early with the fumes of the previous night's second bottle of port swelling his head. A waste of good wine, to drink it with bad thoughts for company, he reminded himself, sitting up cautiously.

Resting for a moment on the bed's sagging side, he levered himself up slowly. Careful to keep his head level, he walked to the washstand, where he picked up the pitcher and drank from one side. Having been heated for use in his ablutions at some point, it tasted as flat as his life looked to him this morning.

Wet, his throat felt far better. He might find it possible to put himself into his clothes and seek out an early breakfast of buttered eggs and strong coffee, a remedy for excess that suited him far better than a hair of the dog.

Half an hour later, he sat in the taproom, eating his meal, consumed by bitter thoughts. Clare's face on the Crescent fields hillside taunted him.

Despite what he had said to her, he couldn't deny he had meant every glance, every word, every touch, every kiss he had bestowed upon her. To deny their sincerity was to deprive himself of their sweet import. He couldn't go back to British Guiana without having that much of her to take with him.

Despite her past, his past, and what his father might

think of them now or in future, he wanted her. Not just desired her, though he didn't lack that response to her lissome figure.

He wanted her in his life as much as in his arms.

But he couldn't dishonor her by revealing either want or desire. He was still a rogue, an outcast, who could offer her no future except exile in a dangerous country, exposed to the uncertainties of his clandestine activities. Both his head and heart felt like a beaten side drum.

Downing coffee strong enough to resurrect the dead, Denzil despised himself for a coward. Better to have owned to his true feelings than to have sent her off down the hill, hurt by his denial of the sweet experiences between them. The least he could do was get himself round to Seymour Street and apologize abjectly.

Lady Clare had shown bottom enough to admit she was wrong to interfere in his affairs and beg his pardon. Begging hers was the least he could do.

Besides, he admitted, in all honesty to himself, he couldn't apologize without seeing her. If all he could keep of the joy Clare brought into his life was what he carried away in his heart, they had best part on good terms.

The coach slowed its unpredictable jolting a fraction, permitting Clare to peek out the smutty glass with less danger of bumping her nose painfully.

"Where are we, can you tell?" Aunt Morrow asked dully.

"I don't know," Clare said. "We're still among

houses, so I'm watching for someone to signal for help."

Nodding listlessly, Aunt Morrow made no effort to duplicate her effort at the glass on her side. Her aunt had seemed in a daze since discovering their captor's identity. She had collapsed on the bench seat, taking little interest in Clare's efforts to escape the rocking coach's confines. Not that assistance would have made much difference to the outcome of those efforts in any case.

Bleak dispassion was utterly alien to her aunt's nature. This dull stupor frightened Clare more than the abduction itself. Now that their captor had a name, she felt less frightened of him, more capable of coping. Lord Morrow was a bully who had beaten his wife, but she wouldn't allow him to touch her aunt again.

Realization struck. "Lord Morrow must have meant to capture you all along," Clare said. "I was never the one in danger. He must have learned you rode a black mare, and our hair is the same color. So when he saw me up on Cinder in the shadows of the homewood, he mistook me for you."

Aunt Morrow answered only with a helpless shrug.

Perturbed, Clare turned back to the glass. "I think I see the Paragon Vineyard between those houses," she announced triumphantly. "We can't be far from the Walcot turnpike. When he stops to pay the toll, we'll cry out for help."

No response met her plan, and Clare looked with concern at her aunt, huddled in the corner, hugging her shoulders. Disturbed by this lack of spirit, she turned back to the glass, peering ahead for a first glimpse of the tollgate.

As she watched, she considered how easily Lord Morrow had captured them. "This hackney was too conveniently at hand in a town that offers few of them," she mused aloud to Aunt Morrow. "We might have been suspicious, had we not been distracted with worry over Lord Guilford. Surely the message about his illness was just bait to bring us out looking for a hackney."

Coming to life enough to grimace, Aunt Morrow said, "Morrow's capable of the deception. He was insanely jealous—with no reason whatsoever—of anyone who showed me the least kindness or even notice."

The five-barred sections of the Walcot tollgate finally loomed ahead. Clare moved close against the door, ready to make her unwilling presence evident to the gatekeeper.

The hackney rolled to a stop. Holding her breath, she watched the toll-taker stroll out at his leisure to collect his due from an early, unexpected traveler. The instant he stopped scratching and raised sleep-swollen eyes, Clare thumped the coach's side, calling to him at full volume.

Through the glass above the forward seat, she caught sight of movement on the box from the corner of her eye. Jerking round, she saw Lord Morrow swing up a blunderbus from between his knees with one hand, aiming it toward the sleepy gatekeeper. The man's yawn became a gape, then he hastened at the double to open the gate. Leaving it standing wide to all comers, he dashed for the safety of his stone gatehouse.

No help was forthcoming from that quarter, Clare

realized, castigating the man as rabbit-spirited to bolt
for his hole. The coach lurched into forward motion
once more. She was nearly ready to curl up in the corner like Aunt Morrow as her hopes of escape vanished
behind them in dust.

How different their last journey along the Bath Road
had been, in their own coach, accompanied by outriders. Then she had decried Lord Denzil's presence. The
rogue's appearance alongside the hackney would be
most welcome now.

The coach bumped into a rut on the hard-packed
road, and she bit her tongue as they pitched up and
slammed down again with force. She caught Aunt
Morrow's unresisting form as she slid over the seat.
Judging from her aunt's listless retreat into herself, it
was up to Clare to save them both, unaided.

Interposed with jangling harness and hoofbeats was
the sound of winded horses blowing out the road's
dust. No one could put his horses along at this pace for
hours. Lord Morrow must stop to change horses
sooner or later. Even his blunderbus wouldn't intimi-
date a yardful of ostlers and sturdy stable lads.
Someone would take him from behind, releasing his
prisoners.

Taking heart from the thought, Clare settled her
aunt against her shoulder and patted her comfortingly.
The two of them had changed roles in recent days,
since Lord Guilford arrived on the scene. Her aunt had
shown a girlish, heedless side of her nature undis-
played before, and in consequence, Clare had felt like
the guardian.

Finding herself in her husband's clutches once more
seemed to have demoralized her aunt completely.

Clare hated and feared Lord Morrow for bringing about
Aunt Morrow's collapse by reappearing in her life.
Even in her fear, she determined to keep her aunt safe
from further brutality. Staring out the side glass, she
vowed to acquit herself well, whatever awaited them
when the hackney halted.

Counting the milestones would distract her from
fear and occupy her mind to better purpose, as she
might hope to know their location when they stopped.
Straining for a view through smeared glass, she spotted milestone l06 in bent, dust-laden grass along the
verge.

By the time milestone 105 appeared, Clare's eyes
felt as dry as the roadside grasses. The clatter of iron-
rimmed wheels slowed as she spotted the marker
standing at an angled intersection with a side road.

The coach veered to the left at a speed the hackney
wasn't built to sustain and stay upright. Clare and her
aunt pitched hard against its right wall. Nothing but a
hedge tavern would be situated along here, off the
main road to London. Hope of help collapsed as surely
as her aunt had.

Picking herself up, Clare left Aunt Morrow heaped in
the corner. The coach swayed dangerously from the
abrupt turn, rocking on its wheels on the rough surface
of the side road.

Shifting to the edge of the seat, she peered around
Lord Morrow's bulk, seeking a hint of the neighborhood they careened through. Rolling hills undulated
toward the horizon like deep swells of the sea, with no
habitation in sight.

The road had grown more narrow and even less
smooth by the time a mean cottage appeared ahead,

situated at a distance from the road. Clare stared at it without expecting assistance from that quarter.

On the box, Lord Morrow hauled on the reins, gradually slowing the horses. He turned their heads toward the cottage. Bumping over a track so rough she and Aunt Morrow were pitched about the coach's interior like cloth dolls, the hackney neared and rounded the stone structure.

Through the front glass, she watched Lord Morrow climb down from the box and disappear from view. Clare guessed he must be securing the reins. She held her breath, hearing mostly her quickening heartbeat. Then heavy footsteps on hard ground approached the door beside her. A scrape like a bolt being shot sounded, and the door swung open on the gloom of the hackney's dingy interior.

Scooting away from the light in dread, Clare shielded her aunt from her estranged husband as best she could, though Aunt Morrow hadn't stirred since they stopped. Lord Morrow peered into the dim hackney, filling the open doorway with his bulk, his expression grim, yet avidly expectant. Clare had seen just that look on hunters' faces, just before they set the hounds to rip the fox apart.

"Come out of there," he ordered, and Clare recognized the voice that had spoken to her in the homewood. More roughly, he threatened, "I'll have you out if I have to climb in and drag you out by the hair."

Aunt Morrow whimpered, and Clare heard an echo of the hedgepad's rough voice at Maidenhead Thicket. She cowered back against her aunt, wishing fervently for Denzil, or at the very least Edmund's pocket pistol, in this meeting with Lord Morrow.

The hackney lurched violently as he set a booted foot on the step and heaved himself inside. The small space filled with menace, cutting off air to her lungs.

As his hairy hands reached toward Clare, Lord Morrow said in a chilling croon, "Two of you, Anna, one young as the day we wed, one a bit older. And the same lovely hair on you both. Two of you to pay back the lost years."

Cringing from his wrenching grasp in sick revulsion, Clare recognized that the man was mad.

At number 26, Green Park Buildings, Lord Denzil stood stunned at the news Hinton had just imparted. "Ill?" he repeated. "Lord Guilford was taken ill?"

"Gravely ill, the message said," Hinton confirmed in hushed tones, holding the hat Denzil had handed over with his request to see Clare. "Apoplexy, no doubt. Lady Morrow said he wasn't expected to live out the morning and had asked for her. She and Lady Clare set out for the Sidney Hotel at once in a hackney."

A roaring like the Demerara River falls in the rainy season filled his ears. His father was in a bad way, not expected to live out the morning.

Clare's prophetic words on the hillside yesterday beat at his skull. She had excused her intervention between Lord Guilford and him on the grounds she hoped they would make peace while his father lived. He was nine kinds of a fool not to have heeded her warning.

"Sir? Lord Denzil?" Hinton peered at him anxiously, still holding his beaver.

Seizing his head gear in a grip that crushed the curled

brim, Denzil shoved it on his head and rushed out of the house without a word. He didn't trust his voice.

Out in the street, he realized his mount was nowhere in view. He had put it into a lackey's hands when he arrived to wait on Clare. The hack was doubtless eating oats in the nearest livery stable, wherever that might be.

Meanwhile, his father lay dying.

He set off at a dead run for the corner of Kings Mead. He must reach the Sidney Hotel while his father still breathed, could still hear him.

Drinking deeply from a bottle, Lord Morrow strode about the two-room cottage. Clare couldn't credit it as a habitat for hogs, let alone a gentleman. Remains of food on the deal table indicated he had been in residence here for some days, probably arriving in Bath shortly after them.

She could make out little of the room's doubtful amenities in the dim light. Shutters secured the few windows, and their captor had fastened the door upon them with a chain and lock, tucking the heavy key into a waistcoat pocket.

Standing before Aunt Morrow where she sat unresisting on a three-legged stool by the cold grate, Clare's every sense was assaulted. The stench of stale wine, unwashed body, and unemptied chamber pot offended her nose. The jumbled disorder of both small rooms confused her eye. She started as Morrow bumbled into the table, sending dirty crockery crashing to the stone floor. The man's menace was tripled in his drunken state, twanging her taut nerves.

She heard Aunt Morrow barely breathe behind her, "Have a care; he's more violent when he drinks."

A show of courage was required with a bully. Stepping forward, Clare addressed Lord Morrow in a reasoning tone. "You had best hand over the key," she said. "You must have stolen the hackney to convey us here, and no doubt it's already being searched for. Adding abduction to charges of thievery won't help your case."

Morrow turned, feeling his way round the table without setting down the bottle. She refused to give ground, though seeing him bare his teeth like a threatening dog tumbled her stomach with fear.

"Doubtless the driver's dead from the clout to the skull with the blunderbus," he said calmly. "He'll tell no tales about the direction the hackney took, or of me."

Clare gripped her hands together to hide their tremors.

"It can't be called abduction," he continued, sounding as reasonable as she had, "reclaiming an errant wife. You're back with me where you belong, where you'll stay 'till death do us part,' as you vowed. Vows are holy. Your lovers can't get at you now. One's dead, and the other will be, too, if he tries to interfere between us again."

Aunt Morrow's indrawn breath behind her gave Clare courage, though ripples of trepidation washed through her at his staggering approach and his continued confusion of her with her aunt. "I'm not your wife, and I haven't the least notion what you mean."

Stopping to tilt the bottle for another draft, Morrow saluted with it when he finished. "Here's to Lord

Deramore. May the worms enjoy him more than you did these many years. Your care wasn't all for your sister's brat, I vow."

Clare realized with horror that the man spoke of her father. He asserted that there had been an improper relationship between her father and her aunt. She was shocked at the very idea. No one who saw Father's polite indifference to Aunt Morrow could credit such a thought for an instant, even if such a relationship weren't forbidden by laws of incest.

Aunt Morrow had been a convenience in Father's life, handy to entrust with his daughter's welfare while he got on with his affairs. While her aunt had spared him the sharp edge of her tongue, she had kept her distance from him as she did from all males, until Lord Guilford's appearance. Lord Morrow's drunken charges horrified Clare in proportion to their utter irrationality.

"Don't be ridiculous," she said firmly. "My father and Aunt Morrow showed each other no more than common civility."

Setting down the bottle, he closed the space between them in two lurching strides. Reaching for a handful of her hair, he yanked her against his chest hard enough to make her cry out.

"Don't lie to me," he said sternly. "You know you make me hurt you when you lie to me. Speak the truth, and I'll go easier on you."

The sound of Aunt Morrow's weeping came from behind her. The painful grip on her hair kept Clare from resisting. Terror tempted her toward capitulation, agreement with any mad thing he said to make him unhand her. She understood how her aunt could have been trapped in a cage of abuse.

"Aunt Morrow has lived an exemplary life," she cried, trying to turn away from the crazed, implacable face thrust too close to hers. She cringed from the emanation of threat more than from Lord Morrow's fetid breath.

"As exemplary as the gown you wear," he sneered, shoving her away from himself violently, so her shoulder blades struck the wall with bruising force. Aunt Morrow slid quietly off her stool and crept toward the table, probably to hide under it. Clare couldn't fault her for protecting herself.

Unaware, Lord Morrow continued ranting. "No decent woman goes about with so few petticoats a man can see her form clearly outlined, and that tight bodice incites the lecherous thoughts of every man who sees you. But you tempt poor sods deliberately, harlot! Cover yourself with a decent dress before I strip that work of Satan off you."

Even knowing the modesty of her morning dress, Clare felt her hand fly protectively to its high neckline. The man's utter belief in his ravings almost convinced her of guilt against reason. Grasping at logic, she said, "You know we didn't come away from the house with baggage. I can't change into another gown I don't have, sir. Besides, this dress is perfectly suitable for a young lady."

"Guilford no doubt told you so. Oh, yes; I know he followed you to Bath. Now that Deramore's dead, you return to your first lover. You shame me, Anna, and you force me to make you pay for it." He took a heavy step in Clare's direction, then another. Tears spilled out, deflected in their downward direction by lined pouches under his eyes. "I never want to hurt you; I love you. But you make me do it."

Unreality and horror seized Clare in a stranglehold. She felt like a rabbit trapped in its hole by a terrier as Lord Morrow stalked her sidling movement along the wall. He raised an arm to backhand her.

Losing control, she cried shrilly, "I'm not your wife, I'm your niece by marriage. Stop bullying me! You had to wait for my father to die before you felt safe coming after Aunt Morrow. I'm not afraid of a coward!"

"You'll make me hurt you, Anna," he repeated softly, matching each step she took. "If I have to catch you to teach you the lesson you've earned, you'll pay for my trouble."

Lost in the morass of his own delusions, Lord Morrow was beyond reason. Despite her brave words, Clare was more frightened than she had ever been in her life.

13

Breath rasping his throat raw, Lord Denzil took the Sidney Hotel's stairs two at a time. Hot and disheveled after running the entire distance from Seymour Street, he halted outside his father's door, unable to knock. He collected himself to deal with what he found inside.

For most of his life, Denzil had resented this autocratic man with his cool air of indifference. Without his father, he would lose the template to measure himself against, even the reason to measure himself in the first place. The opportunity to inspire pride in Lord Guilford's eyes would be gone.

Waiting for his heart's pounding to slow, Denzil recognized that he had perpetrated a hoax upon himself. He didn't hate his parent, and indeed he did need him. A complex tangle of emotions, some corrosive as acid within his gut, tied him to this man. He wanted his father alive, wanted the opportunity to sort out his mixed feelings.

In dread, Lord Denzil set his hand to the door and knocked softly. It opened a few inches.

Having expected Lady Morrow or even Clare to appear, he stood staring through the crack at his father's valet. The man's wizened countenance betrayed no surprise at finding him attending his ill father when he hadn't been sent for. "Barret," he said heavily. "I don't mean to overset him, but I have to see my father. Just let me sit by him quietly, that's all I ask."

The man stared at him blankly, then turned his head to the silence of the room. Barret stood aside, widening the aperture of the door, more than welcoming him within.

Denzil stepped over the threshold and approached his father's bed. Lord Guilford lay against piled pillows on his back, eyes closed, covered to the chest.

Hovering above his father, Denzil felt his throat seize up. He couldn't lose this man. Searching the slack face in the dim light filtering into the room through undrawn curtains, he made out neither pallor nor feverish color.

But on his bed, Lord Guilford looked as vulnerable as any mortal. Denzil had never seen the old man at any disadvantage. This posture of powerlessness, his lack of defenses, stirred irrational fears. If his father weren't strong and well, order and security had abandoned the world.

The sound of even breathing, as if his father slept normally, was surely a good sign. Behind him, Barret swept the curtains apart and early morning sun surged across the bed. Denzil wondered at this lack of consideration.

Lord Guilford's eyes opened, finding Denzil's face at once. He lay perfectly still, showing no indication of surprise at his son's uninvited presence. "Barret, Lord Denzil will join me. Bring another cup and pot of tea, if you please. But you take coffee, as I recall."

Seeing Barret advance with a morning tray, Denzil stood groping for words. Lord Guilford's self-possession was notorious among the *ton*, but surely no seriously ill man observed the social amenities, let alone took tea himself as he lay on his deathbed.

Cautiously, he asked, "Should you have tea in your precarious state? Has a doctor seen you as yet?"

His father sat up, stacking pillows against the headboard and settling himself against them. Only when he leaned at his ease did he say, "A doctor isn't a requirement for every visitor to Bath. Why do you think my state calls for such services?"

Feeling a touch against the backs of his calves, Denzil sat abruptly in the chair Barret had provided. Shock upon shock was too much for continued control. Propping his elbows on the bed, he leaned his forehead into his hands.

"You aren't ill; you aren't dying," he assured himself. Dropping his hands, he stared at his father's quizzical face fiercely. "Thank God you're in health yet."

"My sentiments precisely. Why gratitude to the deity?"

Denzil broke into relieved laughter. "No particular reason, other than my unexpected remorse when I was told you weren't expected to survive. I find I prefer you alive."

Lord Guilford surveyed him without speaking. His gaze was cool and thoughtful at first, then it thawed to a degree Denzil couldn't recall seeing before.

"Leaving aside reports of my impending demise for the moment, I'm gratified to find you don't want me dead," Lord Guilford said dryly. "I can't feel I've given you sufficient reason to wish me well these many years."

For a moment, Denzil was reminded that Clare and her aunt should have arrived here before him. Doubtless they had, and being reassured about Lord Guilford's health, they had returned to Green Park Buildings at once.

Leaning forward eagerly, Denzil determined to seize an opportunity to set things right with his father, as Clare had suggested. "Considering the young rascal I was, I can excuse you for coming down hard on me most times. I wish you could have trusted me more. But that's in the past. What I want now is a chance to redeem myself in your view."

"I wouldn't say that's appropriate," said Lord Guilford.

Denzil recoiled at another cool rejection, feeling the hard chair's back at his shoulders.

"Hold," said Lord Guilford. "Don't poker up before you've heard me out. Impetuosity was ever a sad flaw in your character, but one of few. I mean that I think highly of you as things stand. Dispatches show you've fulfilled every youthful potential I recognized in you years since."

Stunned by a shock greater than any he'd yet had this morning, Denzil asked cautiously, "To what dispatches do you refer?"

"I dip my hand into diplomatic pouches and those that arrive through less formal routes as well."

"Do you sit on a War Office committee?"

"Whitehall, through the back door."

Feeling incredulous, Denzil said, "You're one of us?"

"Considering I formed a part of government security planning before you were born, I believe it more proper to say you work under my aegis," Lord Guilford said wryly.

"I never suspected," Denzil said slowly, passing a hand over his eyes as if the gesture might clear his view. His father's constant absence from the estate during his boyhood, his frequent journeys to London, made more sense now. At the time, he had simply felt ignored.

"We're a close-mouthed lot," said Lord Guilford, pouring milk and tea.

"By necessity," Denzil agreed, ire rising. "However, you might have given me an indication we shared common interests. I might have felt less isolated in exile." *And less ready to risk life and limb to prove myself.*

Lord Guilford set down his tea untasted. "I discussed telling you the whole with the others. We decided you would act the bitter, reckless remittance man more convincingly if you believed yourself truly banished. I realize your position has been uncomfortable. So has mine."

Anger surged anew in Denzil. He hadn't chosen dangerous duty for himself when he reached Guiana as he had believed. He had been set up for it in advance. His fate had been determined by a committee of policy makers—including his father. Younger sons were placed in the church or army at their fathers' discretion every day. He had simply been given to the government under the table.

His father's past actions toward him had been based on different motivations than he had known, perhaps less cruel ones. But his emotions couldn't swing in the wind of change as readily as his knowledge.

"Particularly uncomfortable when Mother died," he said bitterly.

Lord Guilford closed his eyes briefly. "Particularly then," he agreed. "I consoled myself with the value of the information about the French and Spanish you brought on the packet when you heard Elizabeth was ill. I arranged for the messenger at the docks to give you word of your mother's death along with dispatches for Don Felipe. I'm sorry I couldn't deliver the sad news directly."

Head down to conceal his emotion, Denzil nodded. "Your apparent indifference kept me from seeking you out when I slipped onto the estate. Believing you didn't want me there, I stood by Mother's stone near the chapel feeling as much anger at you as grief at her loss."

A long, expelled breath sounded from the bed. "A gameskeeper swore he had seen you prowling the woods about that time, but I believed it to be a poacher. Console yourself with knowing I've felt my failures toward you. I've done what I could to provide for your comfort in Guiana, putting easy purchase of that first plantation in your way. And I've never opened a dispatch without fearing the worst news of you."

Lord Guilford looked old as he made the admission.

The door opened quietly, bringing Denzil to the alert as would an unexpected sound in the jungle. Barret entered with another tray, which he brought with a small table to Denzil's side. At a sign from Lord Guilford, he slipped out as silently as he had come, probably to wait outside.

When the door had closed, Lord Guilford said quietly, "I don't use the covert services to excuse my inadequacies as a father. I'm far from perfect in that regard, as in others. I could have listened to you more when you were a boy."

Feeling bitter, Denzil swept away the thought with a gesture. "Difficult to do when you were rarely at home."

"I suppose affairs of state seemed more urgent to me than a boy's scrapes. By the time I had hauled your brothers out of years of devilry, I had little patience for yours. And I repeated the errors of my dictatorial father." Lord Guilford spoke dispassionately. "We can't change what was. But if the war permits us the opportunity, perhaps in future, matters can improve between us."

Denzil looked up. "I've applied to Bathurst for release from duty. Can't you arrange it? I've reported on allies and enemies in Spanish America for nearly ten years."

"You're a valuable agent, your cover well established for ready movements from Barbados to Guiana to the Spanish Main. Whitehall isn't ready to bring you home."

"How do you know that?" Denzil asked sharply. "Is the decision in your hands or others'?"

"Not wholly mine, or you would have been home long since." Lord Guilford shifted under the covers. "The decision is still on the table, waiting on larger issues. In the meantime, you must continue as you are."

"I can hold on for a time," Denzil said. "The war isn't

over by a long shot." Resentment against his father for years of manipulation still stuck in his craw, even if he had accepted government assignments by choice. Grudgingly, he said, "It affords a measure of relief to know you didn't banish me from the family, as it appeared."

"Never that," Lord Guilford said without inflection. "My pride in your work through the years has been exceeded only by my respect for your character. You said earlier that you wished I had trusted you. Perhaps you see now I've trusted you with the security of England."

Finding an obstruction in his throat, Denzil swallowed coffee. "Thank you, sir," he said quietly. "Perhaps a time will come when we can talk frequently and openly."

"With that degree of understanding between us," Lord Guilford said, "we must remain on guard publicly to retain the cover of estranged father and son."

"The reason you repudiated me in the Pump Room."

"Precisely. Now to other matters." Lord Guilford set aside his cup on the nearby tray. "When you first addressed me this morning, you appeared to think me near death. Will you please tell me the source of this impression?"

Concern for Clare and her aunt flared at the reminder. Quickly, Denzil described his early morning call in Seymour Street. "Doubtless, Lady Morrow and Lady Clare have called here and been informed that the message about your illness is a mistake. But I must return to Green Park Buildings to assure myself they reached home again safely."

His father was out of bed before he finished the

speech, reaching for clothing laid ready for the day. "Instruct Barret to make discrete inquires belowstairs as to the ladies' arrival here. I wish assurance of their safety, too."

Lord Guilford was buttoning his high collar by the time Barret returned to report that no one had inquired for Lord Guilford this morning except Denzil.

The news set Denzil swearing. "The butler said they left quite early in a hackney, yet they never arrived here. I made the journey between there and here on foot; I would have come across them in case of mishap along the way."

Lord Guilford looked a question.

Feeling sheepish, Denzil explained, "Didn't stop to learn where my mount had been stabled before I set off here. I was in too great a pelter over you." Feeling still more anxiety over Clare, he continued, "Now that I think of it, few hackneys serve Bath, with its steep hills. The chance of securing one early in the morning without prior arrangement with a livery stable is slight."

"The available hackney is suspicious. Do you fear they were carried off and robbed?" asked Lord Guilford, chin toward the ceiling as Barret arranged his neckcloth under his collar's ears.

"My concern leans more toward abduction for ransom," Denzil admitted. Dread for Clare's situation inclined him to rush out to search rather than stand about talking. "This failure to arrive here isn't the first disturbing incident involving Clare."

"Tell me," said Lord Guilford, thrusting his arms into a waistcoat held by Barret.

Briefly, Denzil recounted the hedgepad's words about "having her out" of the coach he had stopped at

Maidenhead Thicket. He described the engraved silver pistol by Parker he picked up after the villain escaped.

"I've seen a similar weapon," Lord Guilford said thoughtfully. "The pistol might have been stolen from another victim, however."

"So I thought at the time," Denzil agreed. "Later, Clare was attacked in the homewood on the Linwood estate, by a burly man who said she must 'pay back the lost years.'"

"I don't like the sound of it," Lord Guilford said as Barret eased the sleeves of his coat up his arms. "A pistol similar to your description was once aimed at my head by Lord Morrow. The entire county has heard his drunken threats to get his wife back and make her pay for leaving him. Further, Morrow has gone missing from his sons' protection nearly three months now."

Denzil raised his brows. "His sons' protection?"

"Lord Morrow is known to be quite mad. When he maimed his mistress by throwing her down the stairs, his sons put him under protective custody rather than into Bedlam. I pray God the sham story of my illness wasn't a ruse to lure Anna out where he could seize her. Madness and vindictiveness make a horrific mixture."

"And Clare's with her. In his madness, Lord Morrow mistook her for his wife in the homewood." Denzil felt apprehension he hadn't known on his own behalf, even surrounded by Macusi with curare-dipped arrows.

With a sense she was battling for her very life, Clare ducked under Lord Morrow's arm as he swung at her. Coming up against the opposite wall, she spun to face him, panting from terror and exertion.

"Look at me!" she cried. "I'm not your wife. You don't even know me. Why would you want to harm me?"

He stopped as if considering the question, taking a long pull at the bottle he still held. His expressionless eyes showed no sign he'd seen her for who she actually was. "I don't want to hurt you," he said reasonably. "I never did. But you left me, you have to pay for leaving me." Once more he advanced, stalking her steps as Clare slid along the rough wall, palms against it.

"I didn't leave you," she gasped. "I've never even met you, sir." Her voice shook with an excess of shock and fear, as did her nerves and body.

"Don't lie, Anna!" he bellowed, face suffused with deep color. "I'm not responsible for what happens when you lie."

A wooden doorjamb met Clare's fingers, and she inched to the edge of the opening to the other room. When Morrow rushed at her, teeth bared, she whipped through the door, looking frantically for something to put between herself and the crazed man.

Nothing stood in this small space but a low, narrow cot, covers spilling off its bare mattress. Running to it, Clare yanked up a thin blanket, flinging herself around to cast it toward Lord Morrow as he entered the small room.

The light cover sailed through the air, billowing up and over his head. While he fought his way free of its slight hindrance, Clare jerked the bed away from the wall, turning it on edge with the strength of desperation.

Scrambling round the cot on legs limp with terror, she fell to her knees behind it. Flimsy as was the protection it afforded, she must use what weapons came to hand.

The straw-filled mattress had fallen onto the floor and caught his feet as he moved toward her again. He kicked the ticking out of his way viciously, sending up particles of dust. Coughing, Clare shoved the wooden bed hard, bumping Morrow's booted toes and banging its edge against his shins.

Howling in rage, Lord Morrow dropped his bottle. He lunged across the overturned cot, seizing Clare by the arms. As he dragged her roughly over the bed frame, she realized no refuge was left. One garter gave way and her stocking slipped, like her courage.

Crying out as her shin scraped against the rough underside of the wood frame, she curved her fingers into claws. Morrow could snap her neck in an instant with his enormous hands, but she would fight as long as she remained conscious.

Shaking her with one great hand, Lord Morrow drew back his arm, aiming his fist at her face. Clare squirmed and kicked, desperate to avoid the blow. Indignation, horror, rage, and helplessness came crowding, one on the other.

Then a sound like a dropped melon filled her ears, and Lord Morrow's furious expression dissolved into stunned surprise. Grip loosening on her arm, he half turned away, knees buckling. His hair was wet; he dropped where he stood, groaning.

Aunt Morrow came into view as he went down. She clutched his discarded bottle by the neck, at the ready to strike again. Her caution was unnecessary, for Morrow rolled over and lay still, blood streaming from the head wound.

Clare's labored breathing and her aunt's sobs filled the small room. Her heart pounded her ribs furiously.

A sour scent of wine threatened her unsettled stomach. A dark stain soaked Aunt Morrow's sleeve.

Shudders convulsed her body as Clare realized that her aunt hadn't crept toward the table in the other room to seek shelter. She had sought a weapon and an opportunity.

When her mad husband didn't move, Aunt Morrow skirted his prone form, hurrying to clasp Clare fiercely.

"Are you hurt? I couldn't—couldn't let him harm you!" her aunt said in a rush. "I'm so sorry—even if I've—I've killed him, I *couldn't* let him do to you what he's done to me in the past." Tears tracked her pale cheeks.

Clinging to her aunt as tremors racked her body, Clare couldn't care much about Lord Morrow's condition. "Thanks to you, I'm all of a piece. Oh, Aunt Morrow! I've never been so f-frightened in my life." Their tears mingled as they pressed wet cheeks together.

"I know. Oh, I know far too well," whispered Aunt Morrow brokenly, patting her back.

Heart tripping irregularly still, Clare looked anxiously at the crumpled form on the floor. "Actually, I'm more afraid he's alive than that he's dead. He said he killed the hackney driver, so I'm not sorry you didn't let him hit me. Should we tie him up in case he comes to his senses, such as they are?" She flinched as Morrow's fist uncurled.

"I don't want to touch him," Aunt Morrow said, shuddering.

"Neither do I," Clare agreed, swiping one hand across wet eyes, "but we must have the key if we're to escape this horrid cottage. I'd far rather put my hand in his waistcoat pocket if he's trussed securely first."

Choking on her sobs, Aunt Morrow looked at her husband. "His head's bleeding terribly. Oh, what have I done?"

Clare made an effort to control the aftermath of terror and think sensibly. "For one thing, I doubt you've killed him, for the wound continues flowing freely. Here, I'll put the blanket against his head to stanch it. What can we bind him with?"

Asked a practical question, Aunt Morrow looked about the bare room with distaste. "He has no sheets to tear into strips, I fear."

Clare raised her skirts. "I can rip my petticoat into strips, but I don't know if the linen's strong enough for bindings." One pink stocking sagged round her ankle, and blood trickled from a deep scrape down her shin. She saw the injury with detachment, not feeling its pain.

"You're bleeding," cried Aunt Morrow, as if the minor wound Clare had suffered affected her sensibilities far more than the copious flow of blood soaking into the blanket from Lord Morrow's head. "He did hurt you!"

Her expression grew grim and she straightened her back. "Take off your stockings. Silk is far stronger than linen, and he won't get loose from such bonds in a hurry." Stooping, she unfastened her garters and unrolled her hose.

Clare followed suit, taking heart from her aunt's return to a more normal state. "Our garters would suit admirably to tie his thumbs together. Even if he regains his senses before we've finished binding him, with his thumbs and fingers secured behind him, he can't attack us with as much strength."

"An admirable notion," said Aunt Morrow in approval.

Between them, they rolled Lord Morrow over and pulled his great arms behind his back. When his thumbs and fingers were securely tied, they bound his arms at the wrists and elbows with one pair of stockings. The other pair secured his ankles. Another thin blanket was knotted round his knees.

Finished, they looked at each other with grim satisfaction and relief where they knelt. "I'll get the key," said Aunt Morrow in a tone of determination, reaching into her mad husband's waistcoat pocket to bring it out.

She sat back on her heels, holding the key up before her. "When I saw Morrow on the box of that hackney and realized I was under his control again, I felt as if I were dead. As I did living in his house." She closed her hand round the key. "For a little while, I forgot I had the courage to escape. Come along, Clare. We must get ourselves back to Bath."

"Morrow must be ahead of us," Lord Denzil said, feeling the words like a prayer as he wiped the moisture of a light drizzle from his eyes. "He has to be."

"Don't torture yourself with illogical doubts," said Lord Guilford, urging his mount up beside his son's. "From the inquiries we made on the main roads out of Bath, this is logically the route he took. No hackney was seen on any but the London road this morning. A hackney driven by a man who paid the toll with a blunderbuss can only be Lord Morrow."

"You're right, of course, sir," Denzil agreed. "If he didn't head north toward Bristol, he most likely travels toward London. On horseback, we're bound to come up with him soon. A cumbersome hackney and pair can't do more than five or six miles an hour at best."

Renewed hopes plummeted as he noticed a narrow track leading off to the left. "Unless he turns off this road. Then we've lost them."

"We'll deal with that eventuality when we must. For now, we'll carry on." Lord Guilford increased his mount's pace, despite his calming words.

Denzil urged his father's second hack to greater speed. If anything had befallen Clare, he would literally bury himself in the jungle—after he had buried Lord Morrow in England. Even if his hazardous life wouldn't allow him to take her with him, he couldn't exist without knowing she was safe and well in her world.

His father's quiet chuckle surprised him out of his lowering reflections. Glancing up, he saw two excessively wet, bedraggled females hurrying along the verge, heads down against the slanting rain.

"Clare!" he cried in relief. In the instant he recognized her and Lady Morrow, he realized many of the dark splotches on their dresses were the wrong color to be mud splatters. Dismounting with this disquieting thought, he thrust his reins toward his father.

"Hold these," he said tersely.

"Hold your own reins," Lord Guilford replied, and Denzil found his father advancing toward the ladies alongside him.

Leaving the riddle to puzzle out later, Denzil ran to Clare, dragging the horse after him. He pulled her into the protective cradle of his arms. He couldn't hold her close enough to satisfy his need to assure himself she was safe.

The energy with which she threw herself into his embrace reassured and warmed him. She pressed herself against him wetly, burrowing her face against his shoulder with a glad cry. Her arms clasped him with flattering fervor. Her small hands stroked his back into ripples of desire when he should be concentrating on relief at her safety.

"Are you hurt?" he inquired, letting her loose with reluctance in order to survey her length anxiously. "Surely that's blood on your gown."

"Don't fret. I'm relatively undamaged, though I can't say the same for Lord Morrow." Laughing and crying together, Clare clung to his shoulders with gratifying urgency. "Aunt Morrow was wonderful; she rendered him quite unconscious with his own bottle!"

"A spirited lady, indeed," murmured Lord Guilford appreciatively, nostrils quivering as he looked over Lady Morrow's wine-soaked gown.

Denzil realized his dignified, reserved father was holding Clare's aunt in a close embrace on the public road. And the lady who had frowned at him repressively all summer smiled up at Lord Guilford with more than complaisance.

Dismissing his elders, Denzil concentrated on the lady in his arms. Since she said she wasn't injured, he held her almost as tightly as he wished. Thoroughly soaked, the thin muslin round gown she wore gave a far closer experience of womanly curves than had a wet twill riding habit.

"Some ladies dampen their petticoats," he said. "You never do things by halves, do you?"

"I hardly chose this wetting," Clare said, and blushed adorably. "We trussed up Lord Morrow like a

Christmas goose," she said as if to change the subject. "We had to use our stockings, as we had no other bindings. But you'll have to retrieve him, for his head is bleeding quite freely. Aunt Morrow doesn't want his death on her hands."

"We can lend that assistance, considering you left us nothing more heroic to do," remarked Lord Guilford.

"I'll consider it most heroic if you can make the horses Morrow stole transport us back to Bath. We couldn't tool the coach, the beasts wouldn't let us mount them, and we had decided we must hoof it ourselves," said Lady Morrow, holding out a foot. Her slipper was indistinguishable in color from mud.

"Every time we tried to mount the recalcitrant creatures, they circled away," Clare complained.

"A hackney's prads aren't broken to riders," Denzil explained, admiring her spirit. Being abducted would send most ladies into a faint, and very likely strong hysterics when they came to. Clare not only managed to extricate herself from danger but laughed at failed efforts to transport herself to town.

"I can tool the hackney," Denzil continued, "if you ladies can direct us to it."

"Gladly, if you'll allow us to ride pillion to the cottage," said Lady Morrow. "I refuse to walk another step in this mud if I can avoid it. I also refuse to ride in the coach with Morrow, even with two able protectors along."

"You won't be subjected to such an indignity," Lord Guilford assured her, tightening his arms about her shoulders. "We'll ride inside, for Denzil is quite capable of handling both the ribbons and Morrow, tucked up snugly at his feet on the box. I wouldn't want the two of you exposed to any more common curiosity than can be helped when we arrive in town again."

Reluctantly, Denzil loosened his hold on Clare. They must return to town and reality.

Within days, he would board a packet headed for British Guiana and duty. If he had been unwilling to subject Clare to the hazards of his life there before, he knew now for a certainty he couldn't take her with him. Having just lived through the worst agonies of dread for her safety, he didn't ever want Clare subjected to the least danger again.

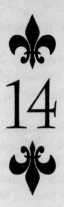

14

Clare wondered that Aunt Morrow could sit reading calmly on the drawing room sofa, awaiting the arrival of the man in whose arms she had stood on the Bath Road. Perhaps the romantic passions didn't affect ladies to the same degree at midlife as they did at nineteen.

Pacing to the window, she hugged her elbows, thinking of Lord Denzil's arms about her yesterday. Circled by his strength and concern, every past dream was fulfilled, while new visions rose for the future.

"You'll wear the colors off the carpet if you continue looking out every two minutes as you have in the last ten," Aunt Morrow observed.

"The gentlemen should have arrived by now," Clare fretted, leaning on the sill to look as far as possible in both directions. Late summer showers had shrouded the street, the green, and the houses across the way in mist.

Placidly, her aunt replied, "Having spent the better part of fifteen years apart from my friend, I'll find his arrival any time before three o'clock quite timely." She turned over another page.

Curious at the term applied to the relationship, Clare turned from the window. "You call Lord Guilford your friend. Yet you certainly don't permit other male acquaintances to embrace you on a public road, and you dismiss other men with decided set-downs."

Looking self-conscious, Aunt Morrow closed her book, keeping a finger in it to mark her place. "I wouldn't like you to think the least impropriety has ever existed in dealings between Ben and me. Elizabeth and I were dear friends, and Ben was never more than that, either, when we were all neighbors in the same county."

Hurriedly, Clare interrupted, "I never meant to imply anything beyond the most proper relations."

"Thank you for that assurance and for defending me on this point to Morrow, doomed as the effort was." Her aunt shook her head and sighed. "Elizabeth and Ben were a refuge of sanity for me at a time in my life when I had no other. But when I met him again in the Pump Room, I saw him in a way I never had before."

"Does he look much different now?"

Smiling, Aunt Morrow tipped back her head, as if looking into the past. "Not so very different, just a few years older. That wasn't my meaning. Actually, when I saw him last, Ben looked very much as Lord Denzil does now. Perhaps Denzil's arrival in London set me thinking about Ben once more. And perhaps that's

why, when he took my hands in the Pump Room, I felt
we were meeting anew, with the familiarity of a shared
past, yet with new possibilities in the present."

Seeing her aunt's bemused expression, Clare revised her opinion of romantic feelings at midlife. This
flowering of new emotion, springing from the seed of
an old friendship, added undeniable beauty to her
aunt's features and outlook. Clare looked ahead to
midlife with Denzil and vowed to cultivate friendship
as well as warmer sentiments.

Reminded of the expected company, she turned
back to the window. "Surely the gentlemen won't daw-
dle about until three o'clock before calling on us." Now
that Denzil had shown his feelings for her clearly, Clare
was eager to spend every second possible in his presence. Her doubts about the rogue's sentiments had
washed away in the rain shower the day before, when
he sprang from his mount to sweep her into his arms.

No gentleman would embrace a lady before his father, her aunt, and anyone who happened along the
public road without harboring feelings that led to a
declaration. She couldn't have mistaken so public a
demonstration of his intentions toward her.

Breathing on the glass, she watched a circle of fog
form against the cool surface. The fogged window reminded her of the coach ride with Denzil, traveling the
road toward Bath.

They had traveled far in affections toward each
other since that day. What had begun as a flirtation on
his part had ended in the loving concern he had dis-
played for her welfare yesterday. And her stubborn in-
sistence on following quite the wrong path, simply
because her father had laid it out for her, had ended in

recognition of her true feelings as she brought Denzil together with his father.

Clare said to her aunt, "Lord Guilford and Denzil appeared on vastly better terms yesterday. I wonder how the reconciliation came about? With Lord Morrow in the hackney, they could hardly stop to tell us the particulars when they set us down here."

Aunt Morrow looked up from her book. "I shouldn't be surprised to learn danger pushed them together."

"An effort to rescue us led them to set aside their differences?" Clare turned from the window.

"The joint effort certainly gave them an opportunity to discuss those differences. Very little true communication takes place when two people are both up in the boughs."

"In the Pump Room, they both appeared too stiff-rumped to make peace between them."

"Edmund's cant accounts for that inelegant expression, I vow," Aunt Morrow said with a grimace. "This must be a matter of conjecture unless they choose to speak of it, but the danger I meant was Guilford's supposed illness. Hearing that his father was near death when Denzil called here must have come as a considerable shock to him."

"No doubt you have the right of it," Clare agreed. "A parent's death reveals unexpected feelings. Perhaps they will tell us the whole of it when they call."

The sound of harness and hooves came to her ears, muffled by the damp mist of the morning. Hastily, she wiped the window to see a curricle with the top up arrive at their entrance.

Lord Guilford climbed down and handed the reins to his groom. He wasn't followed. Alone, Denzil's father crossed the pavement and disappeared under the wrought iron double arch above the step.

Doubt about the rogue's sentiments fogged the reflections of the past moments. "Lord Guilford has arrived," Clare wailed, turning to her aunt.

Aunt Morrow laid aside her book. "I thought you could hardly wait for the gentlemen's visit."

Disconsolate, Clare explained, "He's arrived *alone*. I was persuaded Lord Denzil would accompany his father, when Lord Guilford asked if he could wait on us this morning."

Aunt Morrow said reasonably, "Perhaps Lord Denzil is arriving separately. The two don't lie at the same hotel."

"That's true," Clare said, welcoming this hopeful view.

She greeted Lord Guilford with every proper show of civility moments later. Seating himself on the sofa by her aunt, Lord Guilford inquired after the ladies' health, to be assured they had taken no lasting harm from the alarms of the previous day.

"What of Morrow?" her aunt queried anxiously.

"I've arranged for him to be held under guard," Lord Guilford reassured her. "Don't fear that he will get loose from these fellows. I sent to Bristol for stalwarts who work the docks and use their eyes for the government. They'll do my bidding without question or comment."

"Thank you; I knew you would handle matters discreetly. I've written my sons to come for their father, which will give me an opportunity to visit with them both as well."

"Perhaps you would allow me to arrange private yet

more secure quarters for Lord Morrow, to relieve your sons of an unpleasant task," offered Lord Guilford.

Aunt Morrow nodded. "If the boys agree, I would be grateful. You'll see that he's comfortable, not mistreated, won't you?"

"Morrow's mind is obviously disordered. He was mistaken about killing the hackney driver, for the man is expected to recover from the attack. Contacts in Hamburg can arrange his housing. He won't be situated like a criminal, or as he would be in Bedlam," Lord Guilford assured her. "Which is far better treatment than he deserves. However, I'll feel more at ease about your safety if he's removed from England."

Considering Lord Guilford, Clare wondered at his ability to consign people to foreign countries. He exchanged an intimate gaze with Aunt Morrow, though they sat staidly on the sofa. The two appeared to communicate without words, to achieve a closeness beyond outward expression. She yearned to know Lord Denzil with a similar acceptance and trust, based on many years' acquaintance.

Which was quite impossible, if the vexing man didn't call upon her, at the very least. She wished she sat facing the mantle clock. Surely Denzil should arrive soon. Intruding into the comfortable coze taking place on the sofa, she asked, "Will Denzil follow you here, sir?"

Pulling his attention away from Aunt Morrow with obvious reluctance, Lord Guilford answered. "Denzil asked that I convey his compliments and concern to you both. He rode to Bristol this morning to see what packets might be sailing for Spanish America in the near future."

Sailing! Sitting with a polite smile of attention pinned on her face, Clare felt stunned and forsaken.

The rogue had left Bath without so much as taking his leave of her.

Holding her in his arms must have meant less to him than to her. Perhaps she had read into his actions and features what she needed to find there. Uncertainty plunged her into anxiety.

Lord Guilford continued, "He should return before dinner, as he's engaged to take his meat with me tonight."

Spirits rising, Clare said, "Then you and Denzil have mended fences as it appeared yesterday."

Frowning repressively at her, Aunt Morrow said to Lord Guilford, "You needn't answer pert questions only a saucy miss would ask."

He glanced toward the widow, saying with reserve, "Dinner doesn't alter the fact that my son returns to Spanish America shortly."

"Will he sail at once, do you expect?" Clare marveled at the commonplace tone she achieved, as low spirits reclaimed her.

"One never knows what passage might be booked at any given time," Lord Guilford said. "However, Lord Denzil won't find a cabin available immediately."

Unruly hope wouldn't be repressed as Clare asked, "How can you be certain passage is limited at present?"

"Because I arranged it thus myself," said Lord Guilford. "The same missive that brought guards from Bristol's docks gave instructions that my son be denied passage on any ship leaving port."

Feeling she understood the father no more than the son, Clare observed, "I own myself confused by your change of heart. Previously, you seemed most adamant that Lord Denzil leave the country."

"Publicly, it must seem so, I confess," Lord Guilford said deliberately. "Having observed my son's behavior at first hand yesterday, I believe his interests strongly engaged in England at present. I wish to further those interests."

Even if Lord Guilford were prepared to encourage her future with Denzil, Clare couldn't approve what the rogue would call high-handed interference. She needed Denzil to choose her freely, above every other consideration.

Her chin went up as her heart sank. "If he wishes to leave England, surely he has the right to do so."

"A man may act out of duty rather than desire. Far from restricting his freedom, I endeavor to keep Denzil in England long enough for him to exercise choice."

As usual, Lord Guilford's tone conveyed little to Clare. "How can duty take your son away if he wishes to remain here in England and you don't object?"

His expression bland, Lord Guilford said, "Without going into detail I'm not at liberty to reveal, I can tell you that Denzil has assisted the government in communications with the Spanish Main for years. He's also acquired information on the French through contacts in Barbados and French Guiana."

"Denzil is a *spy*?" Clare gripped the arms of the upholstered side chair she sat on, feeling a sense of unreality despite the texture of tapestry under her fingers.

"We don't apply that term to a British citizen who indulges his tastes for exploration and travel, merely using his charm and powers of observation along the way." A slight smile accompanied Lord Guilford's denial.

"Do you mean he carries dispatches as he goes about his normal business?" she inquired, feeling relieved.

"More than that, certainly."

"Does he simply pass along information which comes to his attention as he travels, or is his life at risk in efforts to gain it?" Apprehension seized Clare again.

"The security of England requires risk on the part of many men," Lord Guilford said evasively, rubbing his forehead with long fingers very much like his son's.

"Denzil can't go back to British Guiana." Clare rose from her chair in agitation. "Spanish America is dangerous enough at best, and you can hardly deny that exposure of his efforts there could mean his death."

Lord Guilford considered her gravely. "If I'm not mistaken, your affection for my son is of a lasting nature."

Hand rising to hide her mouth, Clare sat again. "A lady can't reply to that observation. One doesn't reveal tender feelings if a gentleman has not."

"Too often, significant emotions aren't revealed by those who feel the most strongly. Unspoken messages are too easily misinterpreted when no one speaks plainly." Lord Guilford smiled. "I see no reason a lady who feels a decided preference for a gentleman shouldn't make it known to him."

"Ben!" said Aunt Morrow reprovingly. "You're a pattern-card of propriety in the usual way of things. Why would you fill Clare's head with improper notions?"

"Circumstances sometimes dictate a measure of impropriety, my dear," he said dryly, turning to her. "I don't advocate undertaking it lightly. But when lives will be led in wasteful emptiness if improper actions are not taken, I can see grounds for considering them."

Face flushing delicately, Aunt Morrow sat staring at him with an expression of bemusement. A tremulous smile quivered her lips as she reached for his hand.

Clare felt like a housemaid staring through a keyhole.

She wasn't quite certain what had just transpired between her aunt and Denzil's father, but she felt its import.

Besides, she must set her mind to keeping Lord Denzil in England. He was at risk of his life if he returned to British Guiana and his activities there, whatever they might be called. Denzil truly cared for her, from all indications. She loved him with her entire being.

If she wanted love in her life, she must make every effort to secure it for herself, to give love as well as accept it. Loving meant risking, not waiting tamely for it to be offered like a birthday parcel.

Therefore, only one course of action was right. She must find a way to help the rogue speak his heart to her.

Breaking into the silent conversation of eyes and hands taking place on the sofa, she announced, "Lord Denzil mustn't remove from Bath without taking leave of his friends and family properly. I propose an expedition to Lansdown Hill tomorrow for us four, with Edmund and Sally invited as well."

Sparing her a measure of attention, Lord Guilford said, "The notion might serve, with careful planning for the afternoon's outing."

"I shan't fail to plan," she said with determination.

"But it's rained for the last three days," protested Aunt Morrow. "Had we not best wait on more promising skies before setting out on an *alfresco* party?"

"Improper behavior doesn't wait upon the weather when one knows the proper course for one's life," Clare said, laughing with renewed lightness of heart. "The sun will appear tomorrow. It must!"

15

The sun shown a shade too warm on Lansdown Hill for Clare's comfort next day. By the time the picnic luncheon had been set out on the drag's boot ledge and consumed, the sultry air discouraged walking.

Beside her on the rug, Denzil stirred. "Shall we tramp the hill path to promote digestion?" he proposed to the party.

Aunt Morrow looked to Lord Guilford for response, and he said, "As you prefer, my dear. No doubt we can keep up with the youngsters if they care to stroll."

Edmund lay against a tree trunk with his hands folded across his waistcoat. "Too close to my meal to gallop about." He nodded to Sally Scott. "You'll want to rest before the exertion of a jaunt."

Since getting Denzil apart was essential to her plans for him, Clare pressed the notion despite the close atmosphere. "Morning mists have burned off to the point we surely can see both Bath and Bristol if we stroll out to the viewing point," she urged. "Lord Denzil mustn't leave the area without taking in one of its most famous sights."

A quick glance showed her that the rogue looked as remote as he had throughout the drive and the meal, as if he had already left her in his mind. Determination to salvage the closeness of their shared summer at Linwood grew.

Coming to his feet first, Denzil extended a broad hand to Clare, pulling her up easily. Letting go at once, he turned to her aunt.

"Won't you allow me to assist you, Lady Morrow?" he asked politely, extending both hands.

Nodding, Aunt Morrow accepted his help. "You might as well call me Aunt, like Clare and Edmund," she said with a smile that left Denzil wordless. He simply bowed.

The party ambled toward the hilltop path in pairs, with little conversation. As distant vistas unfolded farther along, Clare envied the closeness of the other couples. Aunt Morrow walked with her hands linked through the crook of Lord Guilford's arm. Edmund assisted Sally over every grassy tussock as if she were ninety.

Clare walked beside Lord Denzil like a hound, looking anxiously at him without receiving notice that she followed at his heels. He didn't appear contented, either with the prospect spread before him across the hills or prospects stretching across time. Returning to Guiana couldn't suit him if he looked this grim and preoccupied.

Pointing out slopes dotted with fat, black-faced sheep grazing on lush vegetation, Edmund said, "Sheep have the right notion—meals should be an all-day occupation. I wonder if a few of Willy's fat rascals are left."

Addressing Sally, he said, "You don't need to exert yourself in this heat, my dear. Let's turn back to the coach and sit in the shade."

Placing a hand on his sleeve, Sally smiled up at him, blue eyes wide. "I should like that above all things."

As her cousin passed with Sally on his arm, he gave Clare a blatant wink and nod. He would make micefeet of her arrangements for the rogue yet.

"Won't you have another cake as well?" Clare asked Lord Denzil hurriedly. "You hardly did justice to them earlier."

Though the gaze he turned upon her looked hungry, he shook his dark head. "I seem to be losing my appetite. But I'll accompany you back to the coach if you wish."

Denzil's lack of enthusiasm for her company was hardly encouraging, but she believed his glum demeanor resulted from hopelessness, not indifference. And a lack of peckishness was a classic symptom of the lovelorn.

Taking leave of Aunt Morrow and Lord Guilford, neither of whom seemed the least reluctant to see them turn back, Clare walked off in company with Denzil. Edmund and Sally already strode ahead, arm in arm.

Though Denzil hadn't offered his arm, Clare took it anyway. His hard forearm muscles tensed to her touch. Looking up quickly, she found him studying her as if the secret to happiness were written on her features. As her glance met his, he looked away over the spectacular view, lips firming. "You're very quiet, sir," she observed.

"That comment invariably robs me of speech," he replied, studying the terrain as if to find his way back to Bath.

"Then we won't talk," Clare said comfortably. "We'll simply walk together and enjoy the remaining hours we can share. Your father says you mean to book passage back to British Guiana in the near future."

His jaw clenched before he spoke. "Cane harvest gets underway soon. I should be there."

"A pity you can't find a good overseer to handle such details in your absence," Clare remarked. His morose expression proved to her satisfaction how little he wanted to leave England.

"A pity," he repeated grimly.

They walked in silence a few steps, then Lord Denzil asked, "Why did Edmund wink at you in that obvious way?"

Clare started at his question, removing her hand from his arm and swatting at a nonexistent insect to cover the reaction. Denzil was too observant, even in distraction. She must remain alert. "He was no doubt signaling us to come along with them, in order to give Aunt Morrow and Lord Guilford a bit of time alone."

"They appear to enjoy each other's companionship," Denzil agreed, glancing back.

As they came in view of the coaches that had transported them and the servants to the picnic site, Clare asked, "Shall we sit with Edmund and Sally under the trees, or might you enjoy walking further?"

"You know I prefer moving to sitting about," he said, "but should we go off and leave them alone?"

"Yes, for the same reason we left my aunt and your father to each other's company," Clare assured him. Getting Denzil away from the others was essential to her plans for him. "The servants provide what chaperonage is needed. Besides, the way Edmund is stuffing himself with cakes, Sally is quite safe from improper attentions for the moment."

Denzil bent forward to look under her chip hat's brim, his expression more animated than it had been all day. "Obviously our elders smell of April and May, but you speak as if Edmund were tying the knot with Sally instead of you."

"So he is," Clare assured him, glad for the opportunity to give him the news. "Edmund spoke to Sir Richard yesterday before tea, and Sally had accepted him before the footman brought up the tea tray."

Denzil's face showed a glimmer of its usual teasing expression. "Took my advice about arranged marriages, did you, and decided to look out a man you could fancy?"

"Precisely," Clare said at once, smiling up at him significantly. She had the satisfaction of seeing the rogue stunned into silence. He walked on beside her, growing more grim-faced as he retreated mentally once more. If she didn't believe in his genuine attachment, she would think him no happier about a future with her than Edmund had been.

"Shall we walk in the shade of the wood?" he asked with an effort at a light tone.

"That suits admirably." She was relieved he fell in with her plans of his own accord. "I want to collect vines to arrange in a bowl for the hall. My gathering basket is in the coach. Will you wait for me here while I get it?"

At his nod, Clare hurried to the two coaches. Waving to Edmund and Sally, she asked a servant for her basket from the boot and turned to rejoin Denzil.

The rogue stood staring, as if memorizing every

movement as she walked toward him. His comprehensive gaze made her feel self-aware and utterly feminine. Denzil's devouring regard made her feel far more a woman than a lady.

Part of her wished to rush to him to stop the disconcerting feelings stirred by his scrutiny. Another self she hardly knew slowed her pace, deliberately invited his attention. Shoulders back in the form-fitting spencer, she lengthened her stride, feeling her skirts sway with a new freedom. In the freshening breeze the light muslin molded itself about her limbs, clinging between her knees in a sensual caress.

He noticed, from the glint sparking his eyes to dangerous blue fire. His fists clenched at his sides.

Denzil's awareness increased her determination to keep him with her, forever. Perhaps walking with him here on the hillside, with the wind touching her face and body as intimately as a lover's fingers, heightened the force of his gaze. Being the focus of his eyes made her feel as languorous as a cat stretching itself. She longed for his sensual hands to touch her every place his gaze did.

Sunlight splintered off his black curls. Lord Denzil stood with booted feet planted firmly, against a backdrop of curving hills receding into the distance. Tall and hard-edged in his dark coat against the soft scenery of Bath's rolling countryside, he exuded strength and purpose. His expressive eyes and lips revealed tenderness as he watched her. He offered a promising vista of the future she desired.

Her plan had to work, or her future held no sunlight. Lord Denzil mustn't be allowed to return to dangerous duty for his country unless he chose it for himself. He had

given enough, and he deserved an opportunity to live
here in England, supported by his family's love. And hers.

As she came up with Denzil, he reached for her basket, and Clare transferred it to the hand away from
him. "Thank you, but an empty basket is no burden to
carry." She mustn't permit either of them to carry the
burden of an empty life.

A path entered the woods up the hill, a short distance along the carriage road. Reaching it, Clare led
the way under the wide-spread arms of tall oak and
ash. In the silence between them, a natural concert
played as a soft wind rustled leaves and bird, called.

"What vines do you mean to gather?" Denzil asked,
catching up to her, even though the narrow path didn't
truly allow space for walking abreast.

"Woodbine," she answered, walking faster along the
faint trail. She felt his presence beside her with every
inch of her skin, both exposed and decently covered.

"Then we need not have come this far into the
wood," he drawled, "for it grew in profusion over a tree
near the path as we entered."

"Those blooms were poor. Honeysuckle farther into
the wood will smell sweeter." She increased her pace
again.

Denzil caught her arm, bringing Clare to a halt
under a sheltering branch. He gestured to a nearby
shrub. "Woodbine grows in profusion on all sides.
You've passed by enough of it to cover the whole of
Green Park Buildings. Tell me what you're playing at, if
you please."

The moment to act decisively had arrived, along
with trepidation and doubts about her abilities to
carry through. Clare pulled away from Lord Denzil's

compelling hold and grasped the basket in both hands to hide their tremors. Difficult as it was to speak the rehearsed words, she wondered that ladies and gentlemen ever formed alliances.

"This is no game. In recent days, I've become aware of certain emotions . . ." But her tongue tripped over the importance of her message. "That is to say," she began again, "I've come to believe that you aren't totally indifferent—what I mean to say is, if you would do me the honor—"

Denzil's expression of stunned disbelief stopped her cold. "I can hardly credit the notion," he said, "but are you proposing marriage to me?"

Put off by this reaction to an effort that had cost her a sleepless night and much anxiety, Clare turned her back abruptly and walked a few steps farther along the path to regain her composure.

Lord Denzil's ready laughter sounded behind her, and a squirrel leapt away overhead at the sound.

Incensed at this unfeeling reaction, Clare turned on the rogue. "You needn't make light of it if I am. If you can't care for the idea, you can simply say so, without humiliating me by laughing."

"Forgive me if I don't know the proper form for a refusal," he said quietly, folding his arms across his deep chest. "Males hardly learn how to answer marriage proposals."

"Refusal?" Clare heard just the one word. Heart battering her breastbone, she reminded herself she had expected no more, despite his obvious regard. "You don't care for me? I believed when you took me in your arms two days since, it had significance for you and for our future."

Entirely sober now, Denzil spread his hands wide. "We have no future. I won't try to deny my sentiments for you this time, Clare. However, because I care for you deeply, I can't ask you to be my wife."

"That's the most provoking statement I ever heard!" she said in exasperation. "I suppose if you didn't like me above half, you could offer for me in a trice."

He smiled ruefully, the curved line of his lips giving her an urge to measure her mouth against his. "You stand to lose everything by allying yourself with a man like me." His tone carried no hope. "I can't take advantage by allowing you to do any such thing."

"I was afraid you would insist on making this choice on my behalf." Clare reached under the napkin lining the basket. "So I shall have to take advantage of you."

Standing on a woodland path with the woman he loved, aching with the effort to deny her what he wanted most, Denzil watched as Clare brought the object of her search into view. She stood pointing what looked like one of Edmund's engraved pocket pistols at him.

He wanted to laugh at the absurdity of the situation, but no sensible man made light of a pistol pointed at his heart. Though considering how that organ had suffered since he renounced Clare for her own good, a ball through it couldn't hurt more.

Recalling her aunt's marksmanship, he suspected Clare's steady hand indicated complete familiarity with weapons. However, he wouldn't want to excite her unnecessarily, as he expected she had aimed at few human targets.

With only the slightest quaver in her voice, she said, "Put up your hands, please, and precede me along the path. A coach will meet us farther on."

Incredulous, Denzil stood his ground. "Are you abducting me? You've taken leave of your senses."

"On the contrary, I know my mind precisely. I'm quite as good a shot as Aunt Morrow, for we take practice regularly. If I have to wound you, I'll do so, but I prefer you undamaged. So please cooperate and walk down this path."

He had no intention of allowing her to carry through with this madness. If he wasn't willing to ruin her life, he was hardly likely to allow her to do so. But Denzil made her a leg before complying with her order. "Am I to assume the carriage waits down the hill, before the road rejoins the main one to Bath?" he asked as he edged past the pistol's deadly bore. "These are my best boots, hardly broken in for long walks as yet."

"This path opens onto the road again soon, long before you will be troubled by blisters. Keep walking, and you'll find one of the drags waiting for us," Clare said breathlessly behind him. "I suspected you wouldn't agree to a normal betrothal, so I arranged transportation to Gretna Green."

He stopped dead on the path and turned. "You're quite serious," he said in wonder. Much as he objected to exposing her to the dangers of his life in Spanish America, this proof that she was set on wedding him was most gratifying.

"Move on," she ordered, gesturing with the pistol. "Your father gave me the idea. He said that improper actions were sometimes justified to avoid an empty life. I don't mean to waste my future, or to have you exposed to dangers which could end yours, over meaningless scruples."

"That hardly sounds like Father. And honor isn't

meaningless," Denzil said over his shoulder as he continued down the path. Removing Clare from family, homeland, and above all, safety, could never be the act of a gentleman.

"Honor is cold comfort when you're lonely." Her voice caught on the last of the observation.

With her father away most of her young life, Clare must have known loneliness, just as Denzil had in exile. He couldn't ask her to endure still more, waiting alone in England for his return. He couldn't know if he would survive an unpredictable term of risky duty. Better that she make a life without him than miss other opportunities for happiness.

Behind him, he heard a sound as if Clare had stumbled on a stone in the path. He turned automatically to assist her and was motioned ahead by the dark muzzle pointed at him. He set off again, hardly aware of his feet on the path.

Ahead, a horse blew out a breath and jangled its harness. Curiosity about a lady's arrangements to carry off the gentleman of her choice tickled his fancy. Sobering, he knew that Clare's regard, although leading to this nonsense, filled an empty place in himself, even if nothing could come of it.

Stepping out of the wood, he saw a familiar coach standing on the verge. From the box, Edmund grinned at them. The little minx had persuaded her cousin to leave his Sally, and Willy's confections, to assist her in this abduction.

Looking up as they reached the drag, Denzil drawled, "I have to refuse to be abducted if Edmund drives. He's cow-handed with a pair, let alone a team."

Over Edmund's protests, Clare ordered briskly,

"Open the door and climb inside." She stood well back as he mounted the step to the coach, as if she expected him to wrench the pistol away from her. He wished he could snatch her into his arms and never let her go.

"Move to the opposite corner and sit on your hands," she instructed as she stepped to the carriage's doorway. While he situated himself to her instructions on the forward seat, she climbed hurriedly into the coach, settling her basket beside her. He could have had the pistol in that instant, had he chosen to take it.

As she sat stiffly on the seat's edge, the wicked little weapon staring one-eyed at him, Denzil felt an urge to go along with her plan. Marriage over the anvil and a fast packet to Spanish America suited the state of his heart and more external parts. A lady intrepid enough to abduct the man she wanted might well survive the rigors of the tropics.

Yearning to fling the pistol out the window and fold her in his arms, Denzil knew he couldn't endure tortures of worry over her welfare in that treacherous land. Especially given the fact of his frequent journeys to supply endless demands for information about the French and Spanish. Undertaking each mission, he knew he might not return. She could be stranded in a strange land, alone.

Jerking into movement, the coach set off down the hill. He hoped Edmund didn't ditch them.

Denzil leaned into his corner as Clare, diagonally across from him, glanced anxiously out the glass. He set one booted foot beside her on the seat. Watching her through half-closed eyes, he savored the way her gaze shifted at once to follow the length of his buckskin-clad leg.

Though she edged away, he believed he could persuade her easily to closeness. Her sensuous display of womanly grace before they entered the wood showed she offered more than fashionable, platonic love. Straightening, he chided himself for thoughts he couldn't make reality.

"Do you seriously believe you can hold that weapon on me all the way to Scotland?" he asked in a conversational tone.

"Though you appear to discount it, I'm capable of planning and foresight," Clare said stiffly. Without taking her gaze or the gun off him, she reached into the basket. Removing a small corked bottle, she continued, "Naturally I've considered the disparity in our sizes and strength. I know I can't be vigilant every moment for days on end. So it's best that you sleep quietly until we reach Gretna."

She tossed him the brown bottle, and reflexively, he caught it. If she thought sleeping in her presence, with or without a pistol, was likely, she was an innocent indeed. "What is this?" he asked, tilting the glass container. "A concoction from your stillroom? Poison?"

"Never fear that the mixture will harm you," Clare assured him earnestly. "I most certainly want you alive after going to this much trouble to carry you off."

He inclined his head, smiling. "Mad as this scheme is, I can't help but be flattered you go to this extreme. I doubt many men have the honor to be abducted by a lady."

Gruffly, Clare said, "Take only one swallow from the bottle. It's mostly laudanum, and I don't want you to have too much at a time, or you'll have bad dreams."

"I feel I'm in a dream now," he said, idly turning the bottle about. "You'll live a nightmare, however, if you proceed with this folly. You'd lose your aunt's good opinion by eloping, besides choosing a man she can't like. Even if you discount the fortune denied you, family is too important to estrange. Believe my experience of that fate."

"Aunt Morrow can hardly scorn the son while getting on terms with the father," Clare reasoned. "Her relations with Lord Guilford will only become warmer, the way she allows him to hang on her sleeve. How can she hold up her nose at a marriage over the anvil, when they can't wed at all while Morrow lives?" Her tone turned persuasive. "If we set up house, the two of them can stay with us as much as they like. They can keep company without occasioning the least comment from the longest-tongued gossip."

"I've heard of marrying to oblige one's family, but an abduction for that purpose goes too far." Denzil leaned toward Clare, and she backed against the squabs. "Unless you mean to marry me purely for love," he said quietly. "A man might want to hear those words as much as any lady."

"I daresay I love you more than you do me." Her lips closed upon the statement firmly, then trembled.

Manfully, he swallowed the words swelling up from his heart, needing expression. He had no right to ask for assurances he wasn't free to give. "Gossip is another stumbling stone. You'll never be received again in the best society if you proceed on this road to Gretna. You'll carry a double curse. Elopements are frowned upon, and both London and Bath society refuse to acknowledge me."

In agitation, Clare said, "What stories can make the rounds—the rogue gets a taste of his own medicine! I don't care what's said of me, if I keep you safely in England."

Denzil tensed at this revelation of her purpose. "Why wouldn't you think me safe outside England?"

The drag plunged into a rut, and Clare righted herself quickly as Denzil dived, not for the gun, but to flatten himself on the seat. "I know how to handle a pistol properly," she objected indignantly. "You don't have to fear I'll shoot you by accident."

"A ball's just as deadly, whether delivered by accident or intent," Denzil protested. "I'll feel safer if you hold that weapon out the window rather than aimed toward me."

"Drink your laudanum, go to sleep, and I'll put it away." The muzzle wavered, and Clare looked less certain.

Determined to have an answer to his earlier question, Denzil returned to it. "Have you and my father had your heads together on the subject of my safety in Spanish America?"

"We discussed your occupation, aside from plantation management and exploration," she admitted, brow creasing.

That his cautious father had spoken of highly sensitive government affairs to Clare, even in the most veiled terms, surprised Denzil. "Then you must understand why I can't ask you to marry me. I could never expose you to the dangers of the tropics, let alone of my activities there."

"You aren't asking me; I'm abducting you," Clare reminded him, waggling the pocket pistol to underscore her point. "If you're exposed to danger, I can hardly sit safely at home in contentment. If you go back to British Guiana, I go with you as your wife."

Looking thoughtful, she added, "Though Lord Guilford said he hardly thought your cover was intact at this point, after the two of you were seen rushing about Bath together, looking for Aunt Morrow and me."

Trust the old man to find a way to thrust a spoke in Whitehall's wheel. Though his father hadn't accompanied him to rescue the ladies in order to render him useless as an agent, he knew how to seize circumstance. Doubtless he could remain in England with Clare now that his cover had been compromised. But he wasn't ready to capitulate.

"That might keep me in England," he admitted. "Though you're no doubt as ready to take on a boa constrictor as a hedgepad, I prefer you not do so."

Voice and hand trembling, she said, "That's quite a large snake, isn't it? You may deal with snakes, if you please, but I still go to Guiana if you do."

"Society will tell you I'm a snake." His desire to protect her from all harm was fierce.

"I know what you are, and if you've made mistakes in your youth, it doesn't signify. I'm sorry I said you very likely had eloped with those ladies; I truly believe what you told me on that score." She looked penitent and adorable, and the pistol definitely listed toward the coach door.

Denzil grimaced. "I'm not at all proud of what I said to you on the Crescent fields hillside. You were in no way at fault for your school-girl experience with a fortune hunter, and I beg your pardon."

Looking irresolute, Clare let the muzzle drop an inch. He shifted on his seat, and the pistol came up again.

Dust had begun to rise in the air, churned up by the carriage wheels. Waving it away with her free hand, she said, "This gabble is just so much stalling. Drink the potion and lean back quietly in your seat, if you please."

"You'll choke on this dust before we reach London," Denzil said solicitously, reaching toward the glass. "I'll let in more air."

"Wait!" Clare protested. "You'll only let in more dust."

By the time the words were out, he had the glass down. Perhaps because a breeze was welcome in the closed carriage, despite the dust, she didn't insist he put it up again.

In an effort at rational persuasion, Denzil said, "Let me open the slider and tell Edmund to go back. Your aunt may not have returned from taking the view. We may not have been missed. Whistling a fortune and your reputation down the wind is no lark to undertake on a whim."

"This is no whim," Clare informed him, chin rising and pistol steady despite the lurching progress of the coach. "I once wished to know romance before settling down to everyday life with Edmund. Now I realize I can have the best of friendships as well as warmer feelings with the same man. So drink the laudanum and accept your fate."

Picking up the small brown bottle, Denzil eased out the cork. He looked at her steadily, raising the vial between them as if offering a toast. Then he tipped the contents out the open window.

"Oh, no!" Clare cried, looking stricken.

"Oh, yes," Denzil replied. It was time to put an end to this farce of an elopement. Taking the pistol from her unresisting hand, he opened the slider and hailed Edmund. "Pull to the verge and stop well off the road. Clare and I need a bit of a natter without pistols to spoil its aim."

Edmund's voice answered faintly, "Thought you'd talk sense into her. I'll just tie up the horses and toddle back to see what's left in the boot. I brought the drag with the luncheon leftovers in it, in case we felt sharpset."

Denzil turned his attention back to Clare as she clasped both hands at her throat. Despite his reputation and experience with females, no lady had gone to such lengths to secure his affection. He loved this intrepid young lady with a smut on her straight nose. He needed to demonstrate that fact in unmistakable terms.

Just as he had done in a coach on the Bath Road weeks earlier, Denzil set a knee on either side of hers. She caught her breath. He leaned across the space between the bench seats, bracing a hand on either side of her lissome body as well. She stopped breathing entirely.

This position brought her mouth enticingly close to his. Though her lips trembled and parted, she didn't draw back.

"If you mean to make me marry you, seduction is the art you must learn, not abduction," he said. "The first lesson is to choose another setting for lovemaking than a coach. Moving, you both risk breaking teeth. Stopped, too little space is available for the full expression of passion."

He reached for the door, unlatched it, and jumped down. Holding up his arms, he invited her out with a smile. She crept to the open door uncertainly, then leaned forward to place her hands on his shoulders. Disregarding the step, she waited for him to lift her down.

Laughing quietly, he swung her out the coach door

and against his chest. Holding her suspended there, he felt his heart accelerate into an irregular rhythm, becoming aware that hers beat as erratically. As tenderness for this woman he loved swelled his chest against hers, their pulses found a matched pace.

Slowly, he let Clare slide down his body until her half-boots touched earth. Letting her loose with one arm, he touched her lips with his forefinger, tracing the perfect curve.

Never removing her gaze from his, she kissed his fingertip, then took it gently into her mouth. Her tongue touched it, teasing with warm promise, and he fought for breath. What a surprise and delight she was to him.

Striving for control, he continued speaking as he turned her toward the woods beyond the verge. "Most important in seduction is to gain willing cooperation. Only if an experience is good for each of you can it be good for both. Further, duress and love never mix. Force is met with resistance, and the reaction you seek is surrender."

Walking far enough into the wood to put Edmund and the coach out of view, Denzil stopped by a stolid oak. Its branches spread a leafy arbor above them; shifting shadows fell over Clare's upturned face like a lace veil.

Warm hands closed upon her shoulders with strength and tenderness. Clare welcomed the rogue's embrace. As he feathered kisses on the corner of her mouth, she turned her head slightly to meet his tantalizing lips with her own, eager to take every delight he offered. He possessed and cherished her deeply with his kiss, until the small sounds of the woods were lost in those rising from her throat. Longing smoldered into urgency, and his need inflamed hers.

Drawing back just enough to allow speech, he murmured, "You see the technique. Offer an invitation. Welcome any response with warmth. Offer further inducement."

"Stop talking and kiss me again," she whispered.

Once more his mouth met hers, and she felt herself awakened to the sweet exploration of his tongue and teeth, challenged to answer his ardor in kind. His strong arms gathered her still closer against his chest, and she grew molten in his embrace, ready to conform to his desire with her entire body and will.

When he released her lips to bury his provocative mouth against the side of her throat, Clare murmured, "Does this outrageous assault upon my person mean you'll give up your silly objections to our marriage?"

"I admire the way you object to outrageousness," he replied, bending to kiss the hollow at the base of her throat in a way that made her pulse bolt. Straightening, he paid the same attentions to each of her eyelids. "You've become entirely too unorthodox to be left unwed, subduing lunatics and abducting men of scandalous reputation."

Kissing her left ear lingeringly, with delicate traceries of the tongue which sent delicious shivers to her elbow, he said, "We'll marry in church like Christians, not over an anvil with a sweaty smith standing by."

Saluting her right ear in the same way, so she clung to his wide shoulders to keep on her feet, he murmured, "A man with a past to live down can't elope like a wild youth."

She should have known that when the rogue paid his

addresses at last, it would be far from an offer in form. Certainly the caresses of his strong hands, which slipped up from her waist to claim new territory, were no more than she would expect from a noted explorer.

Catching his hands, she said, "I realize you're untutored in the art of accepting proposals, but surely you recall that in addressing a lady, you must speak of the nature of your affections."

"I love you like life itself," Denzil said simply. "I love you with the need to share every day with you, whatever comes to either of us. Can you love me?"

"How can you doubt it, when I endeavored to abduct you?" she asked tenderly. "I love you too much to be apart from you ever again."

Launching herself upon Lord Denzil with the full energy of the response he inspired, she bore him back against the oak's broad trunk. Stretching her length languorously against his, she nuzzled his neck under the upward thrust of his jaw, nibbling and kissing her way over his chin to find and claim his mouth. She would never tire of kissing the rogue, whatever further delights he taught her.

When she stopped to breathe for an instant, he opened glowing eyes. "This had best confirm you'll wed me," he said. "Or I may have to make use of that coach after all."

Clare laughed, insinuating herself snugly into his arms to practice the technique of seduction further. "Welcome home to England, Lord Denzil," she murmured, bringing his dark head down to kiss his ear as he had hers. "Welcome home for good."

"That's very good, indeed," he replied, pressing her closer to his heart.

Someday Soon by Debbie Macomber

A beautiful widow unwillingly falls for the worst possible new suitor: a man with a dangerous mission that he must complete—even if it means putting love on hold. Another heartwarming tale from bestselling author Debbie Macomber.

The Bride Wore Spurs by Sharon Ihle

When Lacey O'Carroll arrives in Wyoming as a mail-order bride for the unsettlingly handsome John Winterhawke, she is in for a surprise: he doesn't want a wife. But once the determined Lacey senses his rough kindness and simmering hunger for her, she challenges Hawke with a passion of her own.

Legacy of Dreams by Martha Johnson

Gillian Lang arrives at Lake House, a Victorian resort hotel in upstate New York, determined to get answers to questions about the past that have haunted her. As she is drawn to the hotel's owner Matt O'Donnell, her search for the truth unfolds a thirty-year-old tragedy involving both their families and ignites a dangerous passion that could lead to heartbreak.

Bridge to Yesterday by Stephanie Mittman

After falling from a bridge in Arizona, investigator Mary Grace O'Reilly is stunned to find she has been transported one hundred years into the past to help hell-raising cowboy Sloan Westin free his son from an outlaw gang. They face a perilous mission ahead, but no amount of danger will stop them from defying fate for the love of a lifetime.

Fool of Hearts by Terri Lynn Wilhelm

Upon the untimely death of her father, Lady Gillian finds herself at the mercy of her mysterious new guardian Calum, Marquess of Iolar. While each attempts to outwit the other to become sole heir to her father's fortune, they cannot resist the undeniable desire blazing between them. A witty and romantic novel.

The Lady and the Lawman by Betty Winslow

Amanda is ready to do whatever it takes to uncover the mystery behind her father's death—even live in a brothel in a rugged backwater town in Texas. More disturbing than her new lodgings is the undercover Texas Ranger assigned to help her, with his daring and hungry kisses proving to be the most dangerous obstacle of all.

GLORY IN THE SPLENDOR OF SUMMER WITH

HarperMonogram's

101 DAYS OF ROMANCE

BUY 3 BOOKS, GET 1 FREE!

Take a book to the beach, relax by the pool, or read in the most quiet and romantic spot in your home. You can live through love all summer long when you redeem this exciting offer from HarperMonogram. Buy any three HarperMonogram romances in June, July, or August, and get a fourth book sent to you for FREE. See next page for the list of top-selling novels and romances by your favorite authors that you can choose from for your premium!

101 DAYS OF ROMANCE
BUY 3 BOOKS, GET 1 FREE!

CHOOSE A FREE BOOK FROM THIS OUTSTANDING LIST OF AUTHORS AND TITLES:

HarperMonogram

____LORD OF THE NIGHT Susan Wiggs 0-06-108052-7
____ORCHIDS IN MOONLIGHT Patricia Hagan 0-06-108038-1
____TEARS OF JADE Leigh Riker 0-06-108047-0
____DIAMOND IN THE ROUGH Millie Criswell 0-06-108093-4
____HIGHLAND LOVE SONG Constance O'Banyon 0-06-108121-3
____CHEYENNE AMBER Catherine Anderson 0-06-108061-6
____OUTRAGEOUS Christina Dodd 0-06-108151-5
____THE COURT OF THREE SISTERS Marianne Willman 0-06-108053-
____DIAMOND Sharon Sala 0-06-108196-5
____MOMENTS Georgia Bockoven 0-06-108164-7

HarperPaperbacks

____THE SECRET SISTERS Ann Maxwell 0-06-104236-6
____EVERYWHERE THAT MARY WENT Lisa Scottoline 0-06-104293-5
____NOTHING PERSONAL Eileen Dreyer 0-06-104275-7
____OTHER LOVERS Erin Pizzey 0-06-109032-8
____MAGIC HOUR Susan Isaacs 0-06-109948-1
____A WOMAN BETRAYED Barbara Delinsky 0-06-104034-7
____OUTER BANKS Anne Rivers Siddons 0-06-109973-2
____KEEPER OF THE LIGHT Diane Chamberlain 0-06-109040-9
____ALMONDS AND RAISINS Maisie Mosco 0-06-100142-2
____HERE I STAY Barbara Michaels 0-06-100726-9

To receive your free book, simply send in this coupon **and** your store receipt with the purchase prices circled. You may take part in this exclusive offer as many times as you wish, but all qualifying purchases must be made by September 4, 1995, and all requests must be postmarked by October 4, 1995. Please allow 6-8 weeks for delivery.

MAIL TO: HarperCollins Publishers
P.O. Box 588 Dunmore, PA 18512-0588

Name_____

Address_____

City_____State_____Zip_____

Offer is subject to availability. HarperPaperbacks may make substitutions for requested titles.

H09511